LAURIE KNAPP

A Laurie Knapp Book
Copyright © 11/11/2007 by Laurie M. Knapp

Published in the United States by Laurie Knapp.
ISBN 978-0-578-00052-7

Printed in the United States of America.
First edition October 2008

*To my brother Brian - the last person you'd expect
to see with a book, but the first person who read this one.*

1

Libby Cohen had come close to crossing the yellow line before, staring down into the bowels of the subway tracks and seized by knowing that for this one moment she was completely in control of whether she lived or died.

The arrival of the number 6 train took this power away. Shifting bodies drove her into the car and the air solidified to paste as she 'stood clear from the closing doors' and hooked her arm around a pole so that only the crook of her elbow touched the tainted metal. The two-note chime, sounding like the ominous motif in a horror film, marked the closing of the door and the air became silky and buzzing. *Can't move, can't breathe.*

The train rocketed out of the station. Libby shifted her eyes from one passenger onto the next. The man beside her shuffled his newspaper to match the bucking rhythm of the car. Libby's eyes were drawn past him and onto a woman coughing in thick, gurgling heaves. Her skin was severely pockmarked, and thick, dark hairs descended in spirals from her overstuffed chin. Libby forced the contaminated air out of her lungs and

held her breath as the train swept her into the darkness of a
tunnel and swaddled its riders in sickness and squalor.

All these people: people ruining the air, people stiff or
sprawled over on the red and yellow benches with their heads
bouncing dangerously close to the filthy windows. The glass
was obscured with white paint graffiti and unidentifiable
smears and pasted advertisements that caught Libby's eye and
told her how to live. "Don't Try Black Without The Blue"
would disappear and reappear again as the woman with teased
blonde hair dipped her head in and out of conversation with her
companion, a small girl with scuffed black patent shoes and
colored beads in her hair. Libby counted them. *Eleven.* She
counted again.

The man beside her rattled his papers again, as a voice
overhead impatiently announced the next stop: *now
approaching 27th Street station.* One stop from the hospital, but
Libby could hold her breath no longer. She sucked in the
contaminated air through pursed lips and felt it teeming within
her. The train rapidly decelerated and the platform slid into
view, crowded with people who were seemingly oblivious to
the rapidly diminishing possibility of ending it all in one swift
motion.

As the doors slid open, the car's occupants shifted,
some moving to the door, others moving to fill the open seats.
Libby came face-to-face with a brown corduroy overcoat that
reeked horribly of cigarette smoke. She unhooked her elbow
from the pole and tried to turn away, but the crowd pressed in
and she nearly lost her balance. Instinctively, she grabbed the

pole but drew her fingers away just as quickly as if the surface had been hot. The searing heat remained however and she stretched open her palm and felt the pestilence crawling up her arm, seizing her. Shoulders convulsing, lungs collapsing. She hated the man in the overcoat, but only because it allowed her to purge the restlessness and chaotic anxiety that shook her frame and stole her breath.

The train lurched again and carried its prisoners out into the light, whipping past trees and buildings and yellow-clogged streets and crumbling cement walls decorated with old graffiti from the days before the city was cleaned up. Libby surfed the tracks as the train turned and shook from side to side and turned again and then careened into her stop. The businessman folded his paper and slid it carefully into the front pocket of his bag, then stood and hooked his fingers over the bar above him. As the decelerating train took away Libby's balance once again, he reached down with the offended and offered to steady her. She pulled violently away and burst through the doors and onto the platform.

She pounded past the subway map and the advertisements curled over the sloping walls – "Upset Stomach? Try Sodium Bicarb!" – up each and every gritty step and into the din and confusion of Madison Avenue. There, the buildings rose like the walls of a canyon, confining her to drown in the river of shoppers and businessmen – people living only to buy and sell, buy and sell.

The hospital was just across the street. Libby found her way to the corner. Someone stepped up behind her, jammed his finger impatiently into the call button on the light and then stood with his toes on her heels, breathing heavily on the back of her neck. Ahead of Libby cars staggered, their engines loud and tires crackling on the pavement. Horn blasts ricocheted upward. Libby felt acutely each rhythmic breath sizzling on the back of her neck, and her ankles burned where the man's briefcase brushed them. *Come on, come on, come on…*

The Walk sign illuminated and Libby kicked off the curb, stepping over the curbside collection of graying paper cups and cigarette butts and into the crosswalk. Just three steps ahead was the crack in the road. She had to remember to step over the crack. *Can't step on the crack. God is watching.* They had a deal. If she stayed off the crack, nobody would die.

But a sudden eruption of car horn blasts to her left carried her attention away and when her eyes returned to the ground, she found the toes of her tennis shoes resting insolently on the line of broken pavement. She stopped, frozen, expecting lightning to strike. *I'll just go back. I'll go back and do it again.* "Move lady!" the man behind her bellowed, pressing close again. Beside her, the street seemed to rise and fall like storm-tossed waves, trapping her here with her foot on this crack. Her heart slammed painfully into the front of her rib cage and darkness slid into her vision. "Goddamn it," the man hissed, thrusting his body past her.

First the wind hit and then the black Durango, its coming preceded by the flash of motion reflected in the cars stopped in the adjacent lane. Libby heard the beginnings of a curse word slip past the lips of the man in front of her, but everything was terminated as his body folded over the charging hood, glided over the roof and fell onto the pavement. He came apart it seemed, joints separating, arms and legs dancing wildly as though attached by marionette strings. The black Durango sped through the intersection and out of sight; the wind left in its wake lifted the papers descending erratically from the busted open briefcase. They were ferried to the ground and scattered beneath the dripping chassis of cars parked in front of a now-green light.

The man was dead. Even before moving to his body, Libby knew that he was dead. Amidst cries of "call the police!" and a pressing crowd and her own voice hollowly proclaiming: "It's okay, I work at the hospital," Libby knew that the man was already dead and felt that it was meant to be. There was blood everywhere. Dark red seeping now through the brown corduroy overcoat that reeked of blood and cigarettes.

2

Every day at exactly five past eight, Jon Calahan climbed onto the same stool in front of the same countertop. Every day he wilted beneath the same buzzing fluorescent lights, breathing in the same tinge of acid and the puffs of sterilized air that escaped when a package of pipette tips or tubes was opened. Every day meant filling order after order: 300 milligrams of Plavix here, 40 milligrams of Lipitor there. And every day, he was perpetually aware of the weight of his cell phone in his lab coat pocket, turned on against hospital regulations and anticipating the call.

Jon met techs at the window, talked to nurses on the phone, had lunch with pharmaceutical reps, and had, for the past five years, successfully convinced all of them that his persona was real. To them, he was a well put together young man with a steady job, a thriving personal life, and a past that fell in line with the road most traveled. For five years, he'd allowed himself to believe that things could always be this way. But he knew that one day Andrew wouldn't call. One day he'd be gone forever.

"You need to go out, Jon," his brother had told him. But what did that mean to him other than sitting alone in bars and watching tight groups of single women laugh and dance and occasionally throw glances in the way of charismatic bachelors. They had never met his gaze, never tilted their heads, smiled beguilingly and looked away, never displayed any of the signs that his brother had told him to look for. Jon realized that even if they had, he wouldn't know what to do. He could pretend here at work, but he could never be intimate with someone who wouldn't understand.

At exactly ten past the hour one of the pharmacy techs, a young man named Tony, leaned against the doorframe to Jon's office. This was a posture he had undertaken every Monday morning since Jon had begun working at the hospital and he always posed the same seemingly innocent yet probing question: how was your weekend?

And every Monday morning as he sat beneath the unnatural light, breathing in the over-processed air, Jon would fabricate as much of a lie as his conscience would allow. He would lie, in this case, about the cute blonde who had been squeezing tomatoes at the grocery store and who had made a comment to him about this season's crop.

"Met a cute blonde," he said.

"Yeah? What'd you do?"

"We talked."

"And did you get a little something?" Tony said, adding a sexual pantomime for flourish. He always expected this to be an immediate consequence of a brief conversation with a woman and Jon always humored him. But the words, lacking in decency and so uncharacteristic of the man he was, came out with a grinding friction he could only do so much to hide. With downcast eyes, he smiled weakly and said: "You might say she squeezed my tomatoes."

With that, Jon received his reward: a masculine gesture, the hard slap on the back. Then Tony left with the incident forgotten and Jon went back to his test tubes and his pipettes and the weight of the cell phone in his pocket. Waiting for the one girl to meet his eyes and show him that she was capable of understanding. Waiting for the phone to ring.

*

Libby always felt small on the plastic leather couch. Dr. Sherman sat so far away, with one leg lifted awkwardly over the other and his small-rimmed glasses balancing on the very edge of his reddish nose. Libby wondered how he could judge her sanity when he lived in a state of delusion about his own. One wall of the office was covered with diplomas tucked behind cheap frames. In each corner, silk flowers gathered dust. Everything was fake, from the plastic-mahogany wainscoting to the fabricated expression of interest on Dr. Sherman's face.

"And how have you been lately, Elisabeth?"

He opened every session the same, in the same dry disc jockey voice burdened with false concern. She could feel his eyes evaluating her from behind the plastic lenses. The way she sat, the way she held her shoulders, the motion of her fingers, the subtlest expression on her face. Her affect. Her disgust. Her anxiety. The uneasiness felt in knowing that she would confide her deepest fears and be told that they were ridiculous delusions, products of a mind awash with chemical imbalances.

She decided to answer. "This guy got hit by a car. Right in front of me."

He lifted and lowered his head in a long extended nod. She hoped his glasses would fall off.

"And how did seeing the man's demise make you feel?"

Libby hoped he could see the subtle shifting in the corners of her eyes as they ascended in disbelief. "A guy died in front of me. How am I supposed to feel?"

"Tell me."

He was waiting with his expensive silver pen poised for her to tell him that she believed it was all her fault.

"It was all my fault."

The pen went down. Even with the bushy graying eyebrows shading his downcast eyes, she could see the lids lift with wonder.

"And why would you say that?" he asked. *Because I'm crazy*, she thought.

"I stepped on the crack."

He looked startled. She enjoyed watching her words pierce like barbs through his cool demeanor.

"And why do you think that this was responsible for the man's accident?"

"Look, I told you before. You know already."

"Because you believe that if you step on the crack, someone will be hurt?"

Her face flamed suddenly. Under his penetrating and judgmental gaze, she bowed her head, stared at the back of her hands – the rough, cracked skin. She curled her fingers tightly into a fist and watched as her knuckles pressed white spots into the redness. He wasn't listening. What else did she need to say to him to get him to start listening? It didn't matter what she believed. The better question was why.

"Yes, yes," she murmured, feeling frustration shaking cracks into her own rigid defense. "And I can't sit on the couch after going to the bathroom because the next person that sits there will be contaminated by me. And if I don't check to see that the light switch is all the way down, it'll start a fire. If I don't hit the brakes after hearing the word "stop" on the radio, I'll get into an accident."

"What makes you believe that?"

"That's what I'm asking you! Look, I tell myself every single goddamn time: Libby don't get out of bed, you checked the lock ten times already, it's locked. No, no, I have to check it eleven. But eleven is an odd number, so then I have to check it twelve."

"And why do you do these things?"

"Because it's better than the alternative. Something's moving inside of me, like thousands of fire ants swarming over my skin, stinging – "

Goosebumps rose on her forearms. She ran her hands down them with deep pressure, wiping them away.

"And the feeling goes away once you've checked the lock?" he asked.

"Sometimes it does, sometimes it doesn't. But it's worth getting out of bed to find out."

He paused to make more notes with the silver pen. Her eyes moved away from its rhythmic glint and towards the window.

"I believe things because my mind tells me to believe," she murmured, knowing he was only half-listening now. "Stupid, juvenile things. It could tell me that there was a Japanese movie monster crawling up the side of this building and I'd probably believe it."

"Do you believe that there's a monster out there now?" he asked.

Libby looked back at him and sustained a blink. He'd missed the point entirely. "I'm saying that if my mind told me there was, I'd think it's better to be safe than sorry."

"Would you like to sit farther away from the window?"

She sighed through her nose. He was validating her. She knew it. One of the first mistakes she'd made on her psyche rotation at the hospital was to tell the old man with dementia that his son actually wasn't sleeping on the bed beside him. "Why get him agitated?" her resident had told her. "What's the harm in making him think you believe him?" But from the perspective of the psychotic, it was transparent. Dr. Sherman seemed idiotic for trying to hide behind it.

"I'm fine," she said. Then, to kill the topic, she validated him. "It's gone now."

"Good," he scribbled more notes and then looked up again, his eyes meeting hers much too intensely, waiting.

She pushed him out, got insolent. "Why can't you just say what's wrong with me?"

He laid down the pen. "Elisabeth, we've gone over this before. The things you have been telling me are consistent with obsessive-compulsive disorder. The etiology is not widely understood, but most believe it is due to an imbalance of the neurotransmitter dopamine…"

"Yes, I know all that."

She was sick of hearing about dopamine. It scared her more than theoretical monsters because it was real. What Dr. Sherman didn't know was that as a child, the disorder had crippled her. She was constantly filled with anxiety, fear of sickness and desperate needs to count, hoard, arrange, scrub. At six years old she had told her parents she needed to go to the doctor because she thought she had prostate cancer. She would lie awake at night unable to sleep because the thoughts in her mind would scream at her, command her to do things and then punish her inaction by tightening her stomach and streaming coldness between the layers of her skin.

At sixteen, she'd begun taking a medication for frustrating allergies. It was during this time that she began to conquer the crippling anxiety. She could convince herself not to give in and in brief stages freed herself from the fetters of her mind. But the obsessions and the compulsions were always there, brewing beneath the surface, still striking through not as deep. The triumph gave her courage. She could've been institutionalized, unable to function, afraid to set foot outside her house. Despite a persistent fear of sickness, she had entered medical school. She had placed her hands on faucets and washed dishes in the sink. Everything would be okay because she had freed herself without anyone else. Without Dr. Sherman or the pills he was trying to force down her throat.

And then, during a pharmacology class, she found her allergy medication in her textbook and learned that it did the same things as the pills the doctor had ordered. Dopamine. The chemical, being controlled by the little white pills she took to keep herself from sneezing at dust and dander. They were the source of her strength. She had not cured herself. There was no cure. There were only drugs. There was only a false sense of health, a delusion of freedom. Apart from it, she would be reduced to a dangling puppet without control, even to return to the edge of the yellow line and end the show.

"It's a delusion, Elisabeth."

She looked up.

"That's what we call it," he elaborated. "You believe that the man died because you stepped on a crack. That's a false belief and you know that it is."

"How do I know that?" she challenged. "What proof do you have that our random actions don't affect outcomes? You've heard what they say about butterflies, right? That one flapping its wings in Brazil can cause a tsunami in China?"

"Yes, I have heard of it. It's called the butterfly effect."

"I know what it's called," she snapped. "I wouldn't have brought it up if I didn't know what it was."

She thought she caught a glimpse of triumph in his expression, having succeeded in stirring her up. She was certain that she was much more entertaining to him when she was stirred up.

"Look, we don't really know anything for sure," she continued, "You can't even tell me what causes my disease. So how do you know that I'm not right?"

"Do you question whether or not you believe you are right?"

She sighed forcefully through her nose. "You can't just take everything I say and turn it into a question. I've heard that question before. It's the same one I ask myself every time I'm compelled to do something. I know it's crazy to believe that I'm right, but I have to ask myself what would happen if I decided I wasn't and it turned out I was."

He straightened in his chair. "Elisabeth, I can promise you that your stepping on a crack had nothing to do with the man's death. That's just not possible."

She looked at him, eyes narrowing. "You don't know that. How do you even know that I'm not the psychologist and you're just my delusional patient who thinks it's the other way around? Maybe I'm *validating* you, letting you pretend to treat me when really I'm treating you?"

She wished he would react, wished to see anything beneath the molded face and prescription glasses. But he was robotic. "Do you believe that you are my psychologist?"

"No!" she shot forward, then quickly caught herself and returned to her manufactured slouch of feigned insecurity. "No. I don't. I'm just messing with you."

"Elisabeth, in light of recent events, I'm hoping you will reconsider taking the prescription I've recommended."

"No. I know it can't make this any better."

"It will help with the anxiety…"

"You think this is anxiety?" she laughed harshly. "I'm not anxious. I'm busy. Busy doing pointless things. I need to know why."

"I've told you."

She stood up. "All right, I've had enough. Not today. No more."

"Elisabeth, wait." Dr. Sherman twisted in his chair and pulled a book off of a nearby shelf. "This is a text on anxiety disorders. I can sense that you are a very bright young woman. You might find this helpful."

She took it, even though she didn't understand why he thought she'd trust a book better than his word.

"I'll see you next week, then," he said. He was ending the session early. It didn't matter. She wasn't going to say anything else. All that mattered was that he was satisfied. It meant she could walk out the door and not find men in white coats standing by her car with a giant net.

"Yes," she said, then forced out a thank you.

He bowed down with his silver pen. It glinted. She wanted to touch it. But it wrote her off, told her secrets, caged her in thick dark lines shaped like D's, hooked her in C's, swallowed her in O's.

She didn't need this. If she was really all that crazy, she could talk to herself for free.

3

Libby walked into the hospital the next morning to find that nothing had changed. There was still that singular hospital smell: a mixture of sterilizing chemicals and human sweat. The typical sights awaited her on the daily walk to the emergency room. Televisions playing on low volume in empty waiting rooms. Wheelchairs and gurneys stashed hastily in rooms that had lost their original purpose. Doors marked with red barriers that required her to slide a card or punch a code. Habit and apprehension carried her down each white linoleum hall as she chased the reflection of the overhead lights.

When she entered the ER, she caught Jay coming out of one of the patient examination rooms, swinging his stethoscope back around his neck and looking startled to see her.

"Thought you were going to blow us off again today," he greeted her.

"A guy got hit by a car yesterday."

"I know. They brought him in. He was gone before they got him through the door." He shook his head sadly, a solemn gesture so inconsistent with the Jay that Libby had known since freshman year of college. It never failed to astonish her that he had grown up and she hadn't.

"Yeah, well, I was sort of standing next to him when it happened," she relished, "The cops needed me to make a statement. Then – I guess I just needed some time."

Jay's eyebrows disappeared beneath his choppy hairline, "Are you all right?"

"I'm not the one that got hit by the car."

Jay looked as though he didn't know what to say to that, and so Libby spared him by moving on as though he'd said something spectacular and conclusive. "Did my resident notice I wasn't here?"

"No," Jay smiled. "But if he asks, you spent a lot of time yesterday in the bathroom."

Libby sighed and peered past Jay into the exam room from which he'd just come. "Are there a lot of work-ups?"

"Just one left. I'd say you ought to take it to return to the favor, but she might have an infection."

Libby looked up at him with unending gratitude, hoping he knew how much he meant to her. Jay was the only person outside of the psychiatric community that knew the truth. Or at least Libby's version of it, in which she was perfectly contained and the whole thing was just a mild inconvenience. She had to play that part. Despite a fear of disease, she had chosen a vocation that dealt intimately with it. Jay knew the truth about that too, how Mom and Dad had invested in her and now expected heavy returns. Now, she mused that she would fund their retirement in Cabo and then buy an expensive hand-woven robe to fashion into a noose.

"I'll take care of her," Jay said, laying a hand on Libby's shoulder. She was comfortable under it, though not because she had feelings for him. Rather, it was the opposite. They'd been friends through school, drawn together by Libby's chaos and Jay's love of putting things in order. Libby had never let anyone else in and that was how she liked it. People were confusing, destructive, and selfish. If she let them in, they would want to take her apart. Jay tidied up.

"Anything I can do to return the favor?" she asked.

He sighed, buying time to pick the most innocuous response. "Well, I guess you can go down to pharmacy and pick up meds for Dr. Dugan. He's up in oncology and apparently thinks that since all I do down here is watch the second-hand go round and round, I'm free to do his leg-work."

Libby laughed dryly. "Well, he sure nailed what I do then. When will they be ready?"

"I'm guessing about ten minutes."

He looked uneasy, torn between getting back to his life and continuing to wade in the mire of hers.

"Go on. I'll be fine."

He still looked unconvinced. "We'll talk about this later, I promise."

"Nothing to talk about," she said, curling the edges of her lips up into a forced smile.

"You sure?"

She enhanced the gesture. "Positive."

"Okay then," he returned the smile, though his was fluid and sincere. Libby realized that she had acquired a need to leave everyone else satisfied. It gave her the slightest sense of control. If she couldn't pull herself together, she could at least strengthen her persona.

Jay moved away, directed to the infected patient – the patient he would touch and heal. All of a sudden, Libby's hands burned and she didn't know why. The exam room door closed and she heard Jay's murmured introduction through the door. He belonged here. She belonged in the same way the plastic ferns and pastel paintings and stacks of magazines in the waiting rooms did. Not by choice. Not even for any essential purpose. Just because someone thought they'd look nice in this sort of situation.

The burning escalated. Libby jammed her hands deep into the pockets of her white coat and clenched her fingers, feeling her raw skin sting as it stretched across her knuckles. She meandered over to the nurses' station, paused in front of the chart rack and ran her fingers along the spines, feigning a purpose.

"Dr. Cohen," a voice urged behind her. *Crap*, Libby thought, turning to the voice. It was Darlene, one the one of the nurses that Libby didn't particularly like. Darlene always managed to make it look like she was in the middle of something even if she wasn't. In her presence, Libby's sense of uselessness grew more acute.

"Yeah?"

Darlene allowed her conjured air of importance to fade just briefly, tilting her head and studying Libby from head to foot. Libby, however, did not allow herself to be swayed by Darlene's condescending probing. If the woman had made it her personal mission to drive Libby away from medical practice, she was just going to have to wait in line with fear of disease and lack of basic social skills.

"There's an incoming overdose victim. Dr. Grant is tied up and he's asking you to stabilize him."

Libby felt her face flame-up. She looked towards the door through which Jay had disappeared. *When am I going to be able to do this on my own?*

"Dr. Cohen?" Darlene urged.

Libby swallowed the breath caught in her throat and turned back to Darlene, willing her cheeks to return to their normal pallor.

"Fine. How long until they arrive?"

But her question was answered by the swishing pop of the ER doors opening. Two paramedics entered, flanking a gurney upon which a young man lay. He was clothed in a neatly tailored shirt and trousers, with hair perfectly styled and face without stubble residue. Yet the trace of spittle foaming at the corner of the immaculately shaven chin gave away his dark truth. In another life, he was one of the herd of business-coat wearing, briefcase carrying, clean-shaven young men that piled in and out of the subway stations on their way to making sales and high-teching their way past an old school generation. The only distinguishing feature that separated him from the others, apart from the pallor of drug-induced shock, was a tattoo running up the inside of his forearm. In calligraphic script, it read: Amor Vincit Omnia. Libby wondered what it meant and why it mattered to him, or, why it had not mattered enough to save him from this choice he had made.

"Doctor?" one of the paramedics urged, narrowly missing her head with his arm as he held an IV fluid bag aloft.

She realized he was speaking to her. "What's the story?" she asked.

"26 year old male, overdosed on antidepressant. We found an empty bottle of Tofranil in the bathroom. BP is 80 palp, bradycardic. Tongue is lacerated. He might have had a seizure and bit through it."

"He's going into shock," the other paramedic added, just in case it wasn't obvious from the man's gray, moist skin and dangerously low blood pressure.

"In there," Libby pointed to the nearest trauma room. The trio maneuvered through the door, then brought the gurney beside the bed in the center of the room. With one swift transfer, the charge had been placed in Libby's care.

Three nurses had followed them in and were now looking at Libby with anticipation. She inflated her lungs slowly and then exhaled a stream of orders, following textbook algorithms. Meanwhile, while still keeping a safe distance from the man's sweat-soaked body, she tried to remember what she'd learned about Tofranil overdoses. It was the only thing that could save him; the simplest way to end the cascading problems – the low blood pressure, the slow heart rate, the shock. Yet though she could picture herself in the class where she'd learned the information, nothing was clear. How could it be, when half of her mind was still focused on getting away? She cringed. Another slowly drawn breath tasted of acrid smoke.

"BP is still dropping."

Libby felt the floor beneath her feet sway. She steadied herself, just in time to be hit with a sudden revelation.

"Stop fluids and prepare 1 unit Sodium Bicarb for IV injection."

As one of the nurses ran out to fill the order, Jay appeared at the doorway. His eyes scanned the room rapidly.

"Need any help in here?"

Libby shook her head, keeping her eyes on the blood pressure monitor, watching the digital numbers hovering on the insolently low number.

"What happened to this guy?" Jay asked.

"Suicide attempt," one of the paramedics replied, moving close to Libby's shoulder - far too close.

"Then we're not doing him a favor," Libby murmured, pulling away.

Jay was forced aside as the nurse returned with the medication. Libby held her breath and watched as she injected the solution into the IV already coursing into the man's tattooed arm.

It only took a few moments for the flickering readout to begin rising - by ones, then by fives. Color began to find its way back into the man's ashen cheeks. Libby breathed slowly through pursed lips. He was going to make it.

"Dr. Cohen?"

She looked up.

"Should we admit him to the psyche ward?"

Libby stepped back, staggering under the weight of her guilt, a force generated from the part of her that recognized a fellow resident of her brand of purgatory. In only a matter of minutes, this man would reopen his eyes to the nightmare and realize that he had failed.

"He called 911?" she asked the paramedics.

One of them nodded. "Said he'd tried to kill himself then hung up."

"Then admit him to the general ICU for now and call for a psyche consult."

The nurse looked at her skeptically. She couldn't have known that Libby hoped that the man would talk his way past the consulting psychiatrist. As Libby had just played her own role flawlessly, she understood the importance of this man's masquerade. Perhaps he would live to die another day, but imprisonment here would not deter him. The truth was, this man had not wanted to die. The claws of the world were still deeply entrenched in his back, holding him back from crossing his own yellow line.

*

In a matter of minutes, all the pieces were back where they belonged and Libby was outside the pharmacy, waiting to complete her innocuous task.

The aide at the window had taken Libby's information and then departed into the back room, without even offering Libby a word of instruction. So, itching from the awkward sensation of having no reason to occupy the space she was in, Libby shifted her weight from foot to foot beside the window.

Finally, the back room door opened. A tall young man in a white lab coat emerged, holding a plastic red biohazard bag in one gloved hand. Libby, who was on her way to resume her position in front of the window, began to have second thoughts.

"Dr. Cohen?" the man asked.

"Yes," she admitted, moving closer to the window but still maintaining a safe distance.

Sensing her uneasiness, the pharmacist lifted the bag to eye-level and checked the label as though he'd gotten something wrong.

"10 units of vincristine?" he confirmed.

"Yeah. For Dr. Dugan,"

He set it down on the counter and slid it towards her.

"Do I need gloves?" Libby asked, as the bright red of the bag flashed like warning lights behind her eyes.

"Would you like some?" he asked, taken aback.

"I just thought…" she trailed off, looking pointedly at his own gloved hands.

"Oh," he lifted them, "I have these on because I was filling the vial."

She was silent, prompting him to take further steps to explain himself. "It's chemo – a cellular toxin. That's how it works. You don't want to get any on you."

"So...I should have gloves?"

He gave the hint of a smile, "Well, the bag isn't toxic."

"Right, but." Libby stopped herself. She had a burning question and in any other circumstance, she would have asked it. But in this case...her eyes moved to the pharmacist's nametag. *Jon.* He was young like her, maybe a year or two older. His perfectly combed light brown hair was cut close to his head in the sort of 1950's hairstyle that a man with a girlfriend couldn't get away with. But it was his eyes that captured her; they were withdrawn and piercing all at once. The blue around his dark pupils shone like shallow, unpolluted water. A laugh echoed inside her mind, bouncing off the edges of whirling thoughts that had all come to a sudden halt. She knew why she couldn't pull away. He was dull, he was clean, and more than likely he still thought she was just quirky. If she invited him in, he'd take his shoes off at the door.

"Dr. Cohen?"

Libby tore herself away from his eyes so quickly, it hurt her own. "Yes?"

"Would you like me to get you some gloves?"

She thought about the distant possibility that some of the drug spilled onto the outside of the vial and then was transferred to the outside of the bag. But for some reason, it didn't seem to matter. The question was still in her, scalding her as she dismissed his question with a throaty laugh and then reached for the hazard bag – quickly sliding her hands out from beneath the sleeves of her oversized coat, where she usually hid their ugly rawness. She then gripped the bag by the corner least likely to have been touched by a spill and lifted it into the air.

Seized in that position, she looked up at Jon. He had no idea what a triumph this was. She'd done it all for him, for the slightest possibility that somewhere down the line he'd say to himself, "I need a date tonight, but every girl I know is mentally unstable. But wait a minute! There was that girl who handled that toxic medication with such finesse! I'll give her a call." Wouldn't that be wonderful, Libby thought. I'd finally have proof that something about my life was normal.

She gave him a thumbs-up with her free hand and then instantly regretted it. But he rewarded her with a gentle laugh, then after returning the gesture, departed into the back room. Well, she thought, he's going to look my number up in the directory.

Projecting herself far into a perfect future, Libby started down the hall. The bag, clutched between the tips of her thumb and index finger, swung ominously from side to side as she walked. Libby wondered if she should take an extra precaution and hold her breath, just in case any of the molecules of toxin were flung from the bag and into the air. But it was a long walk from the pharmacy to the cancer ward, so Libby opted for keeping her head twisted as far to the side as she could muster.

Only a few steps later, however, she found her path halted by a sudden collision. As she flung her arms wide to catch her balance, the bag of medication was sent airborne. Libby turned just in time to see it begin a trajectory towards the opposite wall. Knowing that she didn't have time to run, she wrenched her body away and covered her head. Moments later the bag hit, the thud of impact accompanied by the subtle sound of cracking glass. It was the kind of thing that only a person in her condition would hear.

Libby turned back to the scene of disaster, eyes avoiding the bag which now lay several feet from her. The person with whom she had collided murmured an apology and then delivered a "shit happens" smile. Libby didn't have the strength to respond with the customary "this just isn't my day" shrug. Dissatisfied, the other person walked away. Libby's uneasiness swelled.

She had to get the vial back to pharmacy. They'd have to replace it, probably dock her pay. They'd ask her what happened and she couldn't possibly explain it in any way that didn't make her look like a fool. This mistake would pollute Jon's eyes.

Her eyes finally found the red biohazard bag. She couldn't just leave it there, but she couldn't touch it either. The drugs had spilled. She'd refused gloves. *Damnit, why didn't I just take the gloves?*

Think about it Libby, she scolded herself. *If these bags were permeable to chemicals, they wouldn't be very effective.*

That was the war within her. Justification. Common sense justified sanity, while the much stronger voice convinced her that in this case, things were different. Common sense, stoned on dopamine, always backed down.

This time, things might be different.

"Fine," she muttered, conceding yet again though it filled her with a torrid anger. Her fingernails found a rough patch of skin on her thumb and tore. Skin ripped in a satisfying rush of pain. It was what she deserved.

Now what? She dialed the hospital operator. Pharmacy? Extension 111, I'll connect you in just a moment. Ring. Ring. Ring.

A woman answered.

"Hi, this is Dr. Cohen. Is Jon there?"

She didn't know why she'd asked for him. Maybe because this would get back to him anyway and confronting him about it directly would at least soften his new perception of her. Otherwise he'd only remember her as the weird girl whose clumsiness cost him another hour's work.

Jon came to the phone with a little innocent "hello?" that made Libby hate herself further.

"Hi, this is Dr. Cohen."

"Oh, hi," he said, casually enough so that she knew he at least hadn't pushed her out of his memory yet.

"Hey. So, I kind of – screwed up a little."

He was silent. Of course. What kind of idiot would phrase it the way she just had? *Listen to yourself, Libby. What kind of person talks like that?*

"I dropped the vincristine," she said, recovering by adding a detached professionalism to her tone. "I didn't want to open the bag up, but I think the vial broke."

He laughed, the kind of nervous laughter that was meant to cover the lack of a good response. "Okay. Do you want to bring the broken one back and I can replace it?"

"Um…" she stopped herself before asking if she needed gloves. That was how she'd started the first conversation and it hadn't gotten her very far. "Sure. I'll be right there."

She hung up before she could contaminate him. It didn't matter that he had a nice body and would probably bring her flowers and a puppy on their first date, all that mattered was that one decent person in this God-forsaken world thought she was one too. Besides, if Libby Cohen had learned anything from this disease, it was how to find alternative courses of action. There was Jay. And even though the whole point of this had been so he didn't have to take time out of his caseload to deliver meds, she knew he would rescue her.

So she called him, and with minimal taunting he agreed to come. She waited uneasily for him, guarding the red bag and offering half-smiles to passers-by to prevent them from noticing that here was a person who had apparently dropped something and was afraid to pick it up.

When Jay arrived, he easily picked up the bag. She tried not to humor the part of her mind that wanted to find irony in this and instead focused on planning the clandestine drop. Maybe Jon wouldn't have to know that she was afraid.

"Just leave it on the windowsill and run, okay?" Libby said, as the two approached the pharmacy.

"Do I have to run?" Jay laughed. "I might crash into something like you did and then neither one of us will be able to pick up whatever I break."

"Don't even do that right now," she snapped.

They reached the pharmacy window. Jay set the bag down, hit the bell with a grand gesture and then mimed a slow-motion sprint. He was around the corner before Libby had a chance to sort out whether or not to yell at him or laugh.

Jon himself was beckoned by the bell. Libby, still recovering from Jay's exhibition, didn't immediately notice his flustered appearance.

"Is that it?" he asked, his voice seeming rushed and breathless. It got Libby's attention.

"What's wrong?"

He met her eyes and quickly looked away. Color was weaving its way into his pale cheeks in spidery pink lines. "Nothing."

Libby wasn't convinced. If there was one thing she understood well, it was this very thing. Helpless fear being smothered.

"What happened to you between the time we talked and now?" she asked boldly.

He looked up, his eyes widening slightly. Libby understood his apprehension, and knew it was one of her own failings. When it mattered, she said whatever she felt she needed to say, despite social graces. It intimidated most people, and Libby was convinced it was one of her mechanisms for driving them away.

But Jon fell for it. "It was the wrong drug," he said, leaning close and lowering his voice. "I put the wrong drug in the vial."

Libby tried to underscore the severity of this by controlling her expression. Still, she couldn't help feel a shiver of apprehension.

"How do you know?"

"After you called, I went to look up the batch number so I could mark the loss in the inventory. The number wasn't there. I looked it up in the computer and that's when I realized I'd grabbed something else."

"What was it?"

"It doesn't matter." He sighed and leaned away. "It would've been bad. I could've lost my job. I could still lose my job."

He looked up at her. Libby hesitated. She was plagued with never knowing what to do or say. In some cases, however, instinct took over. This, she felt, was one of those times.

"Hey," she leaned forward and laid her hand on his arm. But as his eyes fell onto it, she quickly drew it back into her sleeve. "Look, you made a mistake. It's this thing that humans do sometimes. As far as I'm concerned, you've got someone up there watching out for you and I'm not going to get in the way of that. I'm not going to tell anyone."

She sensed that he was too decent to accept it. He had been the sort of kid who would tell the teacher if he'd accidentally seen an answer on a classmate's test.

"I can't do that. It's just…" his eyes grew vacant, "I really need this job."

She was surprised. He was crumbling right before her eyes. She took a step back, afraid she was transferring her chaos into him. Sure enough, when he met her eyes again, she saw that a hasty cover of whitewash had been painted over the cracks.

"I appreciate your honesty," he said, then rethought this. "Or, your dishonesty. But I'm going to have to deal with this. At least we stopped someone from getting hurt."

"We?"

Jon laughed and felt heat coursing on the surface of his cheeks, a blush he could not hide. *She's beautiful,* he thought, and then wondered where the thought had come from. But she could make him laugh about terrible things. It was a release he hadn't allowed in years and it felt like a fever breaking. He could see her evaluating him, with her patient eyes. There was a vibrant effervescence behind their stark green hue. Even in her awkward stance, hands shoved deep into coat pockets and thin shoulders hunched, he saw her remarkable energy. Her hair was a deep brown, but light played off the chin-length chunks like moonlight glistening on dark water. Though her face was small and heart-shaped, her eyes were big and expressive. Everything about her was soft and alluring. She was like a kitten he just wanted to reach out and pet.

All of a sudden his heart went into overdrive and he knew what he was about to do. As he formed the words, he preceded them with a short gasping laugh and she cocked her head and asked him what was wrong.

"Nothing. It's just - the very least I can do is offer to buy you dinner. I mean – with me. You and I, getting dinner together."

Libby's smile dropped and to fill the absence of an intelligible response, she murmured an inquisitive grunt.

"I'm sorry," Jon's face transitioned from spidery pink to full red. "I shouldn't have. It was much too forward of me."

"No!" she said, and then wondered if that had sounded too enthusiastic. She toned it down, playing it as though this sort of thing happened to her every day. "I mean, no. No it's all right. I just didn't see it coming. But I'd love to. Get dinner, I mean. Who doesn't like food?"

Libby replayed her words and cringed, but Jon's relief was palpable. He laughed and handed her his phone, which she realized meant he wanted her number. *Imagine that*, she thought, and wished that the moment had been caught on film. In a way, it seemed as though it was. She was doing something right for once, but at the same time she was only playing a part.

"I get done kind of late," Jon said, "but we can still catch a quick dinner after nine. Where can I pick you up?"

"305 Park Avenue South. Number 323."

They fell into an awkward silence, and Libby began planning her exit strategy. She knew from past experience that the conversation had reached the point where she was at risk to say whatever incoherent thing came to mind just to fill the space. She smiled, returned his phone in what she hoped was a tantalizing fashion, and began to back away.

He stopped her. "Wait."

Oh no.

"Yeah?"

"I don't know your name."

"Oh wow. That's really embarrassing," she said, and then mentally kicked herself. *Don't tell him it's embarrassing. Maybe he wouldn't have noticed.*

"Well, I should've asked."

"You just did. And – my name is Elisabeth. Libby. People call me Libby. Some people do. People that I know. But now I know you and your name is Jon and…"

Libby shut UP.

"And I will see you at nine…Jon."

"Right," he smiled.

Libby turned away and launched into a brisk exit walk. The fire ants were all up and down her arms by now. *What did I just get myself into?*

She rounded the corner and began the 191 steps to the elevator, and though her mind was clouded with remnants of every ridiculous and embarrassing thing that had popped out of her mouth during the five minute conversation with Jon, she managed to remember to touch the painting of the woman in red, the water fountain in front of the men's bathroom, the place where the railings separated, and Dr. and Mrs. Harold Mayer on the engraved plaque of hospital benefactors.

It made her feel a little better, only in that the fire ants left her arms and burrowed their way into her stomach.

What have I done?

4

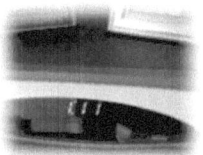

When Jon picked her up it was everything she had expected but the puppy. She'd opened the door to find him retreated against the opposite side of the hall, nervously clutching a bouquet of roses. When he saw her, color rushed out of his cheeks and then surged back in.

He released one hand, looked at it with disdain and then rubbed it furiously across the front of his tan blazer.

"Hi," he said, re-extending the hand and then offering the bouquet. Libby's torn cuticle beds burned, reminding her that she was not soft and perfect. She took the roses first and his hand dropped.

"This is so sweet of you," she said, and then performed the proper ritual of smelling them and putting them in water. While she did this, Jon waited awkwardly in the threshold, shoes still safely within the confines of her welcome mat. It didn't matter. She would let him in. He could probably even sit on her couch. He smelled clean, at least. His hair was slightly more coiffed than she remembered it too, though his face was much less put-together. She could almost feel his anxiety thrumming as she moved past him and into the hall.

He was a perfect gentleman, which Libby knew was rare these days. Not that she had much experience with men of any sorts. Between the demands of medical school and the fear of contact, dating hadn't been a top priority in her life. Still, Libby had experienced enough to sense that, for whatever reason, Jon hadn't done this in a while either. It hit her hardest when he was leaning over her to fasten her seatbelt. His heavy cologne wafted like a sudden front and aroused the butterflies in her stomach. But she felt him, felt his weight as he sank into the drivers' seat, felt his presence infiltrate the healthy space she liked to put between herself and others. It scared her and thrilled her all at once.

As they drove to the restaurant, the conversation remained banal. Libby attributed this to their mutual anxiety. Jon could only talk about the weather and when Libby awkwardly interjected with the standard "getting to know you" questions, he didn't have much to say. This left Libby to fill the space by rambling on about her own answers, though she was certain that Jon could care less which type of adhesive worked best for scrapbooks and which author gave the best social commentary on the 1960's. Thus, she was inordinately thankful when they reached Martini's.

"All set?" Jon said, as he popped open her door and leaned in to unbuckle her. Libby quickly undid herself and plastered on a fake "the past ten minutes haven't been awkward at all" smile.

"Kroger gave this place a great review in the paper," Jon continued, as he led Libby up the stone steps and into the converted townhouse.

Great, Libby thought. *He reads the restaurant reviews.* He probably read the entire paper. Libby only read the comics, and then only in anticipation that one might actually make her laugh. They never did.

"Calahan," Jon gave his name at the hostess desk, which was the first time Libby had heard it. Jon Calahan. Mrs. Elisabeth Calahan. Nice ring. They'd sit together every morning for the next sixty years reading the restaurant reviews together.

The layout of the restaurant was awkward. The entrance had taken them directly into the bar room. A group of middle aged women filled up one side of the long mahogany bar, chatting loudly, laughs made loose and piercing by the house martinis and gin and tonics. In their pantsuits and pearls they seemed out of place in the haze of blue cigarette smoke swirling beneath dim lights. It was only when the hostess led them through the bar that Libby's eyes fell on the one individual who so perfectly belonged. Beyond the long line of women, the bar turned and headed left a ways before colliding with the warped wooden walls. On that end, the man sat with his head bent low and hands resting folded on the tabletop, wreathed by an array of empty glasses. His eyes stared blankly ahead, not focusing on anything or any thought but simply vacant, voided by each glass that had been emptied. More eerie than this, however, was his face – a plastic molded face that had lost its blood and become the color and consistency of putty. Libby didn't understand why seeing this face caused her to drop out of step behind Jon and stop, transfixed, watching him as he raised a cigarette to his swollen lips and sucked in a shallow breath without even moving his eyes.

"Are you all right?"

Jon's voice seemed to come to her from a distance, sneaking through the muted sound of voices murmuring and forks scraping against plates in the next room. Libby tore herself away from the man and turned to Jon, and though he was close to her, she felt the space between them swell. The unblemished eyes were concerned and unable to understand why the girl before him felt that she had been born for moments like this: moments of some sort of lucidity that came and left before she could understand their meaning.

"Thought I recognized someone," Libby murmured, looking past him to the room beyond. The hostess lingered in the doorway, watching them with an annoyed expression.

"Come on," Libby pushed him onward. Yet even as they moved away, Libby felt the man's presence heavy on her shoulders.

It was hard to hide the vacancy in her eyes, or the way she stumbled distractedly into her chair as Jon pulled it out for her. Yet, when she saw the tremors in his hands as he laid the cloth napkin across her lap, she abruptly returned. Here before her was a different sort of enigma. Jon sat down across from her and shifted awkwardly into place, unfolding his napkin and averting his eyes. Libby felt her breath quicken.

"Would you like something to drink?" Jon asked, meeting her eyes briefly before hiding them in the wine list.

Libby hesitated, chasing away an impulsive and awkward response and replacing it with social grace. "What do you recommend?"

"Do you prefer a red or white?"

Libby didn't really know. She drank Diet Coke. This was too much.

Jon, sensing her hesitation, continued. "Depends, of course, on what you're having. A red wine is good with steak. White, I've heard, goes best with fish."

"I usually don't eat fish."

"Oh?" he looked at her over the top of the menu, "Are you allergic?"

"No. I have a fear of fish."

He didn't laugh or smile or make any sort of indication that he didn't think she was serious. Libby furrowed her brow and looked away. What had happened to the guy she'd met earlier that day? Perhaps he still existed. Perhaps it was only she, the oil, who was unable to penetrate the clear waters of his eyes that were afraid to reflect her form.

"We'll try this one." Jon said, closing the wine list and setting it gently down. "Chablis number 8."

"Sounds good."

But it had never come easy for her. She knew all about her own misgivings. Fear of betrayal, perhaps, or fear that if she was not meant to participate in normal existence then love too was out of reach. Of course, she did everything in her power sometimes to avoid intimacy. Jay always told her that her standards were too high, but she had never expected a knight in shining armor. She craved someone who could see through her own.

For 26 years she had been a misfit, a puzzle piece thrown in the wrong box. She yearned to one day discover another mislaid piece among the others; another whose picture was similar to hers, whose shape fit smoothly into her own.

What was rapidly becoming clear to Libby was that Jon was a mislaid piece, but he didn't belong to her picture either. Like the man in the bar, he had stricken her because he was one of her kind, an outlier, an anomaly. Libby wondered if maybe her purpose in life was to round them all up and form some sort of revolution – or at least a support group.

"Tell me about yourself," Jon asked her, unfolding and then refolding his napkin, calming the tremors in his hands.

Libby shrugged. "Not much to tell." *Of course*, she thought. *So much to tell that you can't know.* She pulled her hands out from beneath her napkin and laid them on the edge of the table, looking at her nails. The polish was already chipped from the constant picking. After this was over, she'd go home and it would just be this. For the rest of her life, she'd live with this.

"What do you like to do?" Jon insisted.

"I read a lot."

"Really?" he laughed, easing up a little. "Do you have a favorite author?"

"No. I read a lot of non-fiction," she hesitated, wondering if she was supposed to say she liked glamour guides and chick lit.

"About?" Jon prompted.

She went for it. "I'm kind of a history buff."

"I see" Jon smiled. The reflection of the candlelight swelled in his eyes. "I never did like history – all those names and dates."

"I just feel a connection to the past," she explained, hoping it wasn't too much. "Sometimes I feel like I don't belong in this time."

Jon's smile drooped slightly. It was too much, Libby realized. I'm not supposed to be complicated. The man can't handle it.

"What about you?" she asked. "What do you like to do?"

He laughed tersely, dismissing the question.

"What does that mean?" she asked, narrowing her eyes and smiling in what she hoped was a coquettish manner.

"Nothing. I just – I don't have much time to myself these days."

"Work?" Libby guessed.

The candlelight disappeared from his eyes. "Yes. Work."

"Oh."

The waitress came for their orders. Jon requested the Chablis and then asked for a few moments to decide on an appetizer. Grateful for the distraction, Libby opened her menu and pretended to read.

"How about a shrimp cocktail?" Jon asked.

Without looking up, Libby reminded him that she was afraid of fish.

"Oh, of course. I apologize."

"No problem."

"Have you ever had fried eggplant?"

To Libby, it sounded absolutely disgusting. But she was willing to do anything to end this mindless discussion.

"I love it."

"We'll have that then." Jon closed his menu definitively and laid it back down. Libby noticed the way he treated things with care. The menu so gently folded. The napkin laid so straight.

"So," Libby began, pulling out a last-ditch conversational gem, "How do you like working at the pharmacy?"

Jon was saved the trouble of answering by the muted sound of Ave Maria chiming somewhere beneath the table. He put his hand over his pocket, seemingly hesitating, looking between Libby and some vacant spot behind her.

"Is it yours?" she prompted.

"Yeah," he murmured, voice not seeing to come from within him.

He pulled his cell phone out of his pocket and brought it to his ear.

"Hey," he greeted the caller in a hushed tone, "What's up?"

As the caller responded, Libby watched Jon's eyes slowly drift downward.

"Alright. It's fine. No, I'm on a date. Yes, really." Jon's eyes met Libby's momentarily before re-descending. "No, it's fine. I'll be right there. Just stay where you are."

He flipped his phone shut and slipped it back into his pocket, eyes still on the ground.

"Everything okay?" Libby asked.

"Libby, I'm sorry. I need to cut this date short."

Libby tried to hide her surprise. "Jon, that's fine. Whatever you need to do, go do it."

"I'm sorry, I just – " Jon leaned forward and spoke softly, "That was my brother Andrew. I have to go pick him up."

"Is he okay?"

"Yes, he is now. He's…" Jon fell into silence, eyes moving to the door.

"Alright," Libby stood up, "Come on. We'll go get him. You can take me home later, don't worry about it."

Jon threw a few wadded dollar bills on the table as an apologetic tip and then stood. "Thank you, Libby. I really am sorry."

"It's fine."

Jon nodded, mumbled something to himself and then hurried past her. As Libby followed, the waitress caught her eye and gave her a quizzical look. Libby could do nothing but shrug. She had no idea where they were going either.

Jon continued mumbling to himself as they pulled out of the parking lot. Though Libby didn't want to pry into Jon's personal life, she knew she had to at least channel this anxiety. His face was a bright red and hadn't faded since they'd left.

"Jon, what's really going on? Is everything okay?"

Jon's fingers tightened around the steering wheel and then gradually released. "I've never told anyone this before, Libby. But, I mean – " he paused, forcing out a dry laugh, "One of the reasons I asked you out was because I thought you'd understand."

"Understand what?"

"Abnormality."

Libby wasn't sure how she felt about that.

"I'm sorry," Jon said quickly, sensing her hesitation. "I don't mean it like that. My brother - he has a disorder that they call dissociative fugue. It's a psychiatric condition."

Libby's breath caught in her throat. She coughed. "Really?"

"Ever since we were kids, he has these episodes where he forgets who he is or becomes somebody else. Next thing he knows he wakes up halfway across town. He has no idea what he's done or where he's gone. Sometimes he's cut up and bleeding and he doesn't know why. And I've got to go get him, wherever, whenever."

"Jesus," Libby breathed, "Isn't that dangerous? I mean, what if he goes and sits down on the railroad tracks?"

The muscles in Jon's jaw twitched. She'd hit a nerve.

"That's why I've got to be there. It's either that or they'll put him in a residential treatment facility. I'm not letting that happen. Not after what she went through."

Libby recognized that Jon was no longer really talking to her. The baggage he was unloading was starting to become unbearably heavy and more just kept falling out of the plane. Whether or not Jon believed she'd understand his anomalous existence, she'd come to the conclusion that the best course of action was to forget this evening entirely and make a point to avoid the pharmacy in the future. *Of course*, she thought, rolling her eyes at her reflection in the side mirror. *Why should I have expected any part of my life to remain safely unblemished?*

Jon pulled the car off of the main street and into darkness. Libby could hear the pavement rushing, whispering beneath the tires as they rolled down poorly lit back roads.

"How do you know where he is?" Libby asked, as neon and steel suddenly gave way to crumbling plaster and pools of yellow light.

Jon didn't answer. He leaned forward, eyes scanning the road with intense scrutiny. Libby turned to peer out her window and caught, in passing, the reflection of orange light on two eyes staring out of a pile of boxes in an alley.

Just a block later, Jon pulled the car to a stop at the curb, shifted into park and then laid his hands on his lap, drawing a deep breath.

"You can wait here if you want," he murmured.

"No." Libby undid her seatbelt and let it slide over her shoulder and wind back up, noisily. Jon looked up at her. "I'll come. Where is he?"

Jon shook his head slightly and then pushed open the door. Libby followed. They were outside of what had once been a video store, as advertised by faded letters on the mildewed brick above the door. The windows were boarded up and painted with graffiti, so old that its artists were probably on the straight and narrow now - businessmen somewhere. A single streetlamp cast a flickering pool of light on the ground beneath them, offering nothing to the deep shadows closing in on either side. Libby moved into the light as the wail of a police siren sounded suddenly from nearby.

"Jon," a weak voice called from the darkness.

Jon moved forward and crouched, so that only the back of his suit jacket was still illuminated.

"Are you alright?" Jon's voice was stern, father-like. Libby shifted uncomfortably.

"Yeah. Everything's fantastic."

In an awkward motion, Jon helped his brother to his feet and then moved him into the light. Andrew was leaning heavily on Jon, his eyes on the ground. As his eyes drifted over Libby's shadow, however, he looked up at her.

Libby couldn't understand exactly what she saw in his eyes, but she imagined it was the sort of expression one might have upon waking from a nightmare into a bright room: a vestige of fear dying beneath confusion and then relief.

"Libby, this is Andrew." Jon made the awkward introduction. But Libby barely heard him. Her eyes fell away from Andrew and onto his shirtsleeve, which was dotted with dark blood.

"You're hurt," she moved forward, healer instinct taking over. Andrew shifted his weight off of his brother and twisted his neck to watch Libby as her fingers grazed his sleeve. She curled the fabric beneath her fingers and her skin came into contact with the sticky blood. It would have ordinarily killed her, the fear of blood borne pathogens driving needles into her skin, activating a reflexive withdrawal. But her fingers were steady and her heart, though racing, embraced the first fearless moment she had ever felt in her life.

She rolled up his sleeve to reveal a broad sculpted bicep, resting gently beneath skin that, unlike his brother's, was a flawless golden tone. A black tattoo – something looking like interwoven tongues of flame - wrapped around his arm. Just above it was a two-inch gash.

"How did this happen?' Libby asked, her fingertips hovering just above his skin, outlining the wound.

"I don't know," Andrew said, and with his other hand folded his sleeve down to hide the gash.

"Is it okay? Jon asked, drawing closer.

Andrew's fingers fell, brushing against Libby's. The moment of contact seemed to startle him. He withdrew, eyes stricken and feral. At the same time Libby replied "yes" to Jon, Andrew uttered a whispered "no."

"What's wrong?" Jon pushed further into the light, forcing Libby back. As she stumbled into the darkness, she looked up and found Andrew's eyes still watching her over Jon's shoulder. She wanted to look away, but she couldn't. The very same thing that had drawn her to the putty-faced man in the bar kept her from it. There was a hurried sensation in her chest and a feeling of being on high alert. For just one moment, she had broken the surface. Dark water rose and fell on either side of her, spilling over in waves that threatened to pound her back into the depths of the ocean, keeping her from the sweet air she so desperately craved. But for now, while Andrew's eyes locked onto hers, she drew in desperate, gasping mouthfuls.

"You're fine," Jon said, and then he turned to Libby and wrenched her eyes away from Andrew's. Though Libby wilted from the sudden separation, her heightened alertness detected a sort of innocent confusion in Jon's eyes.

"Nothing to worry about," he said, misinterpreting her fear, "Everything's all right."

"Right," Libby nodded in slow jerking movements. "It's just – this isn't the safest part of town."

"You're right, I'm so sorry," Jon laughed in nervous gasps, "This has to be the worst date you've ever been on."

Libby threw her head back and laughed, a universal female gesture that allowed one to evade lying. "Not so bad."

Not looking entirely convinced, Jon snapped into a desperate retreat. After commanding Andrew into the backseat, he rushed forward to pull open Libby's car door. She climbed in past him, trying to avoid his eyes. She knew how desperate he must be right now, even more so than when they hadn't been able to decide on an appetizer. It was best to pretend that none of this had happened.

Jon shut Libby's door and then hurried around to the other side of the car to help Andrew in. Under his brother's care, Andrew studiously abandoned his volition and let his body slacken over the seatbelt Jon was guiding into place. Accepting his dependence was, as his weary smile indicated, a sort of protest to him.

Once Andrew was settled, Jon climbed into the drivers' seat and hesitated for a few moments before igniting the engine. Libby sensed he was groping for an explanation and wished she could tell him he didn't need one. She just wanted out. Every muddy footprint was burning in her mind.

"He's okay now," he finally said softly. "It just tires him out."

"Okay," Libby said, hoping it was enough. But it wasn't. Jon remained trapped in the oppressive silence, needing to say more – for her sake and his own. "What was he doing?" she conceded, eyes lifting again to the rearview mirror to see Andrew now passed out against the window.

"God only knows. We got lucky this time."

He sighed brutally and twisted the key in the ignition, resuscitating the sputtering engine. Raindrops splattered suddenly on the windshield, each one containing a shifting dot of gold light cast down by the street lamps. Jon turned on the wipers, erasing them.

"Last May he called me from a payphone," he continued, "Said he had no idea where he was, but everyone appeared to be speaking French."

Libby snorted, a last minute attempt to cover a laugh that was probably inappropriate. But Jon's features relaxed into a weary smile, the sort of expression a father might have when discovering that his son had gotten into a fight at school and won.

"Have you heard the expression running amok?" he asked.

"Sure."

"Amok refers to an Indian tribe whose members would lose time and go on spiritual journeys – or at least, what they thought were spiritual journeys. Really, it was dissociation."

Well, Libby thought. He had this down to a speech, complete with gentle explanation, humorous anecdote and cultural allusion. She came complete with speeches too. That's what people on the outside wanted this to be. Quirks, idiosyncrasies. To them it was all about the disease – the symptoms, the consequences. They didn't understand what really mattered: the horrifying sense of being out of control of one's own actions, slave to a mind that ran amok. Captive and captor were one in the same.

Jon's eyes shifted to the rearview mirror and then returned to the road. Whatever he had seen had convinced him Andrew was asleep, for he spoke candidly.

"Libby, I'm sorry. I should've known this would happen."

"It's not your fault. You're doing a good thing by taking care of him, but you have to have a life of your own."

"I know. It's just been like this for so long. I thought – well, I thought I'd take a chance, ask a girl out. Believe it or not, I haven't dated since high school."

Libby hid a smile.

"I just wanted to get away from this all," he continued, "You know, find a nice normal girl, have a nice, normal relationship. Candle-lit dinners. Walks on the beach."

Libby's heart sagged. He wanted normal? She wasn't the way to go.

"Jon, maybe we – " she began.

But he interrupted. "Will you let me try this again some evening?"

From his hurried tone, Libby knew that he was well aware of what she had been about to say. She hesitated, fixating on a scuff of dirt on the dashboard. It really wasn't possible for her to walk away now. There was no spark between her and Jon and little hope of kindling one. He had wanted the same thing she did, to escape insanity by feigning roles in the real world: the happy couple. It just couldn't happen. Not with the persistent chaos that followed her everywhere, and knowing that it was quelled only by her need to demystify the strange boy in the backseat. There was something about him that she couldn't let go of, and as Andrew's presence invaded her mind like a sweet obsession, she told Jon she would take a second date. It was wrong, she knew, but she was no stranger to relinquishing control. Why start fighting back now?

As Jon pulled to a stop outside of her apartment, Libby opened her door before he could get it into his mind to get out and do it for her. She climbed out onto the curb, then turned and leaned into the open doorway. "I'd say thanks for a wonderful time, but…well."

Jon's laugh broke through his tension in staggering gasps. It woke Andrew, who shifted for a moment and then leaned forward into the space between the seats.

"You're leaving?" he asked Libby.

"Yeah. It's late." To demonstrate, she gestured to the clock on Jon's dash. The display flickered back at her, 11:11. Libby felt her heart drop. *Don't tell me that's happening again.*

"Yeah. Nearly midnight." Jon said casually. The time meant nothing to him.

"Sorry for ruining what must have been a perfect date," Andrew murmured, and though it sounded as though he'd been planning the quip for a while, the delivery was lost in his distraction as his eyes also fixated on the clock. Libby couldn't take it anymore. She muttered a quick goodbye and then closed the car door forcefully. Jon beeped the horn and pulled away, sound from the sputtering engine ricocheting between the apartment buildings on her street. She watched the car until it turned the block and then watched for a moment more, pulling the darkness back around her like a cloak.

Safely shrouded, Libby made her way back up to her apartment. She kicked her shoes off at the door and stepped into a room filled with orange light bleeding out from two end-table lamps, one dimmer and with a flickering bulb. The radiator popped and clicked from beneath the window. Dots of rain struck the glass in waves carried by the winds that were ushering in the storm. But she was safe inside. Home. Her four walls, her couch, her pile of shoes, her empty Gatorade bottle on the glass coffee table, her dying plant on the window ledge. Yet suddenly, none of it felt familiar.

5

Sleep was seductive, and Libby craved nothing more than to crawl into bed and wrap the blankets around every limb, trapping the warmth close to her body. Nights such as these, when flickering anxiety churned her stomach, she had always imagined ghostly arms wrapping around her in the darkness. The weight of the pillow beside her became the presence of an invisible lover and in the silence she strained to hear his whispers soothing her.

Tonight, the voice became Andrew's. He had infected her mind. All she could see in the darkness behind her eyelids was his face looking down at her while her fingers outlined his wound. He was everything Jon wasn't. His hair was thicker, choppy like rapids tumbling just over his ears. It nearly covered his eyes too, though not enough that she couldn't see the depth and darkness in them that Jon's eyes had lacked. Jon was lean and tall and his posture was stiff, while Andrew's broad shoulders drooped forward just slightly and made him seem young and at ease. Yet his jaw was rigid and defined, as though containing a natural smile.

Still, she hardly knew him and couldn't understand why he was memorable other than the strange feeling she had that she was supposed to remember him.

Andrew finally released his grip on her as her mind gave in to sleep. Soon, Libby found herself in a familiar place: a recurring dream. As always, she found herself standing before a thick set of doors, beside which stood two men dressed in identical suits. In a grand gesture, they pulled open the doors to reveal a large chapel. Its cathedral ceiling was adorned with carved intricacies that captured and tossed around the light pouring in from the bright stained glass windows. The altar was draped with pastel flowers in bouquets woven together so tightly it was hard to tell where one ended and another began. This sheet of dimpled color was the backdrop to a man who stood in a white robe with purple stole, clasping a Bible.

As the doors opened, he looked up at Libby and the congregation stood, moving in slow motion as they craned their necks to watch her entrance. The women wore wide hats and pearled dresses, while the men wore suits and ties. Each pew was adorned with a garland of white roses. A path of perfect white petals stretched between her and the altar.

Libby took a step forward as violins began to play. There was a man waiting for her at the altar, but she was too far from him to see his face. She moved forward, longing to see him, knowing that if she only could, she would understand. But as she took another step, her veil was pulled down over her face and her vision was obscured.

Then, the dream moved rapidly ahead and she found herself suddenly at the altar. She reached for her veil to remove it, but the man before her took her hands and clasped them in his own. Only his form was visible through the haze of white lace.

The preacher began to murmur the words that Libby never truly perceived. She could only feel: her heart beating furiously, the coldness of the ring sliding on her finger. Then came the pronouncement and the priest's voice, so clear now, telling the man to kiss his bride. With the twisted logic that could only come in dreams, Libby prepared herself to instantly fall in love with the man who had, apparently, saved her from becoming an old maid.

The man's fingers dropped from hers and he took the bottom of her veil. He lifted it gently, and warmth and light rushed in to settle on her face. She opened her eyes to see him, but he leaned forward and pressed his lips into hers and she could see nothing but darkness. This darkness then became the emptiness behind her eyelids and the weight of his lips faded from hers. The euphoria lingered just a moment longer as the dream was lost.

The grief was jarring and she always woke from it. Always stared at the clock. Always found that it was exactly 1:11. Tonight was no different.

Damn.

Her ghostly lover was gone. Shivering, Libby adjusted position in bed and then pulled the blankets more tightly around her. Her feet, however, were forced out of the warm pocket of air they had generated and into a deeper patch of cold. It kept her from slipping back into sleep, and she watched as the clock changed to 1:12.

The numbers on the clock had to mean something, but she didn't know what. Jay told her it was probably nothing. So you wake up at the same time every night. Maybe there's some piece of utility equipment in your apartment that starts making noise around that time. Maybe some guy is always driving home from a late shift and he passes by your window at the same moment every night. Maybe your brain picks up on the fact that the room is suddenly the slightest bit darker, since three ones on a clock produces the least amount of glow. Of course Jay would think like that. But he didn't know how it haunted her everywhere else. On microwaves, on license plates, in phone numbers, in paychecks and bills. Three or four ones, all lined up, so unnaturally. The first time she saw them, she thought they looked beautiful. Then, they just kept coming back.

Suddenly, a high-pitched rendition of Styx's "Renegade" started playing close to Libby's ear, throwing her nervous system into an immediately frenzy. She scrambled violently out of her blankets and grabbed her cell phone.

Before answering, she checked the display. It was Jon. *That was quick*, she thought. Weren't you supposed to wait at least 24 hours for post-date conversation?

"Hey Jon," she answered, trying to sound casual to avoid him the embarrassment of having woken her from sleep.

But Jon's voice was anything but casual.

"Libby, I'm sorry to call you, but I don't know what to do."

Libby's heart, which had just returned to a semi-normal rate, fired up again.

"Jon, what is it?"

"It's Andrew. He – he dissociated again."

"How do you know?"

"When we got home, he went to bed and I took a shower. When I got out, I went to check on him and he was gone."

"Maybe he went to the store?"

"He would've told me."

"You were in the bathroom. Maybe he didn't want to intrude on your…"

"Libby, stop," Jon interrupted forcefully. "He's gone. He took his car, and there's an empty slot on the knife block."

Knife. Even the word was piercing. "What do you mean? Do you think he's going to hurt someone?"

"I don't know. That's why you've got to help me find him. We can split up and cover more ground."

Libby flipped on the light and grabbed a pen from her bedside table drawer. "Okay. What kind of car?"

"A black Dodge Durango."

Libby froze.

"Libby?"

She couldn't get sound out. She couldn't get air in.

"Hello?"

Her head was swimming. She drew in a breath sharply, fighting the tightness in her chest. "Yes. I'm here."

"Call me on my cell if you find him. And be careful. If he has the knife with him, stay away. I don't know what he's capable of when he's like this."

I do.

Jon hung up, and Libby let the phone drop from her numb fingers. Her heart had stopped racing. In fact, it seemed as though it had stopped beating all together. Andrew had killed the man in the crosswalk. This wasn't the reason she had hoped for his strange familiarity.

She slipped a sweatshirt on over her pajamas and headed out to her car. The city was asleep, and as Libby pulled her car out of the parking ramp and entered the night, she felt guilty for intruding upon it. The rain had stopped, but the pavement was still slick. She cringed as the rushing sound of her tires disrupting puddles seemed amplified.

If I were crazy and homicidal, she thought, *where would I go?*

Most likely, the part of town that they'd found Andrew in earlier that evening. Maybe he'd gone back to get the job done. If that were true, Libby suspected that she'd reach Andrew before Jon did. It hadn't taken them long to get back to her apartment from there.

Libby reversed the route that Jon had taken when dropping her off earlier. Again, the city lights dropped away and Libby found herself entering an intense darkness. While the world she had left behind was made black by the absence of light, this darkness was meant to conceal. Libby's headlights barely cut through it.

And then she saw it; the black Durango, parked crookedly in the alley. Its headlights were still on and the beam illuminated the space between the two abandoned buildings. As Libby neared, the light revealed two forms facing each other in a fighter's stance. One of them was Andrew. The headlights glinted on the knife he held raised.

Libby jerked her car to a stop beside the curb and jumped out without even turning off the engine, calling his name. Andrew turned to her voice. The moment lost was enough for the other man to knock the knife out of his hand. Startled, Andrew turned back in time to receive a punch to the face that sent him stumbling into the brick wall. As the man advanced, Libby thrust herself between him and Andrew.

"Get out of the way!" the man shouted, grabbing her shoulders and throwing her aside. Libby tried to stay on her feet, but the force was too great. Next thing she knew, she was down, knees sliding against the rough pavement.

Andrew charged the man and threw a cross punch across his jaw, then kneed him in the stomach. The man doubled over, face close to Libby's, close enough that she could distinguish its features in the dim light.

It was face she couldn't have forgotten. A face like putty.

"Jesus," Libby gasped, pulling away from the man. It couldn't be. What was going on? It had to be a dream. But no – the pain radiating up from her abused knees was real enough.

She stood painfully and turned to see Andrew retrieve the knife from beneath a pile of empty boxes and rain-dotted plastic bags. He faced the still kneeling man, swinging the knife in a wide arc as though to strike a deep gash across his back.

"Stop!" Libby screamed, throwing her weight into Andrew's side. She couldn't let him kill again.

"Get out of my way!" Andrew shouted and then he turned to restrain her.

When he did, however, he got his first real look at who she was. Recognition dawned on his face and a bright intensity rose in his dark eyes. He dropped the knife and took her shoulders, pressing her into the wall. The putty-faced man, seeing an advantage, climbed to his feet and limped out of the alley.

Andrew paid no notice, however. There were tears fighting to reflect light in his dark eyes as he lifted one hand to Libby's face and ran his fingers hesitantly down her cheek, as though afraid she wasn't truly there.

"Meg," he gasped.

And then his eyes clouded over and he dropped to the ground.

6

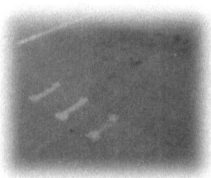

Libby sank down beside him and pulled his face away from the wet pavement.

"Andrew!" she hissed, pressing her cold palm against his feverish cheek, soothing the growing welt on his jaw. He writhed in her arms and then uttered a deep groan. She said his name again and his eyes fluttered open. Wildly, he searched his surroundings and then, having seen her hovering over him, locked onto her gaze intensely. Libby felt gravity funnel, as though it was draining her into him.

"You're okay," she soothed, helping him as he propped himself up on one elbow.

"No. I'm not." He grimaced and pulled away from her, struggling to push himself up into a sitting position.

"What do you mean? Are you hurt?" Libby checked him over. The knife was beside him, blade still clean.

"I just woke up in an alley with the girl that's dating my brother, and -" his eyes fell onto the knife, "Apparently I'm trying to kill someone."

"He got away." Libby offered.

Andrew sighed and leaned forward over his knees, breathing in a shuddering rhythm.

Libby fidgeted nervously, torn between wanting to reintroduce him to reality and wanting to address the things that seemed unreal. She couldn't get that gray face out of her head, and – she looked up, staring into the offensive front end of the black Durango. "Look, this might be hard for you to understand right now, but there's something strange going on here."

"Oh really?" he laughed bitterly, "Look, I don't know why Jon brought you into this, but you don't have to sit here with me and try to figure it all out. Please, just call my brother."

"Come on," she persisted, "Don't tell me that you don't suddenly feel like maybe you're missing some big point here?"

"You're crazier than me," he interjected, though Libby was sure she could detect a catch in his voice.

"The guy you were fighting? I saw him earlier today in a bar. He stood out to me and I didn't know why until now."

"Yeah? And what makes you so special?"

"Because I'm like you. I don't black out, but I have…this thing." Libby finished feebly, finding it harder to share the truth than she'd imagined it would be.

Yet Andrew was stricken, and Libby knew why. It was the very best kind of validation, the kind that fed the basic human urge to find patterns and order in apparent chaos. He felt the way she would if a scientist appeared and told her that due to cosmic forces, it actually was necessary to tap the faucet three times before turning on the sink. "You're keeping the world from falling out of orbit," he would tell her, and meaninglessness and meaning would exchange places.

"Just a coincidence," Andrew murmured, completely unconvincingly.

Libby stopped herself from telling him about the man he'd run down. Albeit convincing, it might also be destructive.

"Before you blacked out, you called me Meg."

He looked blank. "I don't know anyone named Meg. I don't even really remember your name."

That hurt her. But when she told him her name, he murmured a genuine apology before continuing. "I mean, Libby, I apparently do a lot of senseless things when I'm dissociated. Calling someone by the wrong name is the least of my worries."

He crawled to the nearest wall and leaned against it, lifting his knees and folding his body over them. Defeated, Libby dialed Jon, feeling suddenly guilty for not having called right away and foolish for having confronted Andrew with what were obviously her own personal delusions.

"Did you find him?" Jon burst into the phone, bypassing hello.

"Yes. He went back to the alley. He's fine."

"Was he – alone?"

Libby looked at Andrew, who had lifted his head and was now watching her with the desperate intensity of a child watching the doctor filling a syringe.

"No one else was here." Libby lied, without knowing why.

"Good," Jon's relieved sigh crackled the phone. "Stay put. I'll come get him."

Libby folded her phone and slid it back into her pocket, then crawled over to Andrew and leaned against the wall beside him, feeling the wet pavement soaking into her pajama bottoms. The knife was a few inches away. She reached for it and then slid it into her purse.

"This may look bad if I get arrested, but I think I'd better hang onto this for a while," she explained.

"Probably a good idea," he sighed and leaned his head back against the wall. "And thanks for not telling him. Most people get a little uptight about the whole 'crazy person posing a threat to others' thing."

"Well, most people don't know what it's like to be crazy."

He looked at her, reconsidering several questions before finally choosing one. "How long have you been dating my brother?"

She smiled weakly. "Since tonight."

"Oh."

There was a relief in his voice that made her heart begin to race.

"He's a good guy," Andrew continued. "I mean, he takes care of me. I probably ruined his life, but he doesn't complain."

"It's not your fault."

"Well that's the funny thing about being crazy. You believe a lot of things that aren't true."

Libby didn't know what to say. His words engendered a physiological response and her palms became slippery with sweat. Here, right beside her, was a piece from her puzzle. She just didn't know how to tell him – or if she could *ever* tell him. Knowing that nearly brought her to tears, mourning the loss of what might have been perfection. It was the same way she'd felt when her grandmother's house had burned down just a few years before she died. Every painting that her grandmother had ever labored over filled the attic corners and overstuffed closets. Each brushstroke was done with purpose, capturing in colors and lines the passion and hope that went into each creation. They were perfection, never seen by the world but loved dearly by their creator. And then, faulty wiring had sparked and the house had burned with nearly everything in it. Every painting lost, every purposeful stroke melted and stripped away by the heat of the flame. Even at a young age, Libby had been haunted by the tragic loss of singular beauty.

"You'll be good for Jon though." Andrew said, "He needs to get away from all of this."

Libby looked at him, wondering if it was as hard from him to say that as it was for her to hear.

"What about you?" she asked.

He laughed and his head dropped. Libby struggled with what to say, but the sound of tires grinding on the pavement saved her. She recognized the sound of Jon's sputtering engine, and as his headlights swept into the alley, Andrew made a motion as if to get up. But Libby grabbed his arm and pulled him back down, her fingers lingering on his arm before falling away. He had to know. He was *supposed* to know.

"I believe in things that aren't true and I do things that don't make any sense and I don't know why."

"Libby, don't," Andrew began, looking desperate.

"You see this?" She slid her hands out of her sweatshirt sleeves and showed them to him, turning them over so he could see the stretched raw skin over her knuckles and the dark blood dotting the corners of her fingernails. "This is what I do to myself, and I can't stop. I have no control."

A car door slammed. Jon was coming. They could see his shadow elongating on the ground before them. But Andrew took Libby's hands and drew them into the light, running his thumbs over her fingers, caressing the torn skin, hiding her fingers within his own. His skin was soft and familiar. Libby's heart raced, though each beat tripped gently.

"Andrew? Are you back there?" Jon's voice echoed between the alley walls.

Andrew released her fingers and pulled away, curling his hands into fists and lowering them to his side.

"You have to stop. You don't know what you're getting into," he murmured, looking away.

Libby felt the stinging heat of shame coursing through her. Her need to be near him was nothing more than a schoolgirl crush and she was needlessly jeopardizing Jon's trust in her. If Andrew didn't feel the importance of this, then it obviously existed only in her mind. Her fingertips stung, the abraded skin throbbing beneath this seeming insult. Or was it simply the inertia driving them to be touched again?

Jon waited until Libby was safely in her car. As he said goodbye, his eyes lingered for a moment on hers, trying to detect the source of her discomfort.

"I'm sorry to have to put you through this again," he apologized, offering the sort of smile that two adults share when a child does something particularly juvenile. "Next time I call, it'll be under better circumstances."

"Right. Next time." She smiled back, playing the part of Jon's sane companion. Through her windshield, she watched Andrew pull himself to his feet. He leaned heavily against the wall, watching their exchange with an odd expression: the corners of his lips lifted with slight amusement but his eyes held a desperate fear.

"Maybe this isn't the place to say it, but I think you're really special, Libby." Jon said, drawing Libby's attention back to him. "Most girls would've said see ya later alligator by now. So, you don't have to say anything. I just want you to know that I'm really thankful that you're giving me another chance."

Libby's stomach folded into itself several times. His awkwardness was physically painful. What was she expected to say? You're welcome?

"Alright, good night then." Jon smiled and smacked his palms on the roof of her car, then pulled away. Either he'd suddenly become aware of his own inelegance or he knew that Libby saw him this way and wanted to save her the difficulty of hiding it. Either way, he stepped back and waved her on.

As she maneuvered back onto the road, she kept her eyes away from Andrew. Meanwhile, Jon was watching her with so much light in his eyes, it was visible even in the pervasive darkness of the night. He would be her savior, while Andrew was her ruin personified. Her obsession, and nothing more. The desire that drove her to him was the same senseless desire that drove her to check the light switch or count the ceiling tiles or tear her skin. Jon was reality. Andrew was dopamine, and he was right: she had to stop.

*

The next morning emerged pathetically: weak, rainy and filled with reminders of the previous night. Libby had a hard time convincing herself that any of it had actually occurred. Yet the heap of rain-soaked pajamas under the sink gave it all away and filled her stomach with a heavy queasiness that had only grown as the morning progressed. Afternoon found her listlessly picking at a chicken salad sandwich, drowning in the lights and sounds of the hospital cafeteria and feeling an unending urge to throw her head into the nearest brick wall.

"Are you going to eat that?" Jay asked, wiping the last remnants of his own sandwich from his lips. Libby happily shoved the tray across the table.

"Rough date last night?" Jay guessed, pulling the crusts off the edge of the bread.

Libby allowed herself to smile as she watched him, hoping it would pull her back into her own reality. Sitting in the cafeteria watching Jay de-crust his bread, every damn day for the past four years. That was where she belonged.

"Well, let's see. The date was over in about five minutes and I ended up in an alley on the bad side of town. Twice."

"With Jon Calahan?" Jay wrinkled his forehead. "I didn't think he was that kind of guy."

"He's not. He's completely the opposite of *that guy*. But his brother…"

"His brother came onto you?"

"Stop guessing and let me finish," she admonished him, having had enough of baseless assumptions with Dr. Sherman. Jay nodded and obediently crammed a wad of sandwich into his mouth. But then, even though she had the floor, Libby wasn't sure what to say. She couldn't label Andrew as crazy and discuss him with Jay like he was one of their patients. She had no right to pretend that she was put-off by insanity.

And so she dismissed everything. "It was nothing. His brother needed to be picked up, and it sort of ruined the evening."

"Oh," Jay replied, disappointed. "Well, are you going to go out with him again?"

Libby shrugged. "I guess so."

Admitting it made her body tingle, not with pleasure but with the urge to get up and throw herself into something heavy. Crash and burn.

"Are you done?" she asked, with the breathlessness of desperation. She had to get up, had to move.

He wasn't, but he quickly gathered the contents of his tray. "Yeah. Let's go out and get some air."

Libby jumped to her feet, hands clenching. Yes. Air. She needed air. She needed to stop seeing Jon's desperate uncollected face in her mind while feeling the thrill of Andrew in her heart.

"So what's really going on?" Jay asked as they moved through the revolving doors.

Libby didn't answer at first, but pushed forward impatiently and burst onto the sidewalk before the drop-off lane. Jay guided her to a bench that was out of the sun and she sat down, feeling the stone surface abrading her palms and soothing her with a pain that was so much easier to control than the one gripping her heart.

"It's like I finally broke the surface, Jay, and then dove right back down. Like I missed the dying."

"You're afraid that you like Jon too much?" Jay laughed good-naturedly, the sort of laugh that set him apart from her. When she had problems, he fixed them.

"That's not it," Libby frowned, wondering if it was bad that every person she knew tried to psychoanalyze her. Or if it was worse that she depended on it.

"Well, let's deconstruct your analogy. Is Jon the water or the air?"

"It's not a good analogy," Libby grumbled, but really it was. Jay couldn't know that Jon wasn't even part of the picture. It was Andrew that she was afraid to breathe.

"Maybe I'm just afraid to be normal," she sighed.

"Or you're finding out that normal isn't all it's cracked up to be."

She laughed bitterly. He didn't know. How could anyone know? Andrew wasn't normal. He wasn't reality. He was proof that reality was a lie.

"Ever get the feeling that too many weird things happen in life for us to keep ignoring them?" she asked.

Jay thought about it for a while and then nodded. "Do you remember a couple of years back when there was that bad car accident near the park?"

"Sort of."

"The seventeen year old that was killed in the accident was the son of my nephew's third grade teacher. When my nephew found out about the accident, he drew a picture for his teacher, showing her son up in Heaven surrounded by a bunch of elephants. Sounds crazy, right? Well this woman called my sister in tears, saying that she didn't know how my nephew knew, but her son's favorite animal had been elephants. His dream had been to go to Africa and work with them. My nephew's teacher swore she never shared this with the kids, and when my sister asked my nephew where he'd gotten the idea, he just shrugged and said it seemed right."

A car rolled up to the curb. Libby looked up, allowing it to distract her while she took in Jay's story. Maybe it was a coincidence. Or maybe miracles really still happened. As the car pulled forward, Libby caught a glimpse of the license plate. *Of course.* TAG-1111. There they were again, the ones, haunting her, telling her to pay attention. She looked sidelong at Jay.

"Do you think it was a miracle?"

"I don't know," he exhaled slowly. "I wish I could believe that it was."

"Why?"

"I kind of want my own elephants when I die."

Libby allowed herself to taste a deeply drawn breath of cool air, though it failed to soothe the heat of her frustration.

"You know what I think? It's ridiculous. We pump some kind of chemical into a patient's veins and it saves their lives and we go to school for four years to figure out why. We need an explanation for absolutely every stupid little thing that happens on this earth, but we don't seem to give a damn about everything that happens off of it. Forget the fact that everything we have was created from nothing. Forget coincidence, forget miracles, forget déjà vu, forget predictions and instinct and consciousness. If it doesn't fit under a microscope, it doesn't matter. It's like someone walked into a department store, saw a rack of shoes and assumed that that's all they sell. Then they go outside and put up a big sign that says "shoe store" and they tell everyone in the world not to bother going in if you're looking for toasters or ties or dresses or decorative pillows because all they've got is shoes. So everyone believes it, and for some reason this blinds them and when they walk in, they can't look beyond the shoes. Even if some people look out at the untouched expanse of the store and ask what else might be out there, everyone else ridicules them. Why would it be anything but shoes? That's what *they* told us. That's what the sign says. All hail the mighty sign that cannot possibly be wrong."

Jay grinned slyly, "You know, some stores do sell only shoes."

"Jay, I'm trying to make this big existential point. I'm sorry if the metaphor doesn't hold, but don't you at least see what I'm trying to say? Look at your nephew. Look at what happened to me last night."

"I don't know what happened to you last night."

Libby sighed. She couldn't tell him that she'd felt some transcendental connection to a homicidal lunatic. "Well," she finally said, "Suffice it to say that I found the toasters."

Jay was silent. Libby glanced at him to gauge his reaction and found that he looked uncharacteristically disconcerted.

"What?" she accused.

He coughed. "Nothing. I mean, you seem really upset. I just wonder if maybe you're letting yourself be, uh, persuaded by certain factors beyond your control."

Libby threw up her hands and then slammed them back down onto the bench, "Right. Okay. It's the mental illness talking. So give me anti-psychotic drugs and I'll shut up. Or why don't you burn me at the stake, nail me to a cross or pour hemlock down my throat. It's no different, right?"

"So you're comparing yourself to Jesus now?" Jay laughed dismissively. Libby fumed.

"You're not going to listen to me, are you?" she asked, without expecting an answer. She'd done this song and dance before with Dr. Sherman. She shouldn't have expected Jay to react any differently. If it wasn't for TAG-1111 still parked on the curb, she probably would've convinced herself that Jay was right; but for the first time in her life, she dared to stay on, to see where this wild ride would lead her. To the ends of the universe, perhaps, or to a padded cell.

The rest of the day dragged, chained to her ankles, slowly defeating her with the weight of knowing that everything she did was a lie. The immensity of what she had discovered couldn't be held back. She had to tell everyone what she had seen and felt, grab them by the shoulders and shake them and tell them that it was possible to believe in miracles and to fall in love for more than the desire to feel worthy of being loved by another.

But this isn't what her patients expected from her. They expected her to build rapport, to discuss the weather as though it were some new unprecedented experience. They expected a hand laid on their arm for comfort. Libby delivered, but it shook her foundations. And the elevens haunted her all day long.

Meanwhile, Jay watched her like a hawk, waiting for the break down. Libby was aware of his presence in the halls outside her patient's rooms. It was why she did the things that had been so hard before, touching her patients, talking to them in a manner that mimicked Jay's – the hi, how are you's and I hear it's going to be even warmer tomorrow's.

Then they brought Tom in. He was Libby's patient, and when she walked into his room she saw a clean-cut middle-aged man in a business shirt and trousers sitting calmly on the end of the examining table. She said hi, how are you, and he responded with the customary fine, yourself? And then Libby saw the policeman in the corner; a magazine spread open on his knee.

The guard caught Libby staring at him and looked up.

"Doc, meet Tom," he said, gesturing dramatically, "Hey, why don't you tell the nice doctor what you told me Tom?"

"Not if I'm to be chastised again," Tom murmured, eyes shooting daggers at the ground. Libby detected the slight elegance of a British accent.

The guard laughed uproariously, eyes gleaming as though he had been sat down before a towering banquet. "Doc, I picked this guy up on 55th and Broadway, chasing some woman around and trying to tell her that she was going to die."

"She was," Tom interjected forcefully.

"So I look up his record, right?" the guard continued, relishing this as though it were his big fish story, "Turns out this guy's called the precinct a couple times before, trying to warn us about this or that. Regular psychic, right?"

"Well, was he right?" Libby asked, catching Tom's eye. She held his gaze long enough to tell him she could be trusted.

The guard, catching this exchange, laughed harder. "Look, doc, he's no psychic. If he was, he could tell me what my wife is really doing when she goes out for book club meetings."

"As you suspect, she's shagging her fitness trainer," Tom murmured, his voice driving like cold rain. His own fury seemed to startle him, however, and he quickly returned to his graceful demeanor. "And she's not going to stop until you learn the meaning of respect. It doesn't take a psychic to see that."

Seeing the guard's expression begin to flame, Libby stepped in. "Why exactly did you bring him here?"

"Look, it's not my idea. They said bring him here and you'd admit him to the nut ward. Out of my hands, right?"

"Yeah," Libby glared pointedly at him for several moments, then asked, "Do you mind if I have a moment alone with him?"

Both Tom and the guard looked shocked at this request.

"I want to ask him some questions, and we're not getting anywhere with you two having a pissing contest here," she explained, surprised by her own tactlessness.

"I'm afraid I can't do that, doc. It'd be my ass if something happened," the guard eyed Tom with intense suspicion, as if he had already committed the violent act.

"What happens in this room is between me and my patient. He has a right to privacy."

"He gave up that right when he – "the guard trailed off, unable to find anything meaningful with which to implicate Tom. Libby crossed her arms with childish defiance and stared him down.

"Fine," he yielded, "You can have five minutes, but I'm going to be right outside the door."

Libby closed the door on his heels and then turned to Tom.

"Why don't you tell me what's really going on," she said, her voice low and conspiratorial.

"They tend to come in dreams, the visions. I can call some to mind, but they are never as clear. When they started, I didn't know that they meant anything. If they'd even come true, I wouldn't have noticed. Then, six years ago, I had a dream that I was running through the streets of New York City. There was fire and smoke in the air, people running and screaming, papers fluttering down like confetti, the hospitals filled to capacity. It was vague enough to be meaningless until three days later when it came true, and I think you know the date. Do you know how many thousands of lives I could have saved if I had known?"

"No one would have listened."

For a moment, Tom looked at Libby as though she were the crazy one. "Am I to take it that you believe me?"

Libby's eyes swept over the room, taking in all the things that reminded her that she was a professional and this was her place of work – a place of pills and computers and science.

"Maybe I do."

But even as she admitted it, she felt a sweeping weightless feeling in her stomach as though she were falling. It was too much. She'd spent six months in a psychiatric ward working with patients like Tom, people who had stories to tell about alien encounters and government conspiracies and apocalyptic visions. It went against everything she had been taught to believe the stories, much less suggest to the patients themselves that they might be true. Who knew what kind of harm she was doing?

"I can't let you go," she told him.

He sighed, sinking into himself. "I know. I should be more careful. Maybe I do need help. It's just – I'm a decent, ordinary man, doctor. It's easier for me to believe that these visions are true than it is to believe I've lost control of my mind."

Libby stared at him as her intrigue mounted. "What about me, Tom? Do you see anything in my future?"

But before he could answer, there was a sudden loud knock at the door. Libby and Tom both drew back guiltily as it swung open and Jay appeared.

"How are things going in here?" he asked. Libby saw that his critical expression did not change when his eyes moved from Tom to her.

"Fine," she murmured feebly.

"Dr. Cohen, can I speak with you outside?" Jay asked. Then, without waiting for an answer, he looked up at Tom. "It'll be just a moment."

Libby followed him out like a child being pulled by the ear. But before she left, she heard Tom murmur something behind her: "Be careful at the crosswalk." Libby tried to turn back, but Jay moved her away from the doorway and the guard reentered. As he passed Libby caught a smug grin on his face. So he'd ratted her out.

"What's this I'm hearing, Libby?" Jay hissed, hovering close so that she was forced to step back into the wall. He outstretched one arm above her and leaned his weight against the wall, hiding this exchange from the rest of the hospital by the curtain of his sleeve.

"Hearing about what?"

"If a patient comes in with a guard, he stays in the room no matter what."

"I wanted to talk to the guy alone. He wasn't going to say anything if the guard was in the room."

"Libby!" Jay sighed with exasperation. "It's not your job to talk to him. Run a tox screen, make sure he's not injured, and then transfer him to psyche. They'll sort him out."

"If that's the way you want to see it, why don't you ship me off to psyche? Don't I deserve it just as much as that guy?"

"I'm not going to have this argument with you."

Libby felt stung. What right did Jay have to treat her like he was her father? She tried to duck under her arm but he slid it down the wall, keeping her in.

"Jay, get out of my way," Libby warned, "I need to get back to my patient."

"Only if you promise me that you're going to approach this sensibly."

Libby drew in breath to argue, but his words suddenly struck her and her shoulders dropped. Her life was a charade enough already without this. Wasn't it bad enough that she did stupid, pointless things, or that she was a doctor who was afraid of the sick? Now she was here, wearing this white coat and asking her psychotic patient to make predictions for her? She could indulge in her insanity in her own time, but she couldn't let it misguide her at work. The consequences were too great.

Jay, seeing her inner struggle reflected in her changing eyes, softened. "Libby, I'm sorry to come down on you. I'm just worried about you. I don't want you getting too far gone."

She had gone too far chasing Andrew. She had to let it all go. But that thought stung with a physical pang that took her breath away. Her chest collapsed, containing shallow breaths. If she let this go, what would be left? An empty future filled with lies. Pretending she was like everyone else: blind and stupid.

Jay continued to look at her with worry in his eyes. "Why don't you take the afternoon off?"

She wanted to ask him what she thought this would do for her. Was her insanity due to a lack of sleep? Did he want her gone because he believed that, or was it because he wanted to stop her from making messes that he had to clean up?

"Fine," she resigned, though it terrified her. She had a feeling that if she left this place now, she could never bring herself to return.

"I'll take your patients."

She nodded, ready to leave without a last word, ready to convince him that she was weak and needed his guidance. But

Tom's words replayed in her mind. *I'm a decent, ordinary man.* She shared his struggle, and wasn't going to let him down. Thus, she dismissed Jay's paternal smile and returned with her own twisted smirk. "Well then for your own good, I hope you ask Tom about your future."

Jay sighed, smile fading. "Libby, for your sake, I hope you stop thinking I should."

She pushed away from him, but as she walked out of the ER she felt his eyes on her. Everything unnatural about this escape followed in her wake until she was safe in her car and driving out of the hospital parking lot. She turned on the radio, began to sing along to a familiar tune, and kept herself from thinking about the consequences. The hospital descended from view in her rearview mirror and she let it go, and though she was as hesitant as a caged bird set free, she allowed herself to celebrate the knowledge that she'd learned the manner of escape.

She had nowhere to go and knew she couldn't go back to her apartment to sit alone and dwell on the ruin of her mind. For some reason, she found herself crossing into Brooklyn. It was the way back home to her parent's house. She hadn't visited in months, but now that she was openly defying their vision for her future, facing them would be the most privately entertaining thing Libby had ever done. Hiding the truth was never more fun when it was such a shocking thing.

"I had the afternoon off," Libby lied to her mother, who had greeted her at the door with palpable confusion.

"Oh," her mother returned simply, and then stepped back to let her into the small foyer.

"Hope I didn't come in the middle of anything," Libby said, looking around the living room that lay to the right. One corner was filled with dusty boxes.

"No, no." Her mother was nervous, wringing her hands. "I was just cleaning out the attic."

She probably thinks I'm in the middle of a nervous breakdown, Libby realized. She gave an overzealous laugh and said, "Of course I'd show up on a day when you'd put me to work."

The quip relieved her mother somewhat. "You bet I am. I'm just going through these boxes. Your father took them down this morning. It's not very exciting work, but it needs to be done. You can help me decide what to throw out."

"You know me, I can't throw out anything."

Her mother offered a guarded smile, remembering the extent of this. As a child, Libby had hoarded things mercilessly, often bringing home bits of lint or dirt she'd found on the classroom floor. For years, Libby had believed that if she didn't bring these things home to show her mother, something terrible would happen. The obsession had progressed to a hoarding of thoughts as well and Libby spent a terrifying three-day period without sleep, writing down every thought that came into her head. Something drove her to climb out of bed time after time, stumble across the floor to her desk and scribble thought after thought onto the back of an old desk plotter calendar. Arrows to indicate the melodic direction of tunes stuck in her head. Senseless thoughts, memories, complaints. Even the pitch and rhythm of her own sobbing. She'd collected the pages and brought them to her mother who had merely set them aside without a second thought. It was seeing her disinterest in what had been so monumental to her that finally convinced Libby to stop.

Yes, Mrs. Cohen was fully aware of the implications of Libby's harmless comment, and it only heightened her suspicions of why her daughter had appeared on her doorstep in the middle of a work day.

Libby sat down at one of the boxes and wrenched the warped top open, holding her breath against the cloud of dust that was released. Neatly packed within were old photo albums, the spines split and faded in spots. Libby pulled one out and turned it over, reading the gold lettering on the cover: Wedding Memories.

"You keep your wedding album in the attic?"

"Why not?"

Libby peeled open the cover. The plastic covering the photographs had turned yellow, while the photos themselves had faded to pastels. She spotted her mother immediately, sporting an incredible tower of hair. Her father was more difficult to recognize, as he was completely without his gut and graying beard. Libby stared deeply into her mother's face, seeing her own. Her mother's skin was smooth and glowing, and her eyes – now tired – were filled then with joy and possibility. At this point in her mother's life, she had no idea that her future would involve rearing a disappointing child. Yet

Libby wondered if it was obvious to her mother even then that the marriage would soon be loveless.

"God, mom, you were gorgeous."

Her mother brushed off the compliment. "Look at that wild hair. I can't imagine."

Libby turned the page, where the posed pictures gave way to candid reception shots. Her mother and father were dancing in each other's arms. Now, they rarely touched. Libby wondered why she was so desperate to find someone to marry. It didn't seem to mean the same thing as love.

Libby's mother slid over to her, looking more closely at the album. Libby watched as an affectionate smile fought its way to the surface. "I saved my dress for your wedding, Elisabeth. It's up in the attic somewhere, probably a wreck by now."

Libby bristled, knowing exactly what was coming. To save herself the torment of hearing the question, she supplied the answer before her mother could ask.

"I've been going out with someone,"

Her mother was as shocked as Libby thought she would be. "Oh! How long?"

Libby gave an offhand shrug, as though she hadn't been counting.

"What's his name?"

"Jon. He works in the pharmacy at the hospital."

"A pharmacist? There's good money in that, I hear."

"Yeah, well there's more to it than that," Libby retorted, meaning that there was more to dating in general. Her mother, however, misinterpreted.

"You think you're in love?"

Libby looked away from her mother's hopeful eyes, knowing what she wanted. She wanted Libby to bring home a nice boy for dinner, to hear that he made a lot of money and didn't seem to notice that his bride-to-be was a lunatic. But she didn't love him, even if he was determined to fall in love with her. Libby looked at her mother's young face staring up from the photograph. Her mother, of all people, should understand how important it is to wait for the right one. But that was the curse of humanity: mistakes would be made and while the consequences would linger, the lessons learned would be lost in time.

"I don't know," she asked, "How do you know if you're in love?"

In other families, this would be a sort of Full House Moment. But Libby's mother merely frowned and looked away, disappointed. Her daughter had only had one real relationship in her life and it was back in high school, when she had managed to snag a popular boy named James. They had dated for nearly six blissful months, and for the duration Mrs. Cohen could forgive her daughter's idiosyncrasies, knowing that at least they would not keep her from the things a young girl deserved: a date to the prom, a kiss at midnight on New Years. Even when James had suddenly broken her daughter's heart, they had fought desperately to win him back. Those were the most genuinely happy moments she and her daughter had ever shared, and when James had graduated and left Libby behind for good, it had left a terrible hole in both their hearts.

Libby watched her mother's smile wash out as her expression grew distant, then disappointed. Libby sighed and returned to the photo album, flipping more vehemently through the crumbling pages.

One of the photographs caught her eye and drove her to lean closer. It was a shot of a group of men in tuxedos standing in front of a cream colored wall lined with red panels. She'd seen this image before, but not in a photograph.

"I don't believe it. Look, mom, I told you I was there." Libby said, turning the album around and pointing to the photo. All her life, she'd had a strange vivid memory of having her photograph taken in a room that looked exactly like this one. Throughout her life, the clarity of the memory had faded, but despite the fact that no one she asked remembered taking Libby to such a room, she was convinced that she'd been there.

"What do you mean? This was from my brother's wedding, Elisabeth. You weren't there. In fact, I was pregnant with you at the time."

"Well, whether or not I was at that specific event I at least remember this room. I even described this to you before, remember? Cream-colored walls, red panels, being in a photograph with guys in suits."

"This is the reception room off of St. Augustine," her mother's frown deepened, "Why would you have gone there?"

Libby was beginning to get annoyed. She was sick of her mother trying to discredit this one particular memory. Yet it struck her as eerie that she'd had this memory ever since she could remember. In whatever circumstances surrounded her being in this room, she would have been too young to be there alone. Her mother had to remember.

"This isn't an early sign of Alzheimer's, is it?" Libby asked.

Libby's mother deconstructed her daughter's expression, looking for signs of teasing. When she found none, she bristled.

"Elisabeth, I wish you would stop focusing on things like this and focus on – well what about this boy you mentioned? Why don't you bring him around for dinner?"

Libby scowled. "Geez, Mom. You're really good at this, aren't you?"

"Good at what?"

Libby remained silent, holding back. Her mother quite possibly had a trifecta win here, managing in only one comment to insult her daughter's sanity, dating life and ability to manage her future. Yet she hid the anger in her eyes and tried to mirror her mother's eager disposition.

"Get me the phone. I'll call him up right now and ask him over," she said, with no real intention of doing so.

Libby's mother climbed to her feet as quickly as her arthritic knees would allow her and disappeared into the kitchen, calling over her shoulder: "What does he like to eat? I can make vegetable lasagna. Jeanette gave me a fabulous recipe."

Libby felt a pang of guilt. Her mother's faith in her was vulnerable - sweet and child-like. It killed Libby to exploit and then destroy this part of her mother's soul. But she was done pretending. Her mother's mood was never even, but instead cycled between highs and lows. During high school, Libby had to lie about the things she was doing and the people she was with in order to construct an elaborate persona who met her mother's approval. The most impressive feint was a made-up relationship with a fictional boy she called James. The lie became so pervasive, Libby began to feel it as truth and longed for the touch of a boy she had merely imagined.

When it became impossible to maintain the lie any further, Libby authored a sudden breakup. The news had devastated her mother and the new game became allowing her mother to participate in the exciting schemes designed to win him back. It was probably the single most complicated thing Libby had ever done - and that included the four years of medical school. Yet she knew now that it was foolish and futile. Her mother would inevitably return to the lows and, losing all volition, would lie in bed all day and moan about how she had failed as a mother by raising a sick, unhappy child.

Like the dying swings of a pendulum, the highs and lows had lost their magnitude over time. The highs were less high, as joy was tempered and laughter guarded and easily silenced. The lows were less low, as fits of tears and anger became silence: numb, disappointed, interminable silence. The love-hate relationship Mrs. Cohen had with her husband deteriorated into a casual partnership. Libby missed the fighting just as much as she missed the few moments she had seem them share in something passionate.

Yet Libby had never blamed herself. She knew chemicals had screwed her mother over just as much as they had destroyed her own life. Libby had made peace with her own condition and it wasn't her fault that her mother hadn't yet made peace with hers. But today, as she looked down at her mother's wedding dress and thought of it packed away in one of these dusty boxes, she allowed herself to abandon the last few things she knew to be true. Now, without reason, she believed in her mother's fears. There wasn't going to be some great deus ex machina in her future that would descend upon all these ruined lives and put things back in order. God wouldn't come down from the Heavens and say: "You've suffered long enough in this farce. Now let me show you the path I really wanted your life to take."

She knew she didn't love Jon, but she was afraid she was supposed to. Even if she was, she didn't know how to keep him. She would eventually break his heart. Sick temptation would destroy her, as the need to touch Andrew…her fingers clenched tightly. If only she could escape with him! But the possibilities of how far from reality they could go terrified her. *Too far gone.*

As her mother's returning footsteps grew louder, Libby slipped the photo of the red paneled room out of the plastic and left silently with it. She was in her car and down the street before her mother even knew she was gone.

7

There was a message on the machine waiting for her when she got home. It was Jon asking her to accompany him to dinner that night. Unaware that this had been anything but an ordinary day for Libby, he'd decided it the perfect night to win her back. And Libby, weakened by her guilt in not wanting to say yes, said yes.

She slipped into a pair of dressy black pants and a silk blouse, hated it, and changed into a short black dress. Standing before the mirror, she surveyed the costume. All of this reminded her of the part of herself that she'd recently discarded: the desire to satisfy everyone else's expectations. She would give Jon the sort of evening that he deserved. Hell, she might even call home tomorrow and tell her mother all about it. If she could develop feelings for an imaginary boy, she could at least playact fondness for Jon. He was a nice guy, after all, and between him and Andrew, there was probably a disappointed mother in the mix somewhere that he was trying to please.

She was completely unprepared, however, when a long white limousine pulled up to the curb. Bombarded by rivaling excitement and panic, Libby could only stay rooted to the spot, staring open-mouthed at the vehicle that seemed so out of place in the middle-income apartment block. Then Jon stepped out, and Libby was once again taken by surprise. The wrinkled, tan blazer was gone; in its place was a well-tailored dark gray suit coat over a crisp white shirt and a pair of dark blue jeans. Even Jon's ridiculous crew cut was uncharacteristically careless.

A gasped "wow" escaped her lips. "You look great."

Jon laughed and extended his hand to her, "Well, I'll admit I had a little help. A certain brother of mine wants to make sure I don't blow this date a second time."

Her heart skipped a beat. *Andrew*. She saw him reflected in his brother: his ease, his savoir-faire. He had done something she had never been able to: find peace and comfort in chaos and impurity.

Jon deconstructed her expression as she stood stalled before him. He was relieved to see an affectionate glow rise in her eyes. It was the first time he'd seen it since the day they'd met and he felt grateful towards his brother for his help in eliciting it.

He outstretched his hand and smiled invitingly. He would treat her like a princess tonight and she would forget everything. There was something so intriguing about her, making her a precious thing to him. Seeing her crouched in that dirty alley had been intolerable to him.

Libby saw his hand extended to her and reluctantly took his fingers, turning her hand to hide the roughness of her skin. But as he helped her into the limousine, she forgot all anxiety as her childlike excitement swelled. She had never been in a limousine before, and it thoroughly met her expectations. A long leather bench ran around three sides of the spacious interior. The fourth wall contained a bar with glassware illuminated from beneath by blue and purple spotlights. Tiny lights ran across the ceiling like a wash of stars, and they seemed to swell and pulsate as though waves of energy were surging through them.

"Jon, this is absolutely fantastic," Libby said, "But you shouldn't have. I mean, it's probably really expensive…"

He cut her off. "Libby, they say first impressions are the most important thing in a relationship. My aim tonight is to give you such a second impression, you will not even recall the first."

Libby wanted to tell him that she honestly didn't hold anything against him. But then she looked at it from his perspective. Assuming that she was an ordinary person, the events of the previous night would have been too incredible to bear. A first date that ended in the woman trying to keep her date's brother from committing murder in a back alley was not one that generally led to a second.

So she kept it vague. "Well, I appreciate it, but please don't think you have to go to so much trouble for me."

"Nonsense. A beautiful girl like you deserves to be treated like royalty every once in a while."

Libby laughed and bowed her head in modesty. "Well, thank you."

Jon leaned forward and tapped on the partition separating them from the driver.

"Yes sir?" a voice returned on some hidden speaker.

"We're ready to go."

"Yes sir."

The limousine lurched and took off. Jon returned to his seat and winked at Libby. "Top secret location."

"Oh. Is that so?"

Libby hoped it was nothing too extravagant, though a part of her that still liked to be spoiled hoped that it was.

"Would you like a drink?" Jon asked, moving to the bar.

"Sure. What have you got?"

Jon opened up the liquor drawer, revealing rows of tiny bottles that clinked together as the limousine thrummed over the bumpy pavement. He surveyed the selection with a puzzled expression.

"Despite the degree in chemistry, I'm not that much of a bartender," he laughed, "Let's try another drawer. Ah, champagne?"

"Perfect."

Jon removed the bottle and the opener, and then handed two glasses to Libby.

"I'm scared of the pop," she warned, as he began to peel away the foil.

He laughed. "To be perfectly honest, so am I."

Libby covered her ears and moved to one corner of the limo while he moved to the other. Holding the bottle at arm's length, he grasped the loop around the mouth of the bottle and began to twist it.

Libby turned her head and closed her eyes, hiccupping unrestrained laughter as the cork popped and Jon yelled, "The glasses, quick!"

Libby looked up to see suds of champagne rolling down the bottle and wrapping around Jon's hands like ribbons. She rushed to extend one of the glasses over the stream, but Jon's hands shook as he too erupted into laughter and the champagne sloshed over the edge of the glass.

"Stop it, we're making a mess!" Libby scolded, and grabbed his wrist to steady it. The glass filled, frothing.

The driver's voice crackled into the cabin suddenly. "Everything alright back there?"

Libby bit her lip to keep from laughing. Everything's fine."

"Yes ma'am."

She snorted and looked up at Jon, expecting to share a scandalous laugh. But Jon was frozen, his dull eyes locked on the fingers she had gently wrapped around his wrist. She quickly pulled her hand away and buried it in her lap. Jon looked at her, the colored lights from the bar dancing in his eyes.

"Sorry," she found herself saying.

"Don't be sorry."

But she was. His expression was stunned, as though being suddenly bombarded with joy and relief. She'd felt the same way before, but not with Jon.

"Here," she held up the empty glass, diverting his eyes away from her.

His pale cheeks flared as he took the glass. The tiny points of light from above seemed to swell in his eyes as he raised his glass to her and smiled. "To second chances."

Libby toasted him half-heartedly and then threw back the champagne like it was a shot.

He laughed, "Wow. Hard day?"

"As a matter of fact, yeah." Libby poured herself another glassful. Her relationship with champagne had always followed true to the old adage and it had faithfully gone straight to her head. It was a more potent poison than dopamine.

"What happened?" Jon asked.

She looked at him blankly, forgetting that her answer deserved explanation. Of course, she couldn't tell him the truth.

"Well, it's a long story, the climax of which involves me visiting my mother."

"Oh," Jon took a sip of champagne. Libby saw him evaluating her over the rim of the glass and for a fleeting moment she was reminded of her time in Dr. Sherman's office. "Well," he continued, "What's so bad about that?"

"She's just never happy with the way things are going in my life."

Jon smiled. "She loves you and wants the best for you."

"Yeah. I guess so." Libby hid a frown. She was sick of people telling her that the things that upset her weren't worth getting upset over. Vindictively, she forced him to take the floor. "What about your mother?"

Jon digested her question for a moment and then dumped the contents of his glass down his throat. Red-faced, he cleared his throat and then answered softly, "I guess she loved too much."

Libby felt queasy. She didn't know what to say, but sensed he didn't need an answer. As he spoke, his lips curled up into a joyless smile, as though finding amusement in his own pathetic concession to fate.

"My mother was deeply religious. When Andrew started having his black outs, Mom told us that God had a purpose for him. She thought he was periodically playing host to an angel and disappearing on some heavenly mission. It terrified Andrew to be out of control like that, and thinking that God was guiding his every move gave him some comfort."

"Well…" Libby began, but then realized she was afraid to commit to any one response. She and God had a long history of misunderstanding between them. The only comfort she had that her soul wasn't going straight to Hell was the fact that she was afraid that it was. To her, God was a sort of poor weather friend whom she felt no guilt in ignoring until she needed him. Though she didn't wear a cross, go to church, or spout Bible verses in response to society's moral failings, she hoped that God still knew she was on the team. Yet a lifetime of bad luck and failed dreams had left her wondering sometimes if that was just another one of her delusions.

Jon continued. "After Andrew – well, after a certain point, Mom couldn't believe that anymore. She never came out and said it, but I think she realized she had a choice. If she believed in God, she had to believe that Andrew was going to hell. And she loved Andrew too much for that."

Jon's voice caught in his throat and he stopped abruptly. As Libby struggled to understand his words, his eyes drifted to the window. She wondered if he was going to say more. Part of her knew she shouldn't ask him to, but a larger part of her felt a deep need to know.

"Why would she think that?" she asked finally, forcing back the pang of guilt with a large mouthful of champagne.

"It's a long story." Jon murmured vacantly, as though it were an automatic response.

There was a long uncomfortable silence, during which Libby downed the rest of her glass and then dropped back against the leather seat cushion, wishing she too could dissociate and escape this. As the engine droned on beneath her, she wondered where they were going and how, after this, they could possibly act when they got there.

Jon turned back to her suddenly, and her heart floundered in her chest, wary of another shock.

"But it was too much for her," he said, his voice strained, "It drove her mad and she – she ended up in an institution. And I watched her…"

"Jon, you don't have to," she pleaded.

"No." His body became rigid. "I just want you to understand why I do this to myself. I love my brother. He's all I've got left. I saw my mother waste away in that place until she had nothing left to hope for except death. I'm not going to let that happen to my brother."

"But you can't prevent him from blacking out, Jon. You can't keep him safe."

"Putting him in a hospital is as good as killing him, Libby. I can take care of him, just like I always have. This is my family and I can't change that. It's what I was born to do."

Libby moved closer to him. His shoulders dropped and he smiled, as though grateful for the minimal comfort her presence provided.

"God, Libby, how did we end up talking about all of this?"

Libby was stunned, but she did her best to hide this. He had erupted before her. How could he so easily return the cork to the bottle as though nothing had happened and nothing had been lost?

"Do you want some more champagne?" he asked, his lips stretching into a forced smile.

Libby's head was swimming. "No. I think I've had enough."

Jon looked relieved, as though perhaps Libby's intoxication would keep her from remembering the things he hadn't been able to keep from saying. Libby, however, felt those words heavily in the pit of her stomach like a rich meal.

It was just the effect she had on people. Wherever she went, minds unraveled.

The limo slowly drew to a stop. Libby looked out the window, trying to discern where Jon had taken her. They'd pulled up beside a tall brownstone, the front of which was decorated with a line of small jockey statues. *The 21 Club.* Libby couldn't help but smile, and seeing this, Jon was relieved in knowing that he had at least balanced the airing of the family's dirty laundry with both a new suit and a great restaurant choice.

"I'm into this place," Libby said, though she stopped herself before revealing why. The club was a former speakeasy and was filled with the sort of history that Libby liked to immerse herself in. Until now she'd had no one to go in with, however, and wasn't brave enough to dine alone.

The street outside the restaurant was alive with the bustle of a Saturday evening. This is what the world is like, Libby thought, as she watched women in sleek dresses walking arm in arm with their husbands and boyfriends, throwing their heads back in laughter and scattering window light with the diamonds draped from their ear lobes. Their mirth was accompanied by the usual backdrop of city sounds: car horns, sputtering engines, and the clop-clop of thousands of high-heeled shoes rushing from one exciting venue to another. Libby was altogether thrilled to be part of this life and as their driver pulled open the limo door, she forgot all about the tension and the complications within.

Jon stepped out first and then turned to help her. As the sidewalk commotion was briefly quieted, Libby imagined that everyone had fallen into a hush of anticipation, waiting to see what celebrity or famed socialite was about to step out of the limousine. But the crowd had quieted for a reason that Libby had not yet detected. A black car had pulled up to a screeching halt behind the limousine, its front right tire bumping up onto the curb. A man jumped from the drivers' side door, his shirt flayed open to the chest. His eyes were filled with a wild anger and the men on the sidewalk pulled the women closer as he began a seething charge toward the man who had just stepped out of the limousine.

Libby's fingers had just made contact with Jon's when, out of nowhere, the figure barreled into his side. Libby withdrew reflexively, fearful that the bottles and glasses jangling on the bar would shatter as Jon was thrust forcefully into the side of the limousine.

"Where is she?" the attacker demanded.

"I – I don't know," Jon stammered, "I don't know who you are talking about."

"Yes you do, you son of a bitch,"

Libby was terrified, able to see only Jon's back twisting as he struggled under his oppressor's grasp. She thought about the knife still in her purse from last night, but could not bring herself to take it out. What could she possibly do other than introduce it into the equation and cause someone to get seriously hurt? Whatever world these brothers were mixed up in, it was more than any of them understood and that put them at a frightening disadvantage. People were trying to kill them, and unless there was something Jon wasn't telling her, they didn't know why.

Through the open door, Libby saw men in the crowd rush forward finally to separate Jon from his attacker. As they wrenched him away, he stumbled towards the gathered women and the pitch of their screams increased. These were the excited screams of one plunging down a roller coaster hill, however, for the fear they felt at seeing this fight was thrilling, as was watching their dates try to overpower the strong, feral attacker. They didn't share the genuine fear that had gripped Libby, leaving her powerless to even draw breath as the man looked up at her and she recognized his face.

"Meg!" he shouted, spitting blood from a split lip that had been elbowed during the struggle.

All she could do was look at him with her mouth open. He lunged for the limousine and her body took over, pulling her away even as her heart ached to quiet the desperate longing in Andrew's eyes.

"Get out of there!" he shouted to her, "What are you doing?"

"I can't," she gasped, "Who do you think I am?"

Jon's hands gripped Andrew's shoulders, trying to pull him back, but Andrew easily shrugged him off.

"I don't know who I am either and I don't know what the Hell keeps happening to me, but I know who you are Meg"

She felt sick and her head swam from the combined effects of shock and alcohol. He was coming at her like a wild animal, eyes flashing, mouth bleeding, sweat darkening his hair. Yet she was sure that if she just took him in her arms, it would tame him. Every inch of her skin longed to feel every inch of his.

"Andrew, stop!" Jon insisted, trying once again to pull his brother away. "Leave her alone. You don't know what you're saying."

Andrew turned on Jon, eyes flashing with anger. "Get off of me. I don't know who you are, but I know what you're doing to me."

"Andrew, it's me. It's Jon. I'm your brother. I'm not going to hurt you."

Andrew spit blood and scowled. "All I know is that I keep waking up in places where you're at. You're the one screwing with me, and now you're screwing with her."

Desperate to avoid a scene, Jon grabbed Andrew's arms and pinned them together, hoping to restrain him long enough to get him back to the car.

But Andrew grunted, "Get off of me!" and with a nearly inhuman strength, wrenched his arms out of Jon's grasp. The two broke apart for just one stumbling moment, then they rushed back together into a wrestler's embrace. Libby envisioned herself emerging from the limousine and jumping between them, chirping 'break it up boys!' She knew it would do little good, however, and was afraid that if she let Andrew get his hands on her, he'd take her away on one of his homicidal missions and she wouldn't be able to stop him. She felt a sudden cold queasiness in the pit of her stomach, realizing at that moment just why Andrew's mother had believed her son would go to Hell.

Jon was beginning to lose his grip. In another moment, Andrew would have him on the ground. But as though he had been struck from behind, Andrew suddenly slumped forward and fell limply into Jon's arms. Jon's relief was palpable as he pulled his brother close, supporting him as his knees collapsed.

"Libby, help," Jon called, his voice weak.

Libby grabbed her purse and climbed out of the limousine. It was not the exit she had originally imagined. She felt frightened and ashamed, and the look of defeat on Jon's face broke her heart. His eyes shifted to the restaurant and then back to her terrified face, and it seemed as though he sensed all was lost. There would be no third chance.

Andrew moaned and straightened his shoulders but remained in his dizzy slump, unable to lift his head from his brother's shoulder. Libby's hand lifted reflexively, offering the comforting touch she had been so afraid to give her patients. She laid her hand on his back just briefly, long enough to feel the tightness in his muscles and the intense heat pouring out.

"Let's get him home," she said, amazed at how steady her voice seemed.

Jon shifted his brother's weight in his arms and sighed deeply, knowing that he was going to have to make a decision that he would probably regret. She was too good for this. She cared for Andrew with the love one would give a wounded animal and he knew that if he let her, she would shoulder the burden that he had grown so weary of bearing. It broke his heart, because he wanted to be with her so badly and knew he never could. It wasn't fair to ask this much from her.

"Have the limo take you home, Libby. I'm sorry, but we just can't do this."

Libby tried to look like she was absorbing his meaning, but she'd already made up her mind. He thought she'd never encountered anything like this, never felt the weight of this particular burden. But her yoke and his had been fashioned out of the same mold. How could she walk away from that?

"Jon, just get in the car."

She watched the small muscles of his face tighten, an effort to restrain an expression of relief. Jon lowered his head and pleaded silently for Andrew to walk, and Andrew, dazed, allowed his brother to drag him to the black Durango. Libby stood at the open door of the limousine, keeping her back to the multitude of curious eyes that still followed the scene. She watched Jon duck into the drivers' seat of the Durango. As he bowed his head to find the keys, her eyes fell as well, drifting onto the slightly dented front bumper. If the side of the limousine had not been nearby, she would have fallen. The rush of wind and smell of acrid blood dropped onto her shoulders, heavy like a bag of wet sand.

"Tell the driver to take you back to my place," Jon said, from the window of the Durango. Libby moved numbly into the expansive backseat of the limousine, now so horribly empty. She mumbled the instructions to the driver and he turned his head slightly towards her in acknowledgement, shoulders shifting in a way as to reveal the digital odometer, which, ordinarily small and inconspicuous, now displayed a figure that drove Libby's eyes reflexively to it: five ones, all in a row. Libby shook her head, found the bottle of champagne and downed the rest in one breath.

*

Jon was waiting for her on the front steps of his home. He'd long ago abandoned his suit coat and his disheveled form seemed hulking in comparison to the squat Brownstone which framed him. The stone steps upon which he sat were cracking, though they were filled in places with peeling gray caulk. Two ornate iron rails framed the steps and led up to the screen door, which was open and admitting a shallow square of light onto the lawn. It settled cautiously on Jon's shoulders as though afraid to touch him and threw his face into shadow.

Libby came up the front walk uneasily. It bisected one of the larger and neater lawns on the block, which offered enough room for a row of hedges beside the steps and a sprawling oak tree whose branches scraped the upper windows of the building. Each square of the cement path was higher or lower than the last and Libby eyes cautiously traced her path. At the foot of the stairs, she looked up into Jon's darkened face and offered a weak hello.

The bottom half of his face took on all the components of a smile, while his brow remained twisted with worry. "Andrew's inside making a frozen pizza. Hope you like cheese."

Libby lifted her hand to the iron railing beside him. At her touch, pieces of black paint flicked off and fluttered to the ground and Libby realized that it was not iron at all, but aluminum in disguise.

"Want to come inside?" he asked.

"Sure," she said, and she leaned into him, giving him barely enough room to stand. He shot up before her, then bowed his head graciously and offered her a hand. Libby pulled her hand off of the railing and let it drift towards his, but at the last minute, her fingers curled and moved to his shoulder. Tentatively, she petted him. This gesture amused her, but Jon, apparently unaware, pulled open the squeaking screen door and admitted them into the house.

The living room they'd stepped into was unusually warm and bright. The white, undecorated walls made the space seem more expansive, as did the lack of furniture. The minimal assortment was typical of a combination of former dorm room furnishings: a worn black leather couch, a large cereal bowl chair and mismatched tables. The television, flickering in the corner, was a moderate sized flat screen. It was tucked into an entertainment center cabinet, which also housed several game consoles. The area around the television was littered with wires, game cartridges and empty beer bottles.

"Sorry," Jon said quickly, following Libby's gaze. "Andrew spends a lot of time at home, and – well, we usually don't expect company."

Andrew emerged from the kitchen holding two bottles of beer, each with a film of condensation sparkling on the amber glass. After uncapping one on the edge of an end table,

Andrew wordlessly offered the second to Libby. She shook her head no, feeling her stomach still swimming in champagne.

"I made pizza," he said, offering her an apologetic smile. "I know it's not as good as the 21 Club, but I'm sure Jon will be able to get another reservation. We'll also be locking me in the closet during future dates, won't we bro?"

Jon, who had been hurriedly collecting the empty bottles, looked up at his brother and frowned. But Andrew merely laughed and tossed him the second bottle of beer. "Lighten up, Jon. She hasn't run away yet, has she?"

As Andrew's arm dropped, a sudden change came over his face, softening the lines of his jaw. Libby saw his free hand searching for the support of the wall. Jon's eyes remained on his brother, even as he twisted the cap off his bottle with the end of his tie and raised the frothing neck to his lips.

"I'll check on the pizza," he said, after swallowing hard. "Libby, please make yourself at home."

Libby moved to the cereal bowl chair and sat on the very edge. She subtly lifted her eyes to watch Andrew as he moved weakly to the couch. The loss of color in the once gold-toned face was striking.

For several minutes they sat wordlessly, listening to the quiet murmur of voices on the television. Andrew nursed his beer, watching Libby over the rim of the bottle. She wondered how much he remembered of their previous night together, praying he had at least forgotten her embarrassing display of insanity. Her fingertips outlined the broken ridges of her cuticles, reliving the moments his soft fingers had done the same.

"So," Andrew forcefully intruded upon the silence, and Libby looked up to find him aiming his words into the ground. "You must really care about my brother."

She remained silent, unable to answer. Andrew's shoulders subtly lifted and fell again. Though his face lay half in shadow, Libby saw the vestige of a trapped smile fight its way to the surface, as his lips parted and lifted at the corners for just a moment before tightening once again.

The sound of cupboard doors banging shut came from the kitchen and Libby felt a pang of guilt. Indifferent, Andrew set his beer bottle carefully on the coffee table and then shifted it with two fingers until it was at the very edge. He watched it with remarkable intensity, as if its precariousness thrilled him.

As he lifted his arm to retrieve the bottle again, his shirtsleeve fell open at the cuff and Libby glanced a twisted pink scar snaking its way down the exposed flesh. Andrew's arm froze and Libby looked up to see him watching her with curious intensity, almost in the same way he had viewed the bottle.

"Where'd you get that scar?" she asked.

He bent his arm at the elbow and inspected the scar, smiling distantly before replying: "Car accident."

Libby felt struck, again seeing the image of the speeding black Durango. "Do you often drive recklessly?" she asked, her voice unusually hollow.

He remained silent, the space between his eyebrows narrowing slightly.

"Do you remember what happens during your black outs?" she pressed.

He shook his head, still stunned by her sudden forwardness. She looked away. "You said you knew who I was."

"I recognized you?"

"You called me Meg."

"Does it matter?" he retrieved the precariously balanced bottle and took a long swig.

"Yes. You recognize me. Sometimes I recognize…people," she copped out, then punished herself by digging the tip of her fingernail into the bed of her thumb. Suddenly she felt very unclean and her skin tingled where it contacted the chair pad.

"I don't know anything, okay?" Andrew sighed forcefully and slammed the bottle down. Foamy amber liquid geysered out. He swore and shook the wetness off of his fingers.

Jon emerged from the kitchen, balancing the pizza pan and three plates. His eyes moved from Andrew's ferocious stance to Libby's timid one.

"Everything okay in here?"

Andrew ignored him. "When are you going to stop asking me about this? I don't even know what's real and what's not anymore. I remember things that never happened, for Christ sake. For all we know, I could be leading some kind of double life, blacking out of this one and into the next, going home to a wife and kids." He laughed bitterly and buried his face in his hands. "Maybe this isn't even my real life."

Jon set the pizza down and then sat on the corner of a small table near the front door.

"Andrew, look at me. You know this is real. You know I've been with you from day one, helping you sort this out." He said this with the weary impatience of one having made the same speech many times over.

"Alright then, try this," Andrew looked up fiercely, "Have we ever been to a fucking disco?"

Jon remained silent, though the red spider lines in his cheeks seemed to sprout all at once.

"What about a big church with a blue lime stained fountain in the lobby? Does that exist?"

"Yes, that's real. Our Lady of the Angels. We used to go there with Grandma Concetta after Grandpa died. She would pray and we would - "

Andrew finished with him: "Walk the kneelers like balance beams."

His gaze snapped suddenly to an empty point in space. While outwardly, his eyes held a dull lock on this invisible point, his inner eye searched and catalogued. Perceiving this, Libby became acutely aware that his odd expression matched her own.

Suddenly, a foreign voice escaped her throat. "I remember having my photograph taken in a red-paneled room. But I was never..." she trailed off, letting the words hang.

Their presence left her uneasy and ashamed and she looked up at the brothers, expecting to see blankness in their expressions.

But Andrew's face was frozen in a twisted horror. The fullness of his cheeks and elevated Adam's apple revealed a breath that had been halted. Libby felt her own throat tighten and she straightened, her flight instinct pumping her heart and electrifying her spine. *No. He can't possibly remember that too.*

Looking between Andrew and Libby, Jon felt sick. The odor of burnt cheese and cold crust reached his nostrils and enhanced the nausea. Something had been wrong with all of this from the start. The looks that had passed between Libby and his brother since their meeting were difficult to interpret, but Jon had imagined that she was merely curious and he amused. Now, her random senseless statements and urge to know more about his brother's condition aroused his suspicion.

But Jon's spirit had never known the acidic stain of jealousy. Instead, he felt scared and uneasy. In that room, sanity was no longer in the majority and Jon feared what he soon might be led to believe.

"The pizza is cold," he spoke neutrally, and without waiting for Libby and Andrew to react, he grabbed the pan and hurried to the kitchen. As he passed by, Andrew snapped his eyes away from Libby to gauge his brother's expression before he disappeared around the corner. The last thing Andrew wanted was for Jon to believe that these frequent disruptions to his budding relationship were intentional. To his relief, however, he found neither anger nor suspicion on his brother's face.

When Andrew turned back to Libby, he found that she was at the door.

"Where are you going?" he asked, rising from the couch.

She shook her head and pursed her lips, then pulled a photograph from her purse, scribbled something on the back and handed it to him.

"Tell Jon I'm sorry," she said, her hand on the door. "This isn't goodbye. Just – goodnight."

She left Andrew dumbfounded, standing in the center of the room with the photograph clutched loosely at his side. At the sound of the banging screen door, Jon came out of the kitchen.

"Where'd she go?" he asked, voice strained from this added level of mystery.

"Just goodnight," Andrew echoed, and then lifted the photograph. There was the room he had so often remembered, white walls, red panels. They told him he'd never been there, and Jon had laughed, saying that his dissociated self must be much less brooding if he'd managed to be invited to a party.

But that didn't explain Libby's memory of the incident. Moreover, it didn't explain why this strange, intense girl that Jon had brought home was also a victim of a deceitful memory. He turned the photograph over and found a phone number scribbled on the back. His heart dropped out of rhythm briefly and he slid the photograph into his pocket and turned to his brother.

"Did you re-heat the pizza?"

Jon nodded slowly, eyes falling to Andrew's pocket. "What was that?"

"Just some ad taped on the front door."

Jon's lips parted slightly and then rejoined as Andrew's collected confidence counteracted his entropy.

"It should be done in a second," he said, and turned away from his brother to breathe in the scent of Libby, which was slowly drifting away after her.

Outside, Libby hesitated at the end of the sidewalk. The limo was gone and home was across town, but she knew that if Jon drove her home, she'd have to choose between awkward silence and telling more of the lies that had unfairly led him on. She could hear the sound of heavy cross traffic several blocks away, however, and knew she could catch a cab there. So, leaving Jon's small patch of light behind, Libby walked past house after house, obsessively taking one step up each front path. Can't miss a single one. Right foot up. Next one left - forcing a body twist that had her facing backwards and led to a new compulsion. Nine steps backwards, pause, count to nine, eight steps forward, pause, count to eight, seven steps backwards, pause... *come on, I'll never get home.*

A crosswalk loomed ahead and she cried out in convulsive tearless sobs. A lone car slowed to a stop before it, waiting for her to cross. *Oh no...* Four steps forward, pause, three steps backward, two, one...then to nine again. She felt

her cheeks flush with the heat of pent-up rage and as she
stepped slowly through the headlight beams, the driver's
impatience seemed personified in the growling engine.
Frustrated and apologetic, she looked through the windshield at
the driver.

The dictated four-second pause lasted six, until the
putty-faced man laid on the horn and startled her away. He then
burned rubber. Stumbling, Libby watched his taillights waning,
as the howl his tires had left behind echoed off every house on
the block and then returned to her.

8

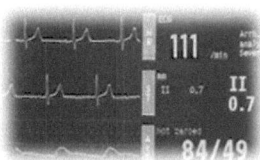

Consciousness came to Jon in flashes. At one moment, he was crouched over the black lab bench top, arms moving skillfully through an array of glass tubes and flasks. In the next, his feet were pounding the pavement, running to God knows where. Then he was jumping up cracking cement steps, fingers driving flecks of black paint from the bars of the screen door as he jammed his key into the lock.

He clung to this latest state of clarity as his body drove him into his living room. *Why am I here? What is this feeling?* The last question he addressed to the sick sensation that overpowered him, as if the walls had unfolded and expanded and air had rushed in to fill the spaces between his cells. Dizzily he stumbled forward, falling towards the kitchen door, off of which he ricocheted to the counter. His head flew back, the walls spun, the light of the overhead bulb streaked in blinding ribbons, back and forth. Then, clarity was once again lost. Suddenly, he was behind Andrew, who was sitting on a beanbag chair in front of the television fighting with a game controller. The screen flickered intensely and Jon lost focus again, returning to see Andrew running down the hall before him, looking back over his shoulder with his mouth wide in the formation of a cry that never reached his ears.

The next thing Jon knew, they were in his bedroom and Andrew was on the ground, floundering against the side of his bed. His eyes were white and rolling like a wounded animal's and when he fell onto his back, Jon saw that he was clutching his waist as though he had been struck. Andrew's eyes stopped their mad flight long enough to follow his brother's gaze, and when he pulled his fingers away from his side, he found a deep pumping gash. The blood, dark and purple, had already steeped through the T-shirt surrounding the wound.

The pace of everything increased, as though suddenly the world in Jon's vision was projected with high-speed film. Andrew's lips, spitting blood and saliva, formed rapid cries but no sound came. Jon remained audibly and emotionally detached, as though he were watching the scene on a projected screen and the sound system had failed. Then in one blinding rush sound and sight exchanged places. The curtain, dark and heavy, fell over the screen and all that was left was the harmony of Jon and his brother's cries building in a massive crescendo, finally breaking and then, with all else, fading out.

At that moment, Jon awoke. His cheek was pressed against the lab bench top, and when he pulled his face away, he saw that he had left behind a patch of moisture that was quickly lost to the air. Several tubes lay on their sides, fallen when he had carelessly let his head drop. *When did I fall asleep?* he wondered, anxiously righting the fallen tubes. His eyes sought the clock; it was just after ten, which meant a long day still lay ahead. Now that the alertness that accompanied sudden waking had left him, he felt the effects of the previous sleepless night. Libby had left in such strange circumstances and he had laid awake, hoping she'd gotten home all right and debating whether or not to call her. He had the sneaking impression that she didn't want to talk to him at the moment, even though Andrew had reiterated that she hadn't intended him to think that way. "She just said goodnight," he had said again, but when Jon asked why she had left, Andrew had remained silent.

Andrew. Jon's mind flashed back to the horrible dream and he shuddered. He didn't think he was the sort of person who had dreams about committing murder, much less stabbing his own brother in cold blood. Still, he could understand the circumstances behind the haunting of his subconscious. The events of the past few days had generated an unwanted feeling of contempt in him towards his brother. The feeling was beyond jealousy, for Jon knew that Andrew would never take Libby from him. Rather, it was the circumstances that were taking both Libby and Andrew away from Jon, and perhaps it was this sickness, represented in the counterfeit form of his brother, that Jon wished to exterminate.

Jon stood up slowly and arched his back, feeling each rib separate as he drew a deep breath and tried to clear his head. He ducked into the lab bathroom and bent over the sink, hungrily opening the tap and splashing handfuls of cool water onto his face. Briefly, blood rose to the surface of his skin and then departed, losing its heat to the air. Thus refreshed, Jon straightened, blinked stray drops off of his eyelashes, and surveyed his haggard reflection. His eyes traveled down the jagged weary lines that had been left behind on his once boyish complexion like tread-marks ruining a fresh snowfall.

Then, his eyes descended a bit further and fell onto a spot of dark red on the collar of his lab coat. He stepped back and looked down, finding the first spot, then another, then a jagged smear. Hesitantly, he pressed the tip of one finger onto the smear and lifted it, finding that a rusted orange had settled into the crevices of his fingertip. When the heavy iron smell hit him, he froze. Blood, still wet. Blood, splattered as if off the tip of a knife. Blood, already seeping through the T-shirt surrounding his brother's wound.

*

Libby had been watching the light change across the foot of her bed. A defined square of bright moonlight had drifted throughout the night before, ebbing into the duller square of new sun, pink in its infancy. After the overture of one soloing bird had led into the morning chorus, Libby had thrown away her bed sheets, set one foot onto the cold hardwood, then decided instead to throw away her obligations and crawl back into the cocoon she had created during the long hours of the night. Why waste such a perfect space?

She had spent the morning drifting in and out of the same dream, losing details when she awoke and regaining them as she returned to sleep. *I'll never go back*, she told herself during one lucid moment. *I'll move away from this place - from myself.* And with that, she returned to the dream.

Yet soon after, her cell phone's ring broke into her fantasy and dragged her back. Resisting, Libby let it ring through to voice mail. But when it rang again several seconds later, she sacrificed the cocoon. As she flipped the lid, she wasn't surprised to see Jon's cell number on the caller ID. She had barely taken breath to say hello before he cut in.

"Libby, it's Jon. Thank God you picked up."

Libby sat straight up in bed, and then watched stars falling down the periphery of her vision. Dizzily she leaned onto her headboard and tried to compose her voice.

"Yeah, I was just sleeping in. What's up?"

"I'm driving over to your place now."

Her eyes drifted to the corner of her room, where a broken cobweb was casting a wavering shadow. She almost didn't want to ask. Andrew had dissociated again, gotten lost, and now Jon was dragging her out of bed to find him.

But Jon's voice was strung tightly. "I think Andrew is seriously hurt."

Her palms, which had once felt the heat of him, instantly blazed. She closed her eyes, seeing him as she had the night before, wrought by the weakness in his form. Her face felt suddenly flushed, or was it the heat of the phone? She wanted to throw it across the room and deny the words that Jon had conveyed to her through it.

"Did you call the police?"

After a long silence, he feebly replied no. Libby felt as though she had been punctured and deflated. "Jon, you have to!"

He fumbled for words, stuttering several responses before finally choosing one. "I can't. I don't even know for sure if he's hurt."

She started to protest, but he abruptly cut her off. "Just be ready."

There was a click on his end and he was gone, leaving Libby in her half-reclined state, one leg still wrapped in her morning's womb while its twin had tasted its first breath of air and found it cold and unwelcoming. Yet so much of her had already drained, she had to reclaim it. Her feet found the cold floor and, thus animated, carried her to the front door where she paused only to grab her keys and slip on a pair of sandals. She pounded down the three flights of stairs to the building lobby and burst onto the porch, facing full assault now from the sunlight, which had previously sent its scouting ray to observe her as she had lain in hiding. Now, dressed only in her faded periwinkle scrub pants and a purple and white Northwestern University T-shirt, she felt exposed and uneasy.

Jon's car arrived quickly. As he screeched to a dead stop, Libby jumped the porch steps and ran down to the street to meet him.

"Where is he?" she asked, edging into the front seat.

He remained silent and floored the gas pedal. Fighting against the inertia, Libby turned her head to look at him.

"Jon, what's going on? Did he call you?"

"I don't know," Jon snapped, his fingers tightening on the wheel, "It doesn't matter. I just..."

He trailed off and as the silence persisted beyond a pause, it seemed as though he had forgotten that he had even said anything to begin with. The space between Libby's eyes burned, bravely containing hot tears of frustration. Why wouldn't he answer?

Jon turned a corner sharply, causing everything on the floor of the car to shift. Libby looked down to find one of Jon's lab coats balled up against her ankle, now slowly unfolding. As it did, the insolent thing bared its marred face for her and she leaned forward, wondering: *is that blood?*

She looked up. Jon was now sitting very erect in his seat, eyes flashing between her and the road.

"Don't touch that," he warned. His voice was toneless, a product of the detached calculations that had led to his response, born from a part of his mind that could sum experiences instantly and produce the only answer that would deter Libby Cohen. "I spilled a sample of HIV positive blood on my coat this morning."

Libby drew herself away, a gesture that allowed Jon to see what he had done. *She'd asked for gloves. She's afraid.* The cinch around his chest tightened, furthering his pain. He'd lied, and he'd done this to Andrew. That was his brother's blood on that jacket, a thing more potent than anything he could invent. But how could it be? How could he have done this?

He felt a sudden stab - a memory, arriving like a frigid knife driving between his shoulder blades. It severed the cinch and his heart, thus freed, began to flee in rapid pounding steps. *Mom was right. Andrew killed that boy as easily as I just...* His fingers tightened on the wheel, while his foot drove deeper into the pedal, delivering another abusive blow to the dying engine. Beside him, Libby gripped the arm rests and squeezed her eyes shut to quell the rising nausea as both her body and mind suffered vertigo while staring down the edge of control.

Jon veered the car to the side and rolled up onto the curb, coming to a crooked stop in front of the Brownstone. For a moment he froze, hand still in its course towards the ignition key. Libby said his name and his eyes fell to the lab coat at her feet, moving from one stain to the next. At the last, the spell seemed to be broken and he plunged out of the car.

Libby followed close behind, watching as he took the steps in one fluid motion and fumbled with his key in the lock. The door opened to dim light and the flicker of the television playing on low volume to an empty room. In the doorway, Jon stalled yet again.

Libby moved past him and into the room, looking around as though she knew what she expected to find. The room looked as though it had the night before, still littered and in bleak disarray, if not more so. Libby turned questioning eyes to Jon, pleading silently with him to end this madness or at least help her understand it. But Jon's gaze was fixed on some invisible point beneath him, his expression as interminably wretched as those ghoulish faces cast forever in their dying cries by the ashes of Vesuvius. There was the bean bag chair, the abandoned game controllers. It was real. It had happened.

Libby tried desperately to get his attention, but he remained transfixed – until a muffled groan reached them both at once and he lunged forward. Libby followed him towards the source of the cry.

Jon reached the corner first and then stopped in his tracks, staring down the hall. Beyond him, Libby saw Andrew lying in a heap against the wall. His knees were bent up against his chest and he leaned over them, his back rising and falling to an immense degree with each forced breath. Libby dropped to her knees beside him and he looked up, exposing the dark stain on the front of his shirt, a color that matched the trail that led from this spot to the bedroom door. His eyes flashed and he lifted his hand, groping desperately for her. The movement brought on new pain, however, and he cried out and pressed his eyelids together tightly. When he opened his eyes again, they were glassy and rolling.

"He's going into shock," Libby said dully, then with more intensity: "Jon, call 911."

He moved to the kitchen. Libby hands hovered hesitantly over Andrew's quivering form. There was so much blood lost. He was draining just as quickly as she, but how could she reanimate him?

Andrew's hand lifted away from the wound, then his chest expanded and he threw his head back, biting down to barricade a scream. It terrified her. Libby took his shoulder with one hand: its feverish heat roiled beneath her skin. She pressed her other hand over the wound, feeling the taut muscles rebound and quiver, feeling the pulse of the warm blood that she could only hope to contain. Andrew reached for her and drove her into him, wrapping his broad hands around her arm, taking in the sensation of life so as to not forget his own.

His face was unnaturally distorted and pale, and even while Libby's own heart quickened, she felt the pulsing beat of his blood slowing beneath her fingertips. Andrew laid his head back against the wall and as his hair fell out of his eyes, Libby saw an eerie calm in them, as though he had accepted resignation.

"Stay with me," Libby commanded, sliding her hand around the back of his neck and turning his face towards hers. The howl of distant sirens reached her ears, help following just behind. She pressed her hand deeper into the wound, searching desperately for life beyond the now slackened muscles and faded pulse. She felt her own heart heavy as a stone in the pit of her stomach.

Jon's shadow fell across them and she looked up to find him in the kitchen doorway, holding the phone at his side.

"Jon, what happened?" Libby demanded, "Who did this to him?"

Jon shook his head slowly, as though he was not in control of the motion. Andrew's gaze resurfaced and met his brother's briefly before growing vacant once again. His body convulsed beneath Libby's hands and then fell still.

"Come on Andrew," Libby pleaded, her hand leaving his neck and burying itself in the moist tangled locks of his hair. She pulled them, shook his head from side to side; but nothing could deter the descent of his eyelids. Jon's shadow elongated suddenly as he fell to his knees.

*

Jay met the gurney at the emergency room door. As he gripped the handles of the bed and pulled it into the trauma room his eyes briefly met Libby's, conveying numerous questions. Libby shook her head slightly and then looked pointedly down at Andrew's graying form. *Not now.*

"Alright people," Jay said, "Stab wound to the lower left quadrant, BP 60 palp, heart rate 150." He signaled to the nurses, "Start a line, please. I need blood sample for type and cross-match."

As Libby watched the huddle of nurses following Jay's orders, her hands began to burn. She'd felt the sensation before in situations such as these. But while her hands had once begged her to stay away from the touch of blood and skin, now they could not lie still. She moved to the supply cabinet and retrieved a handful of gauze squares, which she then pressed over the wound.

"Prep 2 liters of lactate," she found herself snarling to the nurse beside her, who was already in the process of hooking the bag of heavy fluids up to Andrew's IV. The clear liquid began to flow into a bulging vein, balancing the volume of fluid that Andrew's body had lost before his blood could be replaced.

"Libby," Jay urged. She looked up to find him staring at her blood-covered hands. "This is going to need surgery. Do you know what happened?"

Libby spoke softly, "Remember my date's brother?"

Jay's mouth fell open. The blood pressure monitor beeped suddenly and Jay dissociated from his shock long enough to check it, then rebuilt the appalled expression which prompted Libby to elaborate.

"We found him like this at home."

"Any idea who did it?"

"He couldn't say."

Jay sighed, pursing his lips to extend the exhalation. "Well, his pressure is stabilizing. He'll be conscious before surgery. Maybe we can get something out of him."

A clatter from behind Jay caused them both to look up and find Jon, leaning heavily against a counter and hurriedly restacking a fallen stack of instrument trays.

"Does he know anyone who'd want to hurt him?" Jay asked, eyeing Jon suspiciously.

Libby's head jerked up. "Yes. There's this guy who's always following us around."

"Do you think you can identify him?"

She laughed bitterly, "He's pretty distinctive. His face looks like caulking putty."

Jay cocked his head, as though he'd heard wrong. He remained in this position for such an irritatingly long period, Libby snapped at him. "What?"

"Nothing. Just a coincidence. We had a fatal car accident victim come in last night and I remarked to myself that his face looked like it was made of clay."

Beneath Libby's hands, Andrew's arm lifted suddenly. His eyes were wide now and in his disorientated state he reached across his body as though to pull out the IV line. Libby grabbed his hand to pull it back and Andrew curled his fingers around hers. Libby felt herself rising to her toes, as though suddenly weightless.

"What's his name?" Jay asked lowly, restraining Andrew's other shoulder.

"Andrew," Libby said, her voice joined by Jon's, who was now at the foot of the bed.

"Andrew, I'm Dr. Harris." Jay said, in a professional tone that was so unlike his own voice, it startled Libby. "We're going to give you something to help with the pain. You're going to need a belly scan first and then we might have to take you into surgery to fix things up. But you're doing just fine."

Libby cringed; the words she had been taught to say had never before sounded so sickeningly false. She wondered how easily Jay could maintain this farce of professional detachment if he had been there to see the blood loss, or witnessed dying expressed by the gradual fading of color in Andrew's eyes. What would he say to him then?

"Do you understand?" Jay asked. Jon moved closer to his brother, deconstructing his expression and looking for fear behind the dull acceptance that Andrew was showing the others. But the resignation that softened his brother's eyes was genuine. He was no stranger to this.

Jon's relief was short lived, however, when he saw the look that passed between Andrew and Libby as he proved his remaining strength for her and she, transfixed, was drawn closer to him by it. Their fingers were locked together and the muscles in Andrew's arm were taut as he clung to her, the fibers responding to her touch as though the strength he showed had been first derived from her.

Andrew pulled his hand away suddenly, however, and when Jon looked up he found that Andrew was watching him. Libby's eyes darted to Jon quickly and then she drew her own hand back, leaving Andrew's hand to drop at his side. Their guilt only joined the tempest of Jon's own and he withdrew, resigning all further thought to that mechanical part of his being that had kept him moving through a lifetime of stalled moments such as these.

"Give him the pain meds," he commanded dully.

Jay nodded, having already begun to fill the syringe.

"Wait just a moment, doc," a voice interjected from the doorway. Libby and Jon both turned to the source with a vehement frown and then both drew back – though for different reasons. Libby recognized the man as the cop who had brought Tom in.

"Just want to ask him a few questions, if that's all right?" he said, unfolding a notepad.

"It's not all right," Libby protested. The cop looked up at her over his notepad, and, having recognized her, smirked. Apparently he had taken the time since their last meeting to exaggerate his opinion of her. Libby, already vulnerable, shrank under his judgment.

"I'm sedating the patient now," Jay said, eyeing Libby. "You can talk to him after surgery."

The cop pursed his lips and folded his notepad with an enhanced gesture, demonstrating his disdain. "Sometimes," he said dryly, "it's best to talk to the victims before surgery, just in case. After all, there's a certain risk involved, am I right doc?"

He said the words with such ease, it furthered the sense of shock Libby suffered at their meaning. Even Jay's hard demeanor became briefly fluid.

"I can assure you that this is a very simple operation," he said, straightening all of his mediocre height. "You'll be able to speak with him afterwards."

The cop, apparently unconcerned, approached the bed. "Just one question," he asked, edging past Libby. "Did you get a look at the guy that did this to you?"

Andrew's vacant gaze resurfaced and met Jon's. A long silent discourse passed between the brothers before Andrew finally spoke, "No."

Libby felt Jon's body tightening beside her. She understood his frustration. Clearly this hadn't been a random act, which meant that someone was after them. Even if Andrew's non-dissociated self hadn't been able to recognize the putty faced man, it didn't matter. If what Jay was saying was correct, he'd died last night.

That realization struck her, trapping a breath on its ascent. The putty faced man had gotten in a car accident last night, probably soon after she had passed in front of him in the crosswalk. Considering all that had happened in the past few days, it was hard to believe that this was entirely a coincidence.

Jay injected the sedative into Andrew's IV line before the cop could ask any more questions, and Andrew's eyelids began a lazy descent.

"We'll send someone down to pick him up," Jay said, then after patting Andrew's shoulder with textbook reassurance, he drew Jon away from the bed. "I just need to get a medical history from you."

Jon allowed himself to be guided to the far corner of the room, but as the orderlies flocked in and prepared Andrew's bed for transport, he watched with the sort of expression a father might have while watching his sixteen-year-old daughter drive off in his new car.

"We'll take good care of him," Jay promised.

"Yeah," Jon murmured, to fill the space. Libby stepped into his line of sight, forcing him to look at her. Now that the crisis was over, there were quite a few things that needed explaining. Jay, noticing the odd look on Libby's face, posed a hesitant question. "Is there anything else I should know?"

"He has a psychiatric condition," Jon murmured, without even parting his lips. Jay leaned forward and Jon said it again, then added, "It's called dissociative fugue."

"Oh," Jay glanced at Libby, hoping she could silently convey an explanation and save him from appearing ignorant. Libby, however, was not going to offer any further information. In fact, she was appalled that Jon had even mentioned it.

"That has nothing to do with this," she muttered, glaring at him with as much contempt as she dared. She knew Jay's standard solution to any sort of psychological problem.

And predictably, he replied, "We'll admit him to psyche after the operation."

Libby prepared herself to counter Jay, but realized the futility and turned instead to Jon. "How can you let that happen? You told me yourself you never wanted that for him."

Jay lifted his hand to silence her. "Libby, that's enough. Look at what happened. Do you need any more proof that he's at risk?"

"Jay, you don't know anything about this," Libby spat. The condescending softness remained in his eyes, however, and Libby turned her efforts instead to Jon. "You know Andrew didn't do this to himself."

She eyed him with the look a pitbull might offer a sleepy cat, as if to urge: "Wake up and challenge me!" Jon, however, remained in an oddly pale and frozen state. After everything he had said about his mother, he was going to let them take Andrew away without one word of protest. She might as well go with him, what with the red-paneled room and the putty-faced man and her faith in Tom's predictions. She wondered if the poor man was up in psyche right now, having his senses confounded out of him by a lot of doctors who thought they were doing just the opposite.

Very suddenly, she had had enough. Leaving nothing in her expression for Jon or Jay to read, she turned her back on them and walked away. She was done with this: done with the sterile white hallways and the reflection of fluorescent light falling onto the polished floor and sliding forward as she walked, propelling her ahead. She was done wondering where the lights were taking her, knowing all along that it would only be to another hall, another day, another lie.

Jon didn't have the answers and Jay wouldn't let her find them. There was only Andrew, and despite everything that had drawn them together, she couldn't read anything past his incessantly amused expression. She had no idea if the fingers that had clutched hers had only been driven to do so by a wider delirium. How would a man in her same boat respond when she bored a hole in the bottom, letting the feared water bubble in?

But she dropped her head and smiled into the only space of darkness that had escaped the brutal fluorescence. It was sink or swim. She knew exactly what she needed to do.

*

Later that evening, she entered a more subdued hospital lobby. In the main waiting area, a television newscaster droned the nightly news recap to an array of empty chairs. A handful of straggling visitors that passed by gave it no attention; they were bent over into themselves as they headed across the lobby, bolstering their senses before colliding with the outside world and the reality that they were leaving a loved one to spend a lonely night in this deathly prison. As Libby moved past them she thought about Andrew, wondering if he was asleep or awake. His own bed would lie untouched tonight, or perhaps it had already been disturbed in the struggle that had darkened the sheets. There was never meant to be blood on the carpet and the walls. She shivered and pulled her arms around herself, bolstering her own senses before stepping into the elevator and hitting the button for the Psyche floor. She was getting him out.

Her hospital ID got her past the front desk, where she uncovered Andrew's room number and delivered a lie about taking him to radiology. As she walked down to his room, the dark smile crept back onto her face. Of course. She would have expected nothing less than Andrew being in room 11.

The fluorescence that filled the hall leading to his room was as bright as ever, denying the presence of night outside of the four windowless walls that kept these prisoners in. Unlike the other floors of the hospital, the psyche ward was much more eerily contained. The doors to the patients' rooms were all kept shut, so that she or anyone passing down the hall could imagine for a moment that there was nothing behind them but supply closets or bathrooms. Certainly not human beings.

She knocked on the eleventh door and waited for Andrew's voice. When silence returned, however, she pushed the door open hesitantly and stepped into a dim room.

"Hello?" she called softly.

A rustle of bed sheets responded, and her heart hesitated between beats. "Andrew?"

Her fingers found the light switch and plunged the room into stark light. She caught Andrew in the act of hurriedly pulling the sheets around an unkempt gown, whether trying to hide the stained bandages around his waist or the fact that the blue and white checkered drape made him out to be an invalid, just like the other dying souls occupying the hospital's other cells.

"Thank God," he whispered, his voice sounding strained. "This psyche ward was starting to drive me crazy."

He looked at her, a twisted expression, waiting to gauge her reaction to the quip. After all, he hardly knew her at all. She was just some strange girl that his brother had brought home who had an unnatural connection to certain mysterious aspects of his life and – he closed his eyes – who had touched his skin and brought him back.

"What are you doing here?" he asked in a whisper, voice still lost somewhere in the reverie.

She spoke bluntly. "I'm getting you out of here."

His eyelids slid open slowly, admitting the painful light as gradually as possible. He saw that she held her limbs awkwardly, as though uncomfortable in this bold persona she had donned. Andrew was fairly certain that helping a patient escape the mental unit was not part of her job description, so why was she so convinced that she had to do this? Possibly, a small voice in the back of his mind wondered, for the same reasons he felt so compelled to follow.

"Do you think that's wise?" he challenged half-heartedly.

She shook her head but responded in the affirmative, "You'll be fine. The surgery was minor. I can administer the meds you need…"

"I'm not asking you if you think I can," he interrupted. "I'm asking if you think I should."

Libby frowned, having expected him to want nothing more than to leave this place immediately. But years of living as a prisoner in his own home had resigned him to captivity. He could accept the loss of freedom that ensured he would remain safe – not from harm to himself, but from harming others. Even now, as she dug deep into his seemingly blank expression, she sensed the mark of self-loathing that bent his lips into an expression of constant mirth, as though he found his existence to be pathetically comic. From this, she sensed that he knew exactly what he was capable of when dissociated.

"Jon didn't mean for you to be here," she said finally. "He was just scared."

Andrew shifted his eyes away and laughed bitterly. "No doubt he was."

"What does that mean?" she questioned, not understanding his tone.

"Nothing," he looked back, "I just don't think it's a very good idea for me to go back to Jon right now."

Libby wanted to tell him that Jon would understand, but she wasn't sure that he would. Something had really shaken him.

"You can stay at my place," she offered, "Just until Jon comes to his senses."

"I'm sure Jon is in complete possession of his senses right now. I'm just worried what might happen when he loses them again…" Andrew trailed off, seeing the confusion in her eyes and deciding that there was no need for her to know any of this. Jon had to remain perfect in her eyes. Their relationship was the only thing that could save his brother the misery he had caused, even if he wanted the girl so badly for himself. Andrew silenced the thought and tried to hate her for it, but when she spoke again her voice was so honeyed with compassion and fortitude, he could not help but be swept away again by the craving.

"Andrew, we have to find out what's going on before you get seriously hurt."

"I know," he spoke without hearing the words. Instead, he closed his eyes and drew back a bitter memory. He had lost control once too and committed murder in cold blood. That act had torn his family apart and he was not about to let that happen again. If it were happening to Jon now, it had to be stopped. Andrew would sooner die by another's hand than have his brother commit the murder. There had to be an explanation for all of this and it was time to start asking for it.

And then, as though Libby had read his mind, she said, "You know, we're asking the same questions. I can't find the answers alone."

He nodded slowly, offering a solemn consent. She came and took his arm gently. His heart fluttered before he realized what she was doing, as she pulled back the tape surrounding his IV and then, pressing the skin, removed the needle. The tube fell beside him, dripping fluid. He resisted the urge to ask her if whatever was now rolling in bubbles across the waterproof sheets was meant to be in him.

She released his arm and directed him to apply pressure, then fought to unfold a wheelchair that had been stashed beside a cabinet. He watched her work, wondering what it was about her that made her seem so different than any other girl he'd ever seen. Granted, there hadn't been many since he had begun living with Jon, but there were girls he remembered from high school; those four years of fighting with hormones and feeling much like the animal who while dying of some wound, shows sudden aggression to the pack as though to ward off final judgment for this moment of weakness. There had been the girls with big hair and short skirts, girls who laid their manicured hands all over him and spoke to him in pearly tones, driven mad by the dark rebel with the face of a child and the body of a man. He'd never wanted them. They were reflections of everything he hated about his own life - the disconnection with reality. He wanted someone real, someone who didn't know how great she looked, who had a thought in her head and something to say. Libby was that girl. Her simple untended beauty mesmerized him and the more she was with him, the more deeply he longed to find out everything inside of her mind. There was so much there, such a mystery. He had to find a way to unlock the great light inside of her, so it could chase away the darkness that had settled so long over him.

"Can you make it?" she asked, pushing the wheelchair alongside the bed. He nodded and moved gingerly into the chair, lowering his face to hide a reflexive wince.

"Get my things," he said, with what little breath was still trapped in his lungs. It was too painful to draw any more.

She opened the cabinet and found the bag of what clothing hadn't been stained or cut open, then added handfuls of gauze and bandages. She then gripped the back of his chair and pulled him slowly out of the room, taking the corner awkwardly. Andrew pulled his feet in and began to have second thoughts.

They passed a patrolling night nurse as they entered the hall, but Libby merely smiled and delivered the sort of half-hearted wave one might give to another night shift victim. The nurse waved back and moved on and Andrew finally found the means to release the trapped breath. Good idea or not, they might at least get away with it.

Libby stopped at a computer station in a small corridor off the main hall.

"Getting your pain meds," she explained in a whisper, then with flying fingers, logged into Andrew's medical record. She found the prescriptions and fought a pang of guilt upon seeing Jay's name electronically signed at the end of the entry. He would've understood if only she had time to explain. He'd always tried so hard to listen to her. Now she was taking his patient out of the hospital and leaving him to decide whether or not to send the authorities after her. There was no doubt in her mind that he'd know what she'd done.

She shook her head, attempting to banish doubt from it, and then grabbed a pad and wrote out Andrew's prescriptions. She signed her name at her bottom, feeling very much like she was forging it.

"We'll fill this later," she said, handing it to Andrew.

"Can we stop at my place first?" he asked, as she began to wheel him down the hall again. "I need to get a few things."

Her hesitation was reflected in the slowing of the wheelchair. "What about Jon?"

"Working late. He said he'd come to see me when he gets out at eight," Andrew lifted his arm as though to check his watch, if it had not been removed with the rest of his things. Frustrated, he dropped his wrist and let his shoulders cave in. "Well, in any case, he won't be back at the house."

She stopped suddenly, causing him to shift painfully forward. Fearing that she had changed her mind, Andrew's mind raced to find more reassurances. But she had recognized a name on a clipboard which hung near the door they had just passed. *Tom.*

"What are you doing?" Andrew asked, as she knocked insistently on the door. "Libby, we can't free the entire pound."

But a voice from within had invited her in. She left Andrew in the hall and entered the room, feeling very much like she was at the top of a large roller coaster plummet, discovering the severe futility of second thoughts. Was this going too far?

Tom didn't look surprised to see her, which she took as a good sign.

"Nice of you to drop in," he said, his normally airy accent somewhat sodden with whatever sedatives they were using to keep him from countering their reality.

"I'm about to do something crazy," she emphasized the last word.

His tired face lifted into a smile. "Aren't we all?"

"Yes, well," she looked away nervously, "Before I do, I was wondering if you had any particular words of advice?"

His eyelids fluttered and then closed. After a moment of silence, he spoke softly. "Just be sure to get away from the car."

Libby's body tensed. "What do you mean? What car?"

"I – I don't know," he stammered, and when his eyes opened again, she saw guilt in them. "I wish I could tell you more. It's these bloody tranquilizers. They cloud everything."

Libby committed the vague words to memory despite wishing that he had told her something more concrete. Having already forgotten what he had warned her of earlier, she wasn't even sure what had possessed her to believe that Tom had any answers. From her experience, she knew that delusions tended to disguise themselves as the most satisfying answers.

She offered him a feeble thank you, then an apology. She would have to leave him here, despite encouraging the ability that these doctors were systematically destroying, be it psychic or psychotic. The apology covered her awkward retreat and her own lingering doubt as she broke free from delusion's spell and returned to Andrew. It didn't matter. She had him now and was taking him from this place where he didn't belong. Andrew belonged in the arms of every woman and on a pedestal before every man. But only she knew that and she wasn't even allowed to believe it. For all the ridiculous lies her mind had tricked her into believing, her heart wouldn't allow this one simple truth.

"What was that all about?" Andrew asked, as she began wheeling him once again towards the elevators.

"Sometimes, when you're crazy, you do a lot of things that don't make sense," she quoted him, and Andrew almost believed that he could feel her smile.

9

The Brownstone lay dark and silent, convalescing from the madness that had occurred within it earlier. Still, as Libby stepped into the living room for the second time that day, she detected the tangible vestige of the extraordinary events that had proceeded there: the stuffy sensation that accompanied time running out, the acrid tinge of spilt blood. All of it seemed to keep her from entering, like an invisible barrier. Andrew, however, was seemingly unperturbed and glided past the spot where he had laid with little more than a second glance.

As he moved to his bedroom, Libby folded her arms around herself protectively and stepped farther into the living room, looking around for any obvious signs that a struggle had taken place. The front door had not been damaged, at least. She wondered how the intruder could have managed to enter so soundlessly as to not attract Andrew's attention, unless – her eyes moved to the video game controllers at her feet – he had been preoccupied.

She looked up, past the now silent television and onto the careless row of photographs that sat atop of the entertainment center. Imagining that they might offer her some sign that Jon and Andrew's lives weren't entirely without some grounding in reality, she moved closer to examine them. The first two must have been Andrew and Jon's senior portraits. Jon's hair had been cut even closer to his head then, accentuating every bulge and dip in his skull. His eyes were bright and the rosy hue in his cheeks was as defined as ever. The pose had meant to portray him as business-like, and he stood against a backdrop of bookshelves, leaning against a dark red leather executive's chair and offering the slightest of solemn smiles. Yet the youthful energy contained in his bright expression gave him away, while the backdrop was an awkward counter to his gangly frame.

In contrast, Andrew's picture contained him with perfect ease. He stood beside a bright red Mustang convertible, leaning casually against the door with his back to the car, one hand seemingly in the act of flinging an oil-stained rag over the opposite shoulder. While Jon had captured this reflection of passage from youth to adulthood by inelegantly donning a suit and tie, Andrew wore a plain black T-shirt draped low over dark jeans. His hair had been longer then, shearing at the base of his neck and falling well over his ears. The self-amused expression in his face had not changed.

Libby became aware of Andrew's presence behind her and she lifted her hand, gesturing to the photograph.

"You liked cars?"

"Yeah," he replied, his voice distant. "I rebuilt the engines and raced them on Staten Island."

"Against who?"

"Anybody willing to bet their cars on a single race."

"You're kidding. You were willing to give up that much?"

He laughed dismissively. "I didn't care. I knew I wasn't going to lose. There's a certain point beyond which it becomes less about the car and more about the driver, and in that case, I was the only one willing to go so far I could lose control."

"Why?" she frowned, staring deeply into the weary face of the youth leaning against one of his trophies.

"Because that's why I did it," he said, his voice suddenly soft.

She tore herself away from the photograph and looked back at him, recalling the image of the ugly scar on his wrist, seeing once again the speeding black Durango and imagining herself stepping over the yellow line.

Something like understanding rose in her eyes and Andrew stared deep into them, wondering if it were possible that she had felt this way before. She - this precarious thing, this jarring box of light fighting for release. He looked past her and sought the one photograph that he knew could discourage this dangerous hope. It was the image of his mother: a glamour shot taken months before her death. Soon after, they had used it for her obituary.

Libby's eyes followed Andrew's and fell onto the woman's tired visage. Even without asking, she knew that it was his mother. There was something inexplicably unsettling about the image and Libby leaned closer, trying to understand the source of the power it held over her. The woman's face was visibly ravaged by time and disease. Her skin was loose and set with deep lines, crevices that sprouted from the corners of her eyes and her richly painted lips. Her thin neck was draped with folds of weak skin which was discolored and spotted, as though she were a wax figure melting and scorching in heat. The dark hair, cut close to her head, was peppered with gray. Yet for all of the destruction in her figure, the ravages of time and madness, the scene had been composed to reflect elegance and beauty. The background was colorful and abstract. She was dressed in a lace-edged floral print dress, and pearls hung from her neck and earlobes. The make-up on her face was overdone, lending too much blush to the weathered cheeks, painting the shriveled lips in deep red, and framing the tired eyes with bright blue and heavy lines of black mascara that accentuated the short jagged eyelashes. The light of the camera swelled in her eyes, offering a glow that reflected her belief that for just this moment, she possessed a beauty so divine it had to be captured in this timeless portrait. Beneath this glow, however, there was the undeniable darkness of wild fear, the knowledge that as soon as the camera shutter closed, the moment would be lost. She would return to her depression, her destruction, her madness. The plain face, which had borne a troubled life, would return to the shadows and the fantasy would die, forcing her to admit that she was not beautiful or timeless. She would never be like the others.

"What happened to her?" Libby found herself asking, as she felt breathlessly caught in the woman's eternal anticipation.

"She stopped eating," Andrew answered, and she was near enough to him to hear the catch in his voice, "She didn't want to be in that institution, but Dad didn't want to take care of her. So he left her in there until she found her own way out. After she died, Dad blamed me. He knew I was the reason she was there in the first place. I tried to stay out of his way, spending most of my nights down on the Island, but when I was around and he was drinking, he'd come after me. Jon always thought he had to come between us, always tried to protect me, no matter what Dad did to him. Eventually Dad would wear himself out and disappear for a few hours, sometimes a few days. Then, one time, he never came back."

Libby let her eyes cross, picturing the two boys from the photograph standing shoulder to shoulder before a mother's grave and a father's rage. "How old were you?" she asked softly.

"Sixteen. Jon was eighteen and supposed to be starting at Berkeley in the fall, but he told them he wasn't coming and enrolled in NYU instead so he could take care of me. And I've been fucking up his life ever since."

Andrew turned his back on his mother's portrait and moved to the couch, where he sat down heavily and buried his face in his hands. Libby felt tugged in several different directions at once: drawn to him but afraid he didn't want her, drawn to escape but afraid that perhaps he did. Before she could decide, he continued.

"It *was* my fault that she went crazy though."

"No," she said, feeling more pull from the force that urged her to him. She gave in and let her legs carry her to the couch, then dropped into the heat that surrounded him.

"When I was eight," he began in a faraway tone, "This kid named Justin moved into our neighborhood. He was kind of a weird kid and didn't appear to have any friends. I felt bad for him, so I went over to his house one day and asked him if he wanted to play. Last thing I remember before the black out, we're playing in my back yard. I came to later that evening on my bike, probably about a mile from my house. When I got back home there were half a dozen cop cars all up and down the street and my driveway was filled with people. Naturally I wanted to steer clear of that, but my mom saw me and ran over, frantic and saying she thought I'd been kidnapped. She told me that she'd come out into the back yard looking for us and found Justin floating face down in the pool with stab wounds all up and down his back. I saw the pool later. The water was pink.

The cops figured that someone had come into the yard and assaulted us. They had killed Justin and come after me, but I'd managed to escape. Naturally, they said, I'd repressed the memory. And that's what they all believed. It's what I believed too until a month later when I was stashing something beneath my mattress and I found a knife. It was one of the big ones we used to cut the turkey on Thanksgiving. There was dried blood on the handle and on the mattress pad. I was only eight years old, you know. I was scared out of my mind. So I showed it to my mother and she knew what I'd done. I'd dissociated and gone out of my mind, stabbed Justin, thrown his body in the pool, and tried to get away. I was eight years old and already a killer."

Andrew took his face out of his hands and looked at Libby, waiting for her disgust and finding that her face was frozen in fear. Bowing beneath his own self-loathing, he continued. "All those years she'd told me I was blacking out because I was an angel doing God's work. Well, that couldn't possibly be true anymore. And if I wasn't an angel, I had to be a demon." His voice began to crack, thin ice yielding to too much weight. "Toward the end, she couldn't even look at me anymore."

Libby didn't know what to say. She knew that he expected her to deny it, but how could she? His knife was still in her purse. Did he remember that? Did he wonder why the front plate of his Durango was slightly dented?

"Does Jon know?"

"Yeah, and he knows that I'd probably kill again if I had the chance." His eyes moved to Libby's purse, on the table by the door. "Maybe I already have."

"But -" Libby began.

He interrupted, "But he won't let me go to the institution. He thinks it'll destroy me."

She hesitated. "Will it?"

"I don't know. I'm still convinced that there's a reason for this. I'm not a bad person, Libby. I don't think that even my subconscious would kill for no reason." He laughed sourly. "I guess I try to convince myself that maybe I'm doing the world a favor, going after bad guys or something. Like I'm some kind of backwards superhero."

Libby thought about Tom, who believed that his hallucinations were visions that allowed him to save others from impending harm. Was it just a naïve need for a raison d'être or to find apparent order in a life so heavily afflicted with chaos? But what was the reason for her own psychosis other than the justifications her stricken mind conjured? *If I step on the crack, someone will die.* Her mind flashed back to the moment, seeing her hesitation in the middle of the intersection, feeling the man in the overcoat pressing up behind her. Maybe – the thought seized her – maybe, if she hadn't lingered they would have both crossed safely before Andrew's Durango sped through. Maybe the man was dead because of a perfectly orchestrated move between she and Andrew, she stalling the man, he arriving at the exact right moment, both driven by their individual psychoses.

"Andrew, I think I'm a demon too," she whispered, feeling the space between her eyes burn with hot tears.

He broke free from himself and put his arm very suddenly around her as though grasping at an injury. "Why would you say that?" he demanded.

She shuddered violently and his arm tightened around her. "Andrew, it doesn't make sense. Why would a little kid need to die?"

He dropped his head beside her, breathing heat across her cheek. "Hitler was a kid once too, Libby."

But she couldn't take that reasoning as the final word. It didn't matter how many reasons they invented for the necessity of the man's death. The truth of it was, this could not have been a coincidence and it terrified her to think that she was helpless to some higher power that was using her as a means to carry out divine justice.

"Do you still believe in God?" she asked weakly.

His grip on her loosened. "Do you?"

"I guess." She looked up, as if finding God in the corner of the room where she always imagined him to be sitting and watching her. "Maybe the Big Bang and evolution and all that stuff really happened, maybe it didn't. I don't care what happened. I want to know why. Stuff exists, you know? Whether or not it came into being or always existed doesn't matter. There has to be a reason for it."

He laughed bitterly, "People only say that because otherwise their existence is meaningless."

"It doesn't really matter if I personally have a reason to exist. I'm talking about the basest stuff here: matter, energy. That all came from nothing. A big bunch of empty nothing that would have gone on happily being nothing forever until some force came along and made it into something."

He opened his mouth to argue, but she quickly continued. "And don't ask me what made that force, because I don't know. That's God's part of the equation and it's his business."

He laughed, releasing months of stale breath trapped in the bottom of his lungs and enjoying the brief weightlessness it brought. She looked at him critically, as though he was condescending her. But there was nothing but fondness in his eyes and gratitude that she had given him this one glimpse of her intensely alluring being. It was all that he had hoped it would be.

"We share the same memories, Andrew. We – we cause things to happen. The same coincidences are happening to both of us. You always catch the clock at 11:11, don't you?"

The smile faded from his lips and he froze, unable to speak. The silence swelled between them and he feared that it would give away the sound of his heart beating violently against his rib cage, throwing wild punches in a mad effort to survive. He saw the elevens everywhere, like they were a sign that some higher power really was toying with him. Now she was telling him that she saw them too?

"How…" he began, but he couldn't go on. It was too hard to breathe words into the stifling presence of a new reality that had snuck into the spaces within his own.

"I think that's where we start, then," Libby said decisively. "If it's happening to us, it's happening to other people. Let's get back to my place before Jon comes home, and we can Google it."

She stood up abruptly and he followed, wincing as the motion tore at the fresh incision. He longed for the bottle of pain pills in the backseat of Libby's car, though he was only too aware of the transience of their sweet relief. Still, a warm bed and a numbing *soma* was more appealing at this point than questing for the meaning of his life via a search engine.

He slung his bag over his shoulder and followed Libby to the door, hesitating to gaze once more into the face of his younger self. He felt himself once again in the driver's seat, consciousness collapsing as the engine buzzed between his ears, fingers tight on the wheel which jerked away and then, as the tires seemed to leave the road, drifted more serenely. Only in that weightless moment when he had outrun light and sense and time could he soak in the stillness like a wonderful drug until the world caught up again. It was his escape, his flight from life, hurtling at 200 miles an hour down a lonely stretch of road.

Libby looked back at him from the door and he felt a tug in his stomach not caused by the insult to his body. It was the vestigial sting of the chemical dependency he had on those moments, that flight. But when he looked at her, he might as well have been behind the wheel again.

*

She barely spoke to him on the ride home, but it was a comfortable silence. Andrew leaned against the passenger window and slid in and out of the stupor from the pain pill she had given him. As she drove, she let herself unfold into the new terrain, into the sensation of his form and not Jon's beside her. It was so much easier to breathe into the space occupied by him, though guilt sickened her when she imagined Jon walking into his brother's abandoned hospital room. Despite her protest, she understood Jon's change of heart. Though she had only known Andrew for a few days, she now felt viscerally as Jon did the juxtaposition between Andrew's moments of ease and those in which he had lost control and become the sweating, spitting, murderous entity. Jon had realized that this might be bigger than he could handle and Libby suspected the same. What if Andrew lost control while he was with her? She shuddered as the image of Andrew fighting his way into the limousine flashed in her mind.

When they reached her apartment, she supported him to the couch, her eyes insolently falling on the vase of Jon's flowers on the end table. The last time she had had a Calahan brother in her apartment, it was under much different – though equally uprooting – circumstances.

"You can sleep here," she said to Andrew as he slowly lowered himself onto the couch. She went to her closet to get out the extra blankets that she had never had use for before. What would her mother think, she wondered, if she knew that a man was sleeping on her couch? She'd probably be proud, Libby thought, burning with a renewed petulance.

She gave him the blanket and noted, briefly, the presence of his skin on her sterilized leather. He was full of germs from the hospital, no doubt, and it would have killed Libby had she not felt so strongly that she was at a juncture. It didn't seem likely that she would spend any more nights on that couch watching reruns of Full House, her face safely pressed against the leather arm rests that she knew were spotlessly clean. Those nights had been part of an ordinary existence marked by extraordinary beliefs. She felt that no matter where this quest took her, it would lead her to either embrace the ordinary or the extraordinary wholly and apart from the other.

She also knew that the place to begin was with 11:11, so she opened up her laptop and settled into the armchair beside the window, opening it a crack to admit the familiar sounds of the city. Like Jon's bookshelves, she felt that they had become the backdrop this artificial pose she had perfected all these years.

The blank search engine box invited her to cast it all away, and she took a shot in the dark and entered 11:11. Half a second later, over 293 million hits had arrived.

Libby felt a surge of anticipation. Was it really going to be this easy? Was the phenomenon really this common? She entered the first site and began to read aloud to Andrew, her voice hurried and excited despite his somber reception.

"All over the world, millions of people are experiencing the 11:11 phenomenon. Once they become tuned into the series of ones, the numbers seem to pop up everywhere. Many believe that the numbers hold more meaning and some say they feel like something is trying to get their attention – even toying with them. If you see these numbers, know you are not alone. 11:11 wake-up calls are prompts given by 1,111 spirit guardians to remind us of their presence. Some say they are light workers, whose mission is to hold as much spiritual light as possible within matter on earth. During these times of unrest, these spiritual guardians are here to assist anyone who asks them. Once they have your attention, they will continue to remind you of their presence by the 1111 prompts."

She looked expectantly at Andrew, who had stretched out on the couch and was now watching her through half-drawn eyelids.

"Sounds like a lot of bullshit to me," was his profound reaction.

Libby wasn't sure which way to fall off the fence, though she felt a slight push in his direction when, reading on, she discovered a link to receive forwarded emails from the spirit guardians themselves.

And, when after reading further she announced: "Look, we can do the 11:11 sacred dance," Andrew, head buried in her throw pillow, asked if she was shitting him. She wasn't entirely sure if she was. After all, she considered, how could she have expected reasonable answers to unreasonable questions? Maybe spirit guardians really were walking around the earth saving people and, in their spare time, answering emails.

"Seriously, what do you think?" she asked Andrew, forcing him to lift himself out of his daze long enough to grunt indifferently. She sighed and turned back to the screen, trying to imagine the sort of person who had been responsible for this text, these bold blue letters on marble gray that spoke the words of people who believed whole-heartedly in the bizarre. She found it hard to imagine that this population existed in her world, her grocery store and her subway car and her local Starbucks.

Her eyes fell onto a notice at the bottom of the page. *Join your local elevens organization and share your experiences with others. Click here for national meeting locations.*

The list had to include New York City, she thought – and it did. "60th and Third," she read aloud, prompting another grunt from Andrew. "It's an 11:11 club," she elaborated, and he extended his grunt into a moan.

"Libby, you're not serious. Are we honestly going to show up and start socializing with these wackos?"

"Why not? We need answers, don't we?"

"We need real answers, not more of this New Age-y bull shit. What does any of this have to do with what's happening to us? This is just a bunch of people who get off on conspiracies and cults and want to feel like they're special because they were chosen by the light people."

"Well, maybe we were chosen by the light people. It's what you always wanted to believe, isn't it?"

Andrew faltered. "Yeah…but not by *light people*. It just sounds so ridiculous. I mean seriously, Libby, what do they want? Our money?"

"I don't know," she snapped, "But we're at least going to find out. They meet every Thursday at 11 pm. That's two days from today. What do we honestly have to lose?"

"The last bit of sanity we're still clinging to?" he suggested off-handedly.

She sighed brutally, knowing that with his head buried, he wouldn't see her frown. "Andrew, if we don't do this we might as well just go back to the way things were. You return to the psyche ward, I return to work, and occasionally we meet up and accidentally kill someone. Is that what you want?"

He rolled his head back and forth across the pillow, offering a weary no. It was just hard to accept this on top of the recent flight from the mental ward and sleeping on the couch in his brother's girlfriend's apartment. What was he supposed to say when Jon finally caught up to him and asked him why he'd put him through all this hell? *Because*, he imagined himself saying, *it turns out that the girl you were falling for is nuttier than squirrel shit and by the way, we think we're some sort of light people.*

And why was she nutty anyway? She had never really explained what made her like him, other than showing him her battered hands. He felt the pang of a resentment that he'd been trying to suppress. After all, this was his insanity. What right did she have to sympathize with him? Was she nothing more than a conspiracy theorist who had fallen for the mystery?

Spurred by this imagined resentment, he asked a question that he immediately regretted. "What are you going to say when your boyfriend calls?"

Libby looked at him, betrayed. The words, *my what*, formed and then slipped off of her tongue. He didn't really believe that, did he? She stared at him, watching the malice soften quickly into jealousy and then return to the hardness of the accusation. All at once, she wanted to slap him and kiss him madly.

"He's going to find out eventually, you know," Andrew pressed, discouraging the growing glow of affection in her eyes by increasing the sharpness of his tone. "When are you going to tell him the truth?"

"Don't forget, you came along willingly," she bit back.

The truth was, he had never been so willing to do anything in his life. But his pride wouldn't allow her to know that. "I just came along to see what other kind of crazy shit we could get ourselves into. You think I give a damn what happens?"

"I think you do," she said softly, then as his expression remained unchanged, she questioned him more harshly, "What exactly do you think I want that you don't want?"

Nothing, nothing, he thought ardently. *I want everything you want. I want you.*

But he couldn't. "If you go down this road, you're going to hurt everyone you care about, Libby. Don't think I don't know what that's all about."

"And what about you?"

"What about me?"

"Am I going to hurt you?"

His eyes glazed as he fought his way through the confusion in his mind, the many answers he wanted to offer and the many that he could not. In his silence, she shut her computer forcefully and strode from the room. Her bedroom door closed. In a second, a thin rectangle of light streamed out from beneath it and onto the opposite wall. Softly, he addressed it: "You're the only thing that feels good."

Then, surrounded in the cacophony of unfamiliar
sounds, he kept his eyes on that steady patch of light until his
eyelids dropped and the soma took him entirely away.

*

So heavily sedated, Andrew didn't hear Libby's phone
ring at a little past nine. Libby, who had spent the past hour in
her bedroom pulling skin off of her cuticles, lunged for the
phone to silence its ring. She answered, however, with some
hesitation. This had to be Jon.

"Libby where is he?" he demanded, confirming her
fears.

Libby's mouth fell open, not having expected her mind
to have trouble with an answer. But she didn't know whether
the truth or a lie would hurt him more. Though he would be
relieved to know that she was with Andrew, how could he
understand why? If she lied and convinced him that Andrew
had taken flight as usual, he would be stricken with not
knowing if his brother was safe.

Jon, however, had a very clear idea of where Andrew
was. After all, he had seen the way Libby had argued with the
doctor. For whatever reason, she didn't want to see Andrew
locked up. *No*, he kicked himself mentally, as the truth fell
down before his eyes again in a series of blatant images: the
looks that passed between them, the way their hands moved
together, the way she had tenderly covered his wound and then
looked up at him with accusation in her eyes.

"Libby, just tell me the truth. Is he with you?"

Libby's mouth had begun to dry out. She shut it

pointedly and then grasped at ambiguity to stall. "I can tell you that he's safe."

"I'm coming over," he said decisively, and Libby's heart rate tripled.

"No! He's not here, Jon. He – he called me from a hotel. He said he was on the run, and – and to tell you that he was sorry, but he didn't think he should come home right now."

She had recalled Andrew's earlier words, without knowing what they meant or how much they would affect Jon. He fell silent, entirely convinced. Of course, it made sense. Andrew was scared of him right now, and he had all the reason in the world to be.

"Libby, I'm sorry I accused you," he said weakly, "This is all so overwhelming, I didn't know what to think."

"Yeah, well…" she trailed off, retarded by an uneasy churning in the pit of her stomach.

"Maybe it would just be better if we stopped seeing each other," Jon continued, generating his own nausea. "I have a lot of things to sort out right now and I don't want to involve you."

She began to tell him that she was already involved, but he cut her off.

"This isn't any of your business, Libby. Please, for your own good, stay out of it."

And then, with a click, he was gone. Libby lowered the phone slowly, hot tears pooling at the corners of her eyes. She deserved every bit of the anger in his voice, but that did nothing to soothe the hurt. Hearing his voice had convinced her of what she hadn't been able to grasp before. Andrew was right. After years and years of trying desperately to keep her condition from affecting others, she was now letting it tear this family apart. All for her ridiculous quest, her need to find out if the damn digital clock was sending her secret messages from angels.

Finding it unbearable to live with herself, Libby rolled onto her bed and pulled the pillows over her face. The square of moonlight at her feet shivered then fell silent as she too relaxed into a semi-conscious exhaustion. She willed herself to seep into it and disappear as it dwindled into dawn. As she descended, the light from the lamp burned steadily on until very suddenly, her mind drew her back into the present. She sorted out details: I must have fallen asleep, I'm still dressed, Andrew is still here....

She reached for the lamp to switch it off, resigning herself to finish sorting in the morning. As she did so, her eyes fell onto the clock. Moments later, 11:11 was flying across the room.

*

The next two days were spent in awkward tension, with conversation between she and Andrew remaining mindlessly urbane. Jon hadn't called back, though Jay had called several times. Libby let him ring through to her machine, not willing to face another dose of shame. The first day, she cleaned ferociously while Andrew passed the time at her computer, researching more plausible theories and watching her with persistent amusement. The second day, she slept in bed until after noon. By the time she ventured out to the living room, Andrew was gone.

As eleven o'clock approached maddeningly slowly, Libby came under the sinking impression that he wasn't going to come back and she would have to face the meeting alone. At half past ten, however, his insistent knock startled her. She opened the door to find him holding up a set of car keys and smiling impishly.

"Ready for the meeting?" he asked, as though there was no need to excuse his absence or rectify the anxiety she had felt for the past few hours.

"Where were you?" she demanded, barring the door as he tried to slip in.

He jangled the keys in his hand. "Getting us a ride."

Indignant, she stepped back and let him in, but only so she could yell at him without the neighbors hearing. "I have a car, you know. You didn't have to go out and *race*." She spat the word out, then immediately regretted how much she sounded like her mother. She was just shocked at how easily he was willing to go risk his life knowing how much she now depended on it.

"I don't mean to say it like that," she quickly apologized, before he could add the retort that would turn this into a full-blown argument.

"Yeah, well," he lowered the keys to his side, looking like a dog that had just been spanked for a fit of barking that had been intended to protect his master.

Libby snapped her purse up from the door-side table and opened the door behind him. "Come on, we're going to be late. We'll talk about this later."

They descended the stairs in rhythm and then he took the lead, leading her down the front steps and across the street to a bright purple Corvette parked on the curb.

"Nice," she muttered, as he gestured for her to get in, "When we show up in this, they'll know exactly how much money they can scam out of us."

Andrew shrugged and ducked into the driver's seat, "Easy come, easy go."

"That's just the problem. It's not so easy come."

"Well," Andrew paused and threw his arm across the back of Libby's seat, twisting back as much as the incision allowed so he could maneuver onto the street. "That's what you think," he continued, then shifted the growling engine into drive and gunned it.

"Jesus," Libby grabbed for her seatbelt, but found that the entire unit had been taken out and replaced with a roll bar.

Andrew began to laugh, but then, having caught a glimpse of her pale face reflected in the windshield, apologized and let up off the gas. The gesture made her less willing to yell at him, so she settled instead for a brooding silence, watching him skillfully move the car through the late night traffic that had thickened as they moved onto Third Avenue.

The truth was, she felt affronted by this all. She could understand his need to push himself to the limits of control. It was why her body convulsed each time the subway train rushed into the station. Meeting Andrew, however, had given her another more impacting method to lose control. It worried her that she had not had the same effect on him, which then necessarily led to the fear that he was only going along with this whole 11:11 thing to humor her.

Traffic tightened as they moved through the garment district. Heralded by the cacophony of car horns, the Corvette moved flawlessly through the mass of vehicles and pedestrians that migrated chaotically across the intersections. There was a calm indifference on Andrew's face that made Libby fear that he had dissociated again and was primed for another hit and run. Every so often, however, he would snap out of it and throw his shoulders back into the seat while emitting a frustrated sigh. Libby, meanwhile, charted an unfamiliar sensation: solid ground on either side. How could she be so fearless, she wondered, in the most frightening situation she had ever faced?

As the digital clock turned over to 11 o'clock, Andrew slid the car into a space in front of a corner building. Libby stepped out onto the curb and gazed up at the stone structure, which seemed out of place among the office buildings and high-end department stores. It had been built long ago, and for some reason had withstood the test of changing times. Libby shivered, but was immediately soothed as Andrew draped his arm over her shoulders and pulled her closer.

"Best we do this together," he murmured, drawing her onto the sidewalk and towards the large wooden door.

As he pulled it open, Libby half-expected to see a cathedral-like chamber filled with robed men holding torches. Instead, they were admitted into a musty, though innocuous looking lobby. The yellow carpet was threadbare, and the white walls had darkened with time. There was little in the room apart from a drooping fern, a filing cabinet, a reception desk and three mismatching chairs. A signpost directed them towards the set of double doors to the right of the desk, beyond which they heard the murmur of voices.

"Last chance to back out," Andrew warned as he reached for the doorknob.

Libby felt as though she had left her stomach in the car and was more than willing to rush back and join it. But Andrew's presence beside her was grounding and she nodded and gestured for him to continue.

The doors opened onto a large conference room. Rows of folding chairs faced an unoccupied podium, above which a banner reading "Welcome 11:11 O'clock Brethren" had been hastily tacked up. The folding chairs were half-filled and their occupants were all seemingly engaged in conversation with each other. A few faces looked up to see who had entered the room and, after offering Libby and Andrew curious stares, resumed indifference and turned back to their companions.

"Oh man," Andrew breathed beside her, and Libby felt his sentiment course through her. It was an awkward thing to feel so out of place in a society that was so out of place itself. Andrew made a move to guide them to the last row of chairs, but a man nearby caught Libby's eye and beckoned her over.

Libby exchanged a glance with Andrew and then followed the man's insistent gesturing. Andrew reluctantly followed.

"New members?" the man asked.

Libby nodded, staring at the man with what she was sure was an impolite intensity. Though half of the group members seemed drawn out of everyday life, this man was one of those present who seemed as if his entire life was built around cults and conspiracy. He was dressed in a mismatched selection of clothing, worn-down in patches and barely fitting. His hair, black as night and gleaming, was just as patchy and chaotic as his dress. The skin that stretched over his sallow face was dotted with stubble and shadows of dirt and age, so much like the faces Libby had seen staring back at her from back alleys and cardboard shelters.

"My name's Ray," he said, extending a blackened hand towards Libby. Her blood chilled and she stepped back, deferring to Andrew. He took Ray's hand lightly and introduced them both. Ray looked between the two of them, eyes gleaming and hawk-like. "Husband and wife?"

Andrew hastily looked at Libby then shook his head. "No, no. We just met."

Ray laughed, with an almost condescending tone. "Right."

"So what's going on here?" Andrew asked, diverting the touchy subject of their relationship before Ray could pursue it further.

"You tell me, buddy. You know why you're here, right?"

Andrew made a sound as if he was choking, apparently finding it hard to admit aloud that he had been drawn here by an enigmatic relationship with his clock. Libby, seeing his difficulty, answered for him.

"A lot of strange stuff has been happening to us lately and this seemed like the place to start."

The persistently amused gleam in Ray's eyes faded. "Other stuff has happened to you beside the numbers?"

Libby hesitated. "Yeah. Why?"

Ray cast a glance to the front of the room, where a man was now approaching the podium. "Nothing," he murmured. "Sit down. The meeting's starting."

Libby and Andrew sat down obediently behind him and, with the others, watched the man take his place. Unlike Ray, he was one of the members of the crowd who looked as though they had stepped out of ordinary life. He was dressed in a simple white shirt and tan slacks, had thin wire-rimmed glasses, and was crowned by a tuft of blondish hair.

"Welcome friends," he began in a soft effeminate voice, gesturing his hands broadly to the attentive faces before him. "I am so glad you could be here, on this Thursday night, to celebrate our common plight. There are many faces I recognize in the crowd, though some that I do not recognize. To them I extend a hearty applause for having finally discovered the path to enlightenment."

Andrew snorted and looked sidelong at Libby.

"Before we begin our invocation, friends, I would like to speak generally on the 11's, to the benefit of our new members and as a refreshment to our old."

He cleared his throat and scanned the room, gauging the reaction of his crowd. Libby tried to picture this man in the daily roles of his life, wondering if his workday was pervaded with thoughts of fantasy and his home life wrought by these late-night absences.

"The puzzle of the 11s has affected millions," he continued, "And gradually, those touched by the mystery have come to discover how deeply it is imbued in our society. Seeing the 11's is a wake-up call, guiding us towards our personal spiritual connection to the otherworld.

The 11:11 sightings occur during moments of lucidity in the observer, and may lead to a reactivation of the memories we have of our pre-existence. In some, this enlightenment allows communication with spiritual beings. That is the truth we seek here, friends, to find and follow the signs given by our spiritual brethren. Many in this room have shared stories of their contact with the spiritual worlds, whether they have received messages during these moments of lucidity or begged for favors which were, in due course, granted to them."

He fell silent and gazed out at the crowd, as though asking for their input. One woman near the front raised her hand and then stood, addressing the crowd behind her. "I was with a friend when I first saw 11:11. He made a wish on the numbers and told me they were lucky. From that point on, the numbers continued to reappear in my life." She paused, lowering glistening eyes. "Then, I made my own wish: for my brother to be cured of his leukemia. He is in remission now."

Simultaneously and without warning, the crowd chanted, "*I believe*." Libby nearly slipped off of her chair.

"Thank you, Mary," the man at the podium continued. "Friends, every person in this room has a story similar to sister Mary's, as do our guests who were drawn here to us on this day. But perhaps our guests are not aware of the numerous signs that have been given to us as a society. Think of the number of important names whose letters total 11, such as Josef Stalin, Fidel Castro, Jesus Christ, Nostradamus, George W. Bush, and Adolf Hitler. A sign for us, perhaps, to pay attention to these men, these bringers of good or evil. Take out a hundred dollar bill."

Andrew glanced at Libby and smirked knowingly.

"Independence Hall, as depicted on the reverse of the bill, has 11 windows on each side. The World Trade towers, when they stood, resembled a great 11. Indeed, in our time, friends, the events of September *11* were abundant with signs. The numbers of 9/11, or 9 plus 1 plus 1, add to 11. September 11 is the 11th day of the month, the 254th day of the year – the digit sum of which is, you may have guessed, 11. More astonishing than this is the fact that after September 11, there are 111 days left to the year. Friends, the number of letters in New York City totals 11. The first flight to hit was American Airlines 11. There were 92 people on board, while another flight had 65 – both figures, separately, sum to eleven. When the towers collapsed, it was to a height of 11 stories. Not to mention, when the first tower collapsed it did so in a total of eleven seconds."

Libby's head was spinning. She broke away from the speaker for a moment and scanned the crowd, astonished by the identical glazed expressions they wore as they stared up at their leader with admiration, he who had collected these facts and figures for them to behold. Meanwhile, beside her, Andrew was staring at his hands with a bored disinterest.

"The more spiritual of our brethren will find the numbers in their works as well," the man continued, his voice rising to a feverish pitch. "Mormon followers, consider passage *nine eleven* of 3rd Nephi, "I did send down fire and destroy them." Or turn to page 911 of Zodhiate's famous New Testament Dictionary and you will find among the definitions these words and phrases: secretly and unawares, a community of free citizens, heathens, a rich commercial city, and these: the Muslims destroyed the city and today it is a heap of ruins."

"For those of more scientific leaning, consider that the number 11 is the total of the dimensions required by the unifying M-theory which attempts to explain the existence of everything."

The man drew himself into a more grand posture as he continued, "So how do we react to these signs, my friends? Is it enough to notice them and see that there is spiritual play afoot? Or can these signs be collected and used to lead humanity to revelation, or perhaps, to warn of future events? Friends, the tragic bombing in Madrid took place exactly 911 days after our Twin Towers fell, on 3-11-2004, a date whose digits sum to eleven. Many of our kind predict that the next target of attacks will be the Eiffel Tower on the 119th birthday of the monument. Eiffel Tower of course has eleven letters, as does City of Paris."

Libby looked hastily at Andrew, as though expecting him to jump up and order a rush to Paris's defenses. Instead, she found his usual smirk, enhanced as he caught her eye.

"You're not making this very easy," she hissed.

"Making what easy?" he said, not bothering to lower his tone. Several of the people in front of them, including Ray, turned around and glared. Libby wished she had an answer to silence him, but found herself unable to admit that she actually wanted to believe all that she had been told. She felt a separation between herself and the people in this room. They were an ordinary, albeit motley assortment of people who attributed the numbers on the clock to granted wishes and tired conspiracy theories. Her own connection with eleven was entirely random; merely a backdrop to what was a much greater mystery.

Andrew had not stopped watching her as her inner struggle was so clearly reflected on her changing expression. He worried that perhaps she ardently wanted to believe this, thus ending their quest at what he perceived to be an obvious dead end. Never until now had he realized what a risk he held in desiring the light she held locked inside her. When and where she finally released it, it could very well slip through his fingers and be lost to him forever. He didn't know her well enough to be assured that she wouldn't release it here.

"Libby, I think we should get out of here," he murmured, interrupting her struggle at what he deemed was a moment of vulnerability.

She looked at him and perceived the softness in his eyes, the vestige of a child who had not yet looked upon the injustice and horrors of the world and had his visage hardened by them. For the first time in several days, she suspected that he truly did want to find answers. She wondered if perhaps she had been wrong to try so hard to find reasons not to trust him.

"Fine, you're right," she conceded. She grabbed her purse and together they stood, both planning excuses to offer in case their departure was noticed. But as the speaker continued, the audience was left enraptured, unable to perceive their furtive exit. Only one greasy head turned as the doors closed behind them.

*

Outside the building, Andrew took a moment to enjoy the sight of the Corvette neatly parked beneath the lamplight. At least one thing had gone right this evening. Embellishing, he unlocked the car with the remote.

"I could get into this," he said, laughing as the headlights flashed.

Libby sighed, lingering at her door as Andrew moved around to the driver's side.

"What?" he prompted.

"Nothing," she laid her hands flat on the roof of the car, feeling the coolness of the metal soothe her raw skin. "I just don't know where we're going to go from here."

Andrew sighed and laid his own hands on the car, fingers creeping across towards hers. The space between them flared and Libby drew her hands away quickly and glanced over her shoulder as if expecting Jon to be there.

Instead, she saw a dark figure coming rapidly towards her from the doorway of the building. As the figure stepped into the streetlight, she recognized Ray. Moments later, he barreled into her. The shock of it all left her senses powerless and she submitted to the attack, allowing gravity to pull her down to a painful landing on the edge of the curb.

As sight returned, she looked up in time to see Ray's hand raised above her, primed to strike. But as her eyes widened, she saw a second figure descend upon her, snapping Ray's fist out of its descent. Ray jumped to his feet and turned to face Andrew, who had rolled over the hood of the car the moment Libby went down.

"Are you *nuts*?" Andrew cried, stepping closer to Ray and straightening to his full height, "Oh wait, let me rethink that."

Ray snarled, "Buddy, you got no idea."

Libby climbed to her feet and sought shelter behind the car. This was exactly what they had suspected would come from socializing with lunatics. Either that or Ray was another putty-faced man, attacking while Andrew was in his non-dissociated state and unaware of how to defend himself.

But as Ray moved forward to throw another punch, Libby discovered that she had nothing to worry about. Despite an increasingly stunned expression, Andrew moved with automatic motions. As Ray lunged, he blocked, snapping Ray's arms out of the air and twisting them to gain the advantage. Ray, growing desperate, delivered a wild swing which Andrew easily ducked beneath. On his ascent, he got under Ray's shoulders and flipped him skillfully over and onto the ground. He then kneeled over Ray, pressing his shoulders into the pavement, back rising and falling with each labored breath.

"Libby, call the cops," Andrew commanded, tossing his head to shake the hair out of his eyes. Ray squirmed under his grasp, but Andrew had the clear advantage.

"Oh you *are* good," Ray snarled, body growing still as he seemed to concede to defeat.

Libby was digging through her purse, feeling for the smooth metal body of her phone. Her eyes had remained on Ray, however, allowing her to see him slip his hand casually into his pocket.

"Andrew! Left hand!" Libby delivered the vague warning and was surprised that Andrew was able to interpret it. He slid one hand down and tightly pressed Ray's hand to the ground. Ray's fingers tightened and there was the dull sound of cracking glass. Unexpectedly, he wrenched his body aside. Andrew, struggling to regain control, framed Ray's shoulders once again. But in the moment of confusion, Ray freed one hand and lifted it to Andrew's forehead. His skin glistened in the lamplight as drops of water rolled down his arm.

"*Exorcizo te, omnis spiritus immunde, in nomine Dei,*" Ray murmured rapidly, tracing his finger on Andrew's forehead before he could react.

"What is that?" Andrew demanded, grabbing Ray's hand and pulling it into the lamplight.

Ray, however, had suddenly lost his fight. Stunned, he let his hand hang limply in Andrew's grasp.

"You're not one of them," he breathed, letting his head drop back to the pavement.

"Not one of *what* you crazy fuck?" Andrew spit, releasing Ray's hand forcefully.

"It's holy water."

"*What?*"

Ray scowled, "If you get off me, I'll explain everything."

Andrew wasn't sure if that was the best course of action. He glanced at Libby, whose eyes were buried in her phone, unwilling to look up and find him asking her what to do. He looked down at Ray again, watching the man fight to placate his naturally feral expression. Whatever Ray's explanation was going to be, he figured, it couldn't be any worse than what they'd heard in the meeting.

"Fine," he rolled off of Ray and then pulled him to his feet, leaving the man stumbling to regain his balance.

Once recovered, Ray brushed off his perpetually soiled clothing and then straightened, trying to match Andrew's intimidating height.

"C'mon," he gestured up the street, "I know a place. Good coffee. Good pie. A piece of Em's pie could get any man to talk, buddy."

He smacked his lips at Andrew pointedly and Andrew frowned, suddenly suspecting that Ray was nothing more than a bum with a pretty good trick up his sleeve. He glanced back at Libby, who was now approaching in cautious steps, led through uncertainty by this one ray of hope. He held in a sigh. If she wanted this, he was going to have to go along with it. Maybe she'd be right. Maybe any sort of answer was better than none.

"Fine," he conceded to Ray, "How far is it?"

He hoped Ray would say it was too far to walk, for he longed for a chance to get back in the car and to that point, give Ray a ride that demonstrated that he was not to be messed with. Ray, however, replied that the diner was a mere two blocks away.

"Follow me," he gestured, beginning to march up the sidewalk with an air of importance.

As Libby climbed onto the sidewalk, Andrew looped his arm through hers protectively, unable to forget the sight of Ray throwing her to the ground. Libby, however, seemed to tense at his touch as though she wanted to pull away. It was all part of her mystery, Andrew reasoned, letting his arm drop and keeping his eye on Ray and wondering how soon he would be able to tell if he was leading them into a trap.

Libby bowed her head and walked on beside him, guilty and wishing she could tell him why; as she had opened her phone to call the police, a missed call alert bore Jon's name.

*

From its run-down exterior, Libby expected Em's Diner to be equally seedy inside. As Ray led them in through jangling doorbells, however, she discovered to her great relief that the place was immaculately clean. One wall was lined with windows and plastic booths, while a long bar table stretched in front of the other.

The diner held only one customer. She sat at the very end of the bar, her massive body precariously perched on the stool. Her dress fell to the floor in many grungy folds, which admitted the sight of only one arm that leaned against the counter, supporting what looked to be a hand rolled cigarette. As the door jangled shut, she twitched but did not move her head, then raised the joint to her lips and inhaled wearily.

"Sit anywhere," a voice called, and as Ray directed Libby and Andrew to the first booth, a waitress emerged from the kitchen. She was costumed in typical fifties diner garb, wearing a short pink dress and white apron that hung loosely on her bony shoulders. She looked as if she had been born and raised in this diner and the long years of grease and cigarette smoke had ruined her, leaving her skin wrinkled and stained yellow.

"What can I get for you?" she asked, wheezing through what must have been developing emphysema.

Ray rubbed his hands together, laid them flat on the table and then looked up at the waitress. "I'll have one slice of apple pie, three inches across at the widest point, and regular coffee with two and a half creams, one third packet of Equal, and two thirds Sweet 'N Low, all added to the cup before the coffee."

He looked at Andrew and Libby, who wore identical wide-eyed expressions. "Something for yourselves?" he asked

They shook their heads in unison, both registering the sudden drop in Ray's credibility.

As the waitress walked away wordlessly, Ray leaned back against the booth and folded his hands behind his head, looking between Andrew and Libby as though sizing them up.

"Sorry about attacking you on the street," he finally said.

"Yeah," Andrew grimaced, "Though you're not the first."

Ray unfolded his hands and then inspected his fingernails with intense scrutiny. "I suppose," he began without looking up, "You're wondering why?"

Libby and Andrew leaned forward expectantly, but the waitress returned at that moment and slid the cup of coffee and pie plate in front of him. Ray thanked her and then carefully unwrapped his table setting, freeing his fork. This he laid on the narrow point of the pie slice, sliding the tines back and forth until he had reached a satisfactory spot to cut the perfect piece, measured by some standard in his mind alone. He lifted the bite to his mouth, lowered it between his withered lips, and chewed with an agonizing slowness. The motion accentuated every line of his face, which was as sallow and crevassed as an overripe peach.

Andrew watched, strained by the tedium of every bite and feeling a twitch of inertia every so often in his legs that threatened to propel him off of his seat. Questions formed in his mind but the breath dissipated in his throat each time Ray raised another bite to his mouth. Eventually Andrew turned to his own practiced mental dissociation, thrusting all but his visceral body into the driver's seat, drifting around blind corners with burnt rubber smoking his field of vision and filling his lungs. He felt a weight come off of his lips as a smile naturally blossomed, humor in watching the ironic ruin of his life.

Beside him, Libby began to shift nervously, her motion coursing through the plastic bench seat and into him, making every part of him aware of her presence. But she felt cold now and it killed him. He had come so close to finding the prize, growing warmer, hot, hotter now, almost there. But one wrong turned had left him without a clue, growing lukewarm, colder, cold at every step in any direction, turned around, having lost the thrilling nearness to victory. It killed him, as his weightless smile imagined discovering itself against the weight of hers.

"Where do I begin?" Ray's drawl cut into his reverie, pulling him harshly back into the stark reality of the diner.

"Tell us about the elevens," Libby offered, "Do they really mean anything?"

Ray smiled, commencing what Libby imagined was a favorite and practiced speech. "Well, honey, numerology has existed since ancient Greece when our friend Pythagoras was walking around, inspiring future geometry teachers and cult leaders. The numbers are meaning represented in a way we're just not used to. Remember that, alright, because I'm going to have you two talk to Gabe, and Gabe is going to tell you all about meaning. Alright?"

Libby and Andrew nodded obediently.

"I could on and on," Ray said, in the sort of tone that indicated he was about to. "See, I used to believe all this shit about the light workers and the September eleventh conspiracies, but it's bogus. I'm telling you. The people that designed nine eleven didn't plan it so that eleven would show up. All this bullshit they feed you is nothing but what brainier folks call post-hoc reasoning. Say you wear a pair of red socks while buying a lottery ticket which later comes up a winner. By post-hoc reasoning, you might say that the red socks were lucky, even though you didn't put them on that morning because you thought they'd help you win the lottery. You follow?"

Libby nodded impatiently, "Yes, but…"

Ray cut her off, "See honey, you could pick any old number and find just as many connections to 9-11 as they like to tell you. Trust me, kids, I did it once. Take ten. The Pentagon collapsed at 10:10 am, as did Flight 93 in Pennsylvania. They tell you about the planes that had a number of passengers that add up to 11, but they neglect the plane that hit the Pentagon, which had 64 people on board, summing to ten. There were 425,000 tons of concrete in the center of the World Trade site, which adds to eleven, but is that any more significant than the fact that 23.5 acres of earth was excavated to create the site - numbers which add to ten? There's more too, kids. Ten television stations broadcasted from ten antennas on the mast of one of the towers. Towers one, two and seven fell, which adds to ten. The elevators could carry 55 people – sums to ten, or a total of *ten* thousand pounds." He laughed suddenly, more of a hacking cough. "Look, kids, if that doesn't convince you, you can do that name hooey too: Dick Cheney, George Bush, Washington, *World Trade* – all ten letters."

"So if you don't believe in this, why do you go to the meetings?" Libby challenged, somewhat defensive of the small part of her that had been swept up by the conspiracy theories.

"That's a much bigger question, honey, which I'm not so sure I'm at liberty to answer at this point, follow?"

"No," Andrew said sharply, "We don't follow."

Ray looked disappointed. "Look, like I said, I don't know for sure if you kids are mixed up in this business or not, but I can tell you one thing. These 11:11s are chaos numbers, follow? They're not just from angels, they're also from demons. Once people know about them, they start to see them everywhere. Then they start to wonder what they mean and pretty soon they're turning up at groups like the one we just left, making conspiracies, wishing on stars, and worshipping false idols. Next thing you know, they get possessed. That's where I come in."

"You're a priest?" Libby guessed. Andrew looked at her like she had said something stupid and ought to keep quiet in case it happened again.

But Ray was intrigued. "Not a priest, but why do you ask?"

Libby felt her face growing warm and tried to hide it by looking down. "I don't know. That stuff you said before, that was an exorcism, wasn't it?"

Andrew's heart began to kick him from within, snapping his attention to his inner eye where he saw his mother being restrained by two hefty guards, screaming at his father in an inhuman rage, "He's a demon! He's from Satan! Charles, take him to the priest, if not for his sake than for mine..." Andrew suddenly felt very clearly the spot on his forehead that Ray had crossed with holy water.

"How did you know that?" he asked Libby weakly.

Libby looked down, driving her eyes into the speckled tabletop. She was certain they wouldn't believe her if she told them that she had no idea why, the moment Ray had uttered the Latin words, recognition had flashed into her mind.

"Honey, you said you saw something more than the elevens," Ray said, sensing a need to break the intense silence.

"Yeah," Libby murmured. She tried to catch Andrew's eye, but was immediately repelled by his hot glare. "He, um, he sort of blacks out and does things to – to hurt people."

Andrew bristled. "Libby, stop."

She closed her mouth pointedly and looked at Ray, who was running his finger along the rim of his coffee cup, deep in contemplation.

"I've been doing this for many years, kids," he finally said, "Regular people can't see them, but I can. When I saw you, I thought you might be like the others."

"Like what others?" Andrew asked, emphasizing each word darkly.

"The crazy people," Ray laughed bitterly. "Diagnosed with fancy words. Multiple personalities. Schizophrenia. Dissociation."

Andrew's head jerked up, and Ray's bitter smile widened. "So that's your story?"

Before Andrew could answer, Libby cut in. "What about obsessive-compulsive disorder?"

Ray nodded. "Bet you've got no idea how many demons you've killed just by going back to check the locks a hundred times, or how many he's killed one when he's blacked out."

Libby felt stricken. "What if something I did because of my OCD caused a man to be stalled in an intersection and he…" she hesitated, looking at Andrew, still afraid to tell him that he'd killed a second time.

But Ray spoke. "And he unconsciously came barreling along for a classic hit and run, right? You're both working for the same side, kids. Same mission, even if you don't know what it is."

Andrew snapped his head to the side, looking at Libby with his dark eyes wide. The way she looked away from him was answer enough.

"No," he breathed, barely forming the word.

But Libby shook her head. "It was you, Andrew. You hit a man in your car and I saw it. It was before we'd even met."

Andrew jumped out of his seat so quickly, Libby felt the air he displaced rush through her. Without a word of explanation, he stormed towards the door of the diner. The woman with the joint looked back over at her shoulder, maintaining a watch on him as she drew in another drag.

"Andrew, where are you going?" Libby called, in as low and inconspicuous of a shout as she could muster.

"I've had it with this," he said, then he yanked open the door and departed to violently jangling bells.

"Go after him," Ray said, as Libby looked back at him desperately. "And here," he reached into his vest pocket and pulled out a faded card, "This is how you get in contact with Father Gabriel. He'll be able to explain this better than I can."

"What about you? How can we find you?"

"If you need me, you'll be able to find me," he said, then gestured vaguely to the woman with the cigarette, "Right now, I've got some business to take care of."

He laughed dryly and looked up as he muttered, "Sure makes my job easy when you bring 'em to me."

Libby stalled, wanting to ask him more.

"Go on," Ray urged, as the light streaming through the blinds was interrupted by Andrew's passing form.

Libby thanked him and then hurried to the door, her eyes briefly meeting with the cigarette-smoking woman's. As the door bells heralded her own exit, she thought she could see the glow of red flame flashing in the woman's eyes.

Outside, she found Andrew crossing the intersection to the next block. She called his name and hurried after him, but he strode on without looking back. She began a frustrated sprint, lifting her knees high to quiet the sound of her sneakers on the pavement. Halfway down the next block she was near enough to him to grab the back of his shirt, tightly driving her fingers into the folds of his collar and stopping him like a dog on a choke chain.

"Let me go!" he snarled, wheeling around and looking at her with the same feral intensity she had seen in his dissociated visage.

"You're not…" she began, drawing back.

"I'm not dissociated, if that's what you're asking."

He wrenched out of her grasp, but to her relief did not flee. Boldly, she asked him what was wrong.

"Nothing," he snapped. But she wasn't fooled. She stared at him with an expectancy that irritated him. Who did she think she was, he wondered, messing with his head like this? He drew a breath, stalling, trying to remember what Ray had told him. He'd been too upset to register the words, but he knew it wasn't the down-to-earth explanation he'd been hoping for. It was more insanity. More nonsense about how he was meant to be a killer.

"Andrew, if what Ray is saying is true, then we're *good*," she pleaded, reaching for his arm.

But he drew sharply away. "People are dead because of me, Libby. That's all that matters. This bullshit about doing God's work is what drove my mother mad and it's going to drive you mad too. Stay away from me."

"How can I? This isn't just your problem, Andrew. I'm part of this too."

"Oh right. Because what, you wash your hands too much and count shit?"

He grabbed her hands and yanked them into the streetlight. She tried to pull away, but he held them fast. "This is what you show me? If you think you know what it's like to be me because your hands bleed then you're crazier than I am."

He threw her hands back to her and she let them dangle, paralyzed. She couldn't speak, couldn't think, couldn't move.

"I don't want any part of this anymore," he continued to rage. "If you want to chase these fantasies, go ahead. But leave me and my brother out of it. It's shit like this that destroyed my family in the first place and I'm not going to let that happen again."

He turned and began to walk away. Libby used what strength was left in her to revive her senses and called after him, but it was useless. Andrew walked on without looking back, turned down an alley and disappeared into the darkness.

10

Libby stared down the street for several minutes, hoping to see him come back into the light and imagining the dialogue of their tearful apology. But as the unusual silence of the night continued unrelenting, she realized that he wasn't coming back.

Fighting tears, she caught a cab on Third and headed back to her apartment. Still, as she climbed the steps and passed through the front door she felt a thrumming inertia driving her back out onto the streets. She couldn't just go in there and pretend that none of this had happened. The same feeling that had urged her to touch the portrait of the lady in the red dress and Dr. and Mrs. Harold Mayer's engraved names was begging her to turn around and run until she had left everything remotely familiar behind. Her stomach ached, thinking of Andrew's words and the way he had grabbed her hands. She lowered her eyes and watched her feet make their now habitual path around the stains in the carpet. Where could she draw the line between what should and shouldn't be forgiven?

As she crested the steps and stepped onto her floor, she came face to face with the one important factor that she had forgotten: Jon was waiting by her door. Libby stopped in her tracks, wondering if it was too late to duck back into the stairwell.

But Jon took a step towards her and called her name.

"What are you doing here?" she asked, forcing a smile as if this had been a pleasant surprise.

He wasn't fooled. Her hesitation was proof enough that she knew exactly why he was here. He'd called every hotel in the city that Andrew could have gotten to on foot. If he'd gone further, he could have only done so with Libby's help.

"Why are you doing this?" he demanded.

Libby shushed him and pushed him to her door. She fumbled with the lock, stalling for time to come up with an excuse. But she couldn't even answer his first question, and when he sat down on the edge of her couch and repeated it, she could only stare back at him silently.

"At least tell me he's okay," Jon insisted, voice rising in pitch.

Libby's shoulders arced over a long exhalation. "He's resourceful, Jon. I'm sure he can take care of himself."

Jon's eyes flashed. "No, Libby, he can't. That's the problem. I don't care what's going on between you two, but you're wrong if you think you can handle this."

"I'm not the one handling this," she said, beginning to lose hold of the feigned composure, "He's trying to sort out some things. I'm sure he'll call you if he needs you. Just give him time."

"What about you?" he asked, squinting at her as though he could alter his vision and see inside of her.

Libby's hands ached where Andrew had grabbed them. "I'm not part of this," she murmured darkly. "I made a mistake, but I'm getting out now."

Poised to argue, Jon drew a forceful breath. But as tears swelled in Libby's eyes, he withdrew. "Look, I'm sorry to keep coming at you like this."

Libby looked away.

"My mind is playing tricks on me," he continued, his cheeks flushing in patches. "I thought there was something going on between the two of you. It's stupid jealousy, I guess. Like you two had this big secret you weren't letting me in on and it scared me. Maybe I was wrong to think that my brother trusted me explicitly and that you were sticking around because you wanted to be with me."

"Yeah," Libby hesitated, coughing to cover the silence. "I mean, I'm sorry you were led to feel that way. To be honest, I don't know if it's really going to work out between us, Jon." Her eyes dropped to a vacant spot as she once again pictured Andrew's rage filled eyes and felt the sting of his fingertips pressing into her wrists. Looking up, she met Jon's gaze and found her reflection wavering in his clear and unpolluted eyes, "And I can promise you that there is nothing at all going on between Andrew and I."

He didn't say a word, though the clear pools began to overflow and spill into the corners of his eyes, the imaginary water becoming real.

But as the clear water rose to the surface, a murky darkness emerged from the depths. In the space of a blink, all of the transparent purity was replaced with mud. Libby drew back slowly, her nerves thrumming on high alert. Something wasn't right.

As she moved away, Jon rose to his feet and came towards her, moving automatically like a dead man walking.

"What are you doing?" she asked in a small voice, skirting to the side and backing into the hall that led to the kitchen.

He stopped, staring deeply into her for a moment. In the next moment, he was on top of her. She screamed and ducked under his arms and into the hallway. He stumbled into the kitchen and slammed into the metal garbage can, which overturned with a deafening clatter.

Seizing the opportunity to escape, Libby ran for the door, wishing she had her phone, a weapon – anything. She thought about the knife in her purse and stopped in her tracks, wishing she had more time to think. Could she really use it against Jon?

She turned back and saw him emerge from the kitchen, moving swiftly towards her with the dark fury in his eyes eerily illuminated like the reflection of headlights in the eyes of an animal. And he was an animal, feral and charging with teeth bared and body contorting as he clawed the space between them.

"Jon, stop!" she cried, feeling behind her for the doorknob. She knew he could outrun her. There was no escape. He lunged for her again and she darted away, running back into the living room.

The back of her legs bumped into the coffee table; she felt the cool glass top against her feverish skin. There was no further retreat. Jon lunged, grabbed her arm and yanked it upward. It was all she could do to stay on her feet as a ripping, burning pain shot through her chest and her fingers went numb.

"Stop!" she cried, beating her free hand against his chest, scratching his face, pulling his hair. He drew his free hand back and smacked her across the jaw. Lights flashed, her teeth clamped tightly over her tongue and something like a swelling emptiness filled the space between her jawbones. She screamed for help, but he silenced her with another blow. The room began to spin. Her vision flashed, darkening and then relighting once again on small pieces of the scene: the bulging veins in the side of Jon's neck, spit flying from the corner of his mouth, rage burning in his eyes. He grabbed her by the front of her shirt, and dizzy, she lost her balance and let him drag her off her feet. With inhuman strength he held her suspended before him and then thrust her towards the ground. Her breath flew from her lungs as her back hit the top of the coffee table. She heard the shattering of glass and felt the swooping, terrifying feeling of falling farther than she expected. Then, on the ground, she felt each and every piece of glass that pierced her skin, radiating cold, sharp pain. Her heart beat so forcefully her chest ached and her vision began to dim. She had to breathe. She closed her eyes, concentrating on drawing a breath into the collapsed lungs, but the movement only drove more pointed edges through her skin.

His shadow was still on her and every inch of skin that it touched was electrified. He was going to finish her off.

"Please," she gasped, losing precious air.

Jon's shadow seemed to swell as darkness seeped into her vision, leaving only one point visible and all she could see was his eyes, polluted and polished black.

And then as if a wave had crested over him, the muddiness was very suddenly washed away. In the next moment, his advancing form grew limp. His knees collapsed and he dropped to the ground beside her.

A spasm of relief stole the last of her breath. She laid her head back against the broken glass and cried in cat-like howls, gasping for air and growing high on the rush each scream delivered She directed each desperate cry to God's corner of the room: "Why are you doing this to me? I don't want this life. Take it back! Oh God, just take it back!"
She did not hear the door bang open or feel the air change as someone entered the room. But suddenly he was there. His hand pressed her cheek as he dried her tears, drew her hair back from her eyes, and found them with his own. He breathed her name and his fingers slipped behind her shoulder, feeling the broken glass and the stickiness of blood.

"Listen to me," he said, his voice deliberate. But over her cries, she could not hear him. She was lost to fear, willing to let it take her and dissolve her and throw her pieces to the wind. Seeing this terrified him. Her light had begun to surge, ready to explode, ready to be lost.

"Libby, it's me, it's Andrew. Listen to my voice," he demanded more sharply, slipping his arm under her and lifting her away from the debris of broken glass. "You're okay. I'm not going to let anything happen to you."

The words came through, but she didn't want to believe them. The future, with or without him, was abhorrent to her. She'd asked too many questions. This was the result.

Then, somehow, she was in his arms and rising as he stood. She went limp and allowed him to carry her into the bathroom, where he fought with the light switch and then set her gently on the edge of the counter. He slipped his hands beneath her shirt and lifted it over her head - delicately, reverently. She felt no indignity.

"Hold onto me," he murmured, voice soft and caressing. She leaned forward into him, her shoulders still convulsing with hiccupping sobs. He turned on the tap and wet the corner of a towel with warm water, then gently wiped each wound. Carefully he pulled the shards of glass from her skin, the jagged edges cutting his fingertips. She could feel it in him each time the reflex to withdraw surged through him and was repressed. Her hand lifted and clung to him as to a rock in a river current or to driftwood in a churning sea. She leaned all of her weight into him and he held her there, steady and unmoving.

The wounds stung, but over and over he told her it was all right until she believed him and her grip on him relaxed. He had rooted through her drawers until he found bandages and he laid one across each wound, hating their reflection in the mirror behind her, hating that he hadn't been there to keep her from being broken.

"It's not as bad as you think," he said, lowering his head to hers so that his hair tickled her forehead. "Will you be okay?" he pleaded.

She nodded. He straightened and pulled her shirt back over her head, then held her as she swayed between his firm grasp on her shoulders. Cautiously, he asked her what had happened.

She coughed, voice finding its way through the destruction left by her screams, "Jon attacked me. He was possessed."

Andrew's eyes flashed and the grip he had on her tightened, vise-like. "I should've known this would happen," he said.

"Why?"

He threw his head back and sighed brutally. "He was the one that attacked me, Libby."

Her eyes fell to his stomach, finding the wound and recalling the first moment she had seen it. Had Jon known? Was he one of *them*? She suddenly remembered the spots of blood on Jon's lab coat.

"I don't know what it means," Andrew said. His grip relaxed on her, testing her ability to support herself. She curled her fingers beneath the countertop and held her weight on her hands. Andrew stepped back, ran his hands through his hair and then grasped the back of his neck, drawing his head down to face the ground. "I don't know if he's dissociating, or – " he let his arms drop and lifted his head, "Or if Ray was right and we're supposed to kill demons and he's…"

"Jon isn't a demon."

"I know, but…" he hesitated, not sure he was ready to accept that what he was about to say was a real possibility. "What if a demon has possessed him in order to get to us?"

She drew away from him, recalling the doubtful smirk he had held throughout their encounter with Ray and the other elevens worshippers. She wondered if he was humoring her still. And yet the perpetual mirth seemed gone from his eyes.

"Libby, I know I was an asshole," he said, sensing her hesitation.

"Yeah," she said, "You were."

The darkness in his eyes glistened, sending out a ray of light that swam through her. "I know you probably won't be able to forgive me, but – I just want you to know, I didn't mean any of it." He hesitated, bracing himself for the truth he didn't want to admit. "I was scared."

Libby's eyes widened. "Don't you think that I'm scared too? It's like we have to give up on everything we've ever known to be true and maybe all that's going to happen is we'll lose our grip on reality entirely and go over the edge."

He inhaled slowly, feeling the breath weaving through the depths of his lungs. "It's more than that, Libby. I'm scared because I've never felt this way before."

"Like what?"

"Like the most important thing in the world is slipping through my fingers. It's like…" he trailed off, rooting out the sickness and trying to find words to describe it. It was like breathing in used air, or conducting a choir that was constantly under pitch. There was this persistent sensation that things were just not quite right, and growing worse with time.

She had to know. It was why he had come back for her after abandoning her in the street. As he'd walked through the hidden despair of the alleyways, he had felt too much at home. Yet he knew that he could give Libby everything and she would brighten it, charm it, and transform into something warm and real and good.

He braced himself again. "I want you, Libby. Every part of you – your mind, your body, your heart."

Libby felt a twitch at the corners of her lips, a smile wanting to spring. She held it back, waiting for his eyes to return to hers. There was so much she didn't know about him, and she feared that what they considered a spiritual connection was nothing greater than the physical chemistry of lust.

And yet she wanted him more than she'd ever wanted anything before and it terrified her. He was the piece of the puzzle that fit with her own, but the picture they formed together was frightening and unreal. She couldn't give herself away, not to this abandonment of sense and reason that came with overwhelming desire. All her life she had thought love meant sharing her heart with another. Now she understood that she would have to give it entirely away. How could she trust anyone to give it the superior protection is was accustomed to? It could come back damaged and polluted.

A muffled groan infiltrated the silence between them, throwing them both into high alert.

"You have to get out of here," Libby said, eyes on the door.

"Libby, no," Andrew fell silent and she looked back at him, finding him paralyzed with betrayal. He had given his heart to her and was unsure if she had taken it. Libby slipped off the counter and stepped up to him, mingling her heat with his. "Go. I'll tell Jon that you were dissociated and attacked us. He already knows what you're capable of."

"Are you crazy?" he snapped. Libby's mind insolently flashed back to the moments of his earlier accusation.

"No?" she guessed.

"He tried to kill you, Libby. Now I'm supposed to leave you alone with him?"

"If he wakes up and finds you here, he's going to want an explanation. You know your brother. Would he believe us?"

Andrew hesitated, stalling the inevitable answer which was so very clear to him from the start. "No. After mom, this is the last thing he wants to hear."

"Do you think he has any idea what he's done?"

"I don't know," he answered, returning to his blurred memory of the hospital emergency room and the awkward tension between them. Up until now, he'd thought it was because while in his delirious state, he hadn't been able to hide his feelings for Libby and Jon had picked up on them. Now he wondered: could Jon have known? Was possession different than dissociation?

"We need to see this priest guy," he said. It felt like swallowing sand but he had to admit it to her. Libby hid a smile. So he had been paying attention after all. "I'm serious, Libby. I hate to admit that Jon turning all Linda Blair makes any sort of sense, but if it's true then I have to wonder what I'm turning into."

Libby refrained from answering, knowing that anything she could tell him would raise more questions than they had time to address right now. She wasn't even sure that the priest would be able to explain why Andrew's demon fighting dissociated self thought she was someone named Meg. Or, for that matter, whether or not she really was someone named Meg.

Jon groaned again, and Libby grabbed Andrew's shirt between her fingers and pushed him to the door.

"I'll meet up with you later," she promised.

"Get him out of here," he insisted as she ferried him through the living room and past Jon's stirring form. "I'll follow him home, and then..." he trailed off. What could he do? He'd told her everything and it didn't seem to matter. She still didn't trust him. Her words replayed: *He already knows what you're capable of.* Of course: how could he expect her to forget that she had seen him kill? She was right to withhold her light from him. Jon would treat her like a queen, while he would only lead her down back alleys and get her broken and bruised.

It was wrong and it killed him because he wanted it to be right. He wanted her to love him when she was sober of the attraction. But it was too much. He was scorned and in love, happy and ashamed, hopeful and afraid. She knew him, or she didn't. She loved him, or he was unworthy of being loved. Without her, there were no answers. With her, there were only more questions. He had to leave her, and then suffocate his mind and drown it in whatever potent combination of adrenaline and ethanol would allow him to forget that he was incapable of forgetting her.

He lingered in the entryway and Libby reached past him to pull open the door. As she did, she asked him, "Then what?" and he looked down at her blankly.

"You're going to follow him home, and then what?" she elaborated impatiently.

As the dazed look in his eyes faded, she saw that it carried the light within it away, drawing it down to a single point.

"I don't know. I think I need to disappear for a while."

The sudden change hit her like a punch in the stomach, stealing her breath.

"Why?" she coughed.

He didn't tell her the truth: that maybe it would better, that maybe he needed to feel the engine thrumming under him again, to seize control and then throw it away, to pray for a messy yet convenient ending. "I have a lot I need to sort out now."

She felt for the wall behind her, needing it to maintain the straight posture that made her out to be calm and indifferent. Inside, however, she felt as though she had collapsed down to a single drop of blood.

He had to sort things out? Where did that leave her? She knew the brutal truth: it would never be as easy for him as it was for her. He needed old pacifiers to get through this shock. Her hand rose to her chest. All these loveless years she'd imagined that heartache was nothing more than a metaphor. Now she wondered, scientifically, how this pain could truly exist.

"How long will you be gone?"

"I'll call." He stepped through the door and began to pull it shut behind him, until there was but a thin sliver of light left between them. She rushed forward and seized the door, pushing him into the hall and spilling out after. He wanted to lose himself, speeding down abandoned streets, chasing a cure for the numbness? She would give him something to feel.

As his lips parted to form a question, she sought them. Her heart gave one last resounding beat and then stopped, leaving her drunk and dizzy as his hands pressed into her back, sliding upwards, drawing her in and binding her to him.

But when her lips were just inches from his, his head fell back.

"Go back inside," he said, mouth so close to hers she could feel the breath of each word striking her.

She drew away and found that his eyes were vacant, focused on the hall behind her. Her stung lips closed, while the offended heart began to beat again as his grip on her released. She fought to find words, but before she could even draw breath he had moved past her and down the hall. As suddenly as he had come, he was gone. She wondered if any of it had been real.

In her stupor, she was startled as Jon's terrified voice cried out suddenly for her. She bolstered herself with a deeply drawn breath and stepped back into the apartment. Jon was on his knees staring at the blood-smeared glass shards, his naturally pale face an even more ghostly shade of white.

"What happened?" he gasped.

Numbly, Libby navigated the prepared lie. "Andrew was dissociated Jon. He burst in, started shouting at you like he did outside the 21 Club and then pushed you into the table. Don't you remember?"

Jon stretched his arms out and looked at them, searching for blood. Finding none, he looked at Libby skeptically. "Are you sure I fell into the table?"

Libby was in no mood for skepticism. "Are you sure that you spilled a blood sample on your lab coat?" she snapped.

Libby knew instantly that the outburst had been a mistake. Jon's expression went blank for a moment - the calm before the fury - before he jumped to his feet and faced her combatively, eyes flashing. For a moment, Libby was afraid that he'd been possessed again.

"What are you saying?" he demanded.

"Nothing," she said, in a tone that pointed to just the opposite.

"Alright, that's enough," he threw his hands up and stepped over the broken glass, heading for the door.

"Where are you going?" she feigned eleventh hour innocence. But it was too late.

"Lately things are getting worse for Andrew and I, and all I know is that it began when you started trying to interfere. It ends here."

"I'm involved now too," she protested. "As much as I'd like it to be over for me, I'm stuck."

"No, you're not. I don't know whether or not you actually care about me or if you're just attracted to my brother, but that doesn't make you responsible for either one of us."

Libby pocketed the hurt, saving it for later. Right now, there was some truth that had to be told, painful as it might be. "You don't know everything, Jon. I'm just like him. I've got obsessive-compulsive disorder."

He scowled. "The hand-washing thing?"

"Oh my *God*. Can't anyone get past that?"

"Does it matter?" he threw open the door. "I'm sorry to break up your little support group, but this has to stop. If you have any feelings at all for me, you'll tell me where to find my brother. Otherwise, I don't want to see you again."

"I honestly don't know where he is."

Jon looked pained. "Please, Libby."

His hang-dog look tore at her. Andrew wouldn't want her to hurt him like this. "Jon, I'm sorry. I lied to you about a lot of things. I do care about you and I never meant to hurt you. The truth is, I helped Andrew out of the hospital because he was trying to find answers to a question that I've been asking myself all my life."

"What's that?"

"Why am I like this? Why did you take one look at me and know that I'd understand what it was like to be abnormal?"

His tortured expression deepened, "And what kind of answers do you think you're going to find?"

She knew the motivation for the question, and as such, reluctantly dismissed it. "He told me he needed to disappear for a while. I think you know why."

He drew back his next plea and his lips, now idle, silently caressed the one and only question he wanted answered. *Have I lost my brother?*

But he couldn't trust her with it. She was beyond comprehension now. Somehow she knew what he'd done. And – his eyes traveled to the broken glass – he suspected she still wasn't being completely honest with him. For all he knew, he had been the one to attack Andrew this evening and not the reverse, a thought that raised another question he couldn't trust Libby with. *What's happening to me?*

He had something he wanted to say, but he didn't want to hurt her. So he blunted his expression and walked out of the apartment, unconcerned with whether or not she considered things settled. But once the door was shut, he faced it and whispered the words into the wood-grained plastic: "You were the worst mistake of my life."

Inside, Libby's eyes fixed on the door until they became dry. Her anger was ruined by guilt and weakened by humiliation. The dimmer of her two lamps began to flicker as it often did. The changing glow was reflected on the mess of glass shards at her feet. Impulse overcame her and she did what she did best. Dustpan, broom, vacuum. Every shard removed, piece by piece. The carpet inspected for lingering grains. Then, vacuuming over the spot, once, twice, ten times, on and on into the long and lonely night.

11

There was no word from Andrew for two weeks. Libby spent the fortnight with the pangs of inertia, feeling as though there was something that needed to be done or some action that needed to be fulfilled. Inaction drove her mad and she spent a sedentary week trolling the internet for more information, frequenting the sorts of web sites that she embarrassed to have God, in his omniscience, see her visit. It was divine porn, heartfelt Satan worship and demon fetishism, and she was left wondering how much of it was actually legitimate.

At the beginning of the second week, she surprised herself and decided to go back to work. Somehow she found herself tracing the familiar route, all along justifying her way into retreat until she was already through the doors and unable to turn back. She was chasing the fluorescent lights again, swiping key cards and being admitted to places where she clearly did not belong. Yet the part of her that was grieving the loss of her protective façade was earnestly hoping that she would be welcomed back. Put the mask back on again, Libby, it pleaded. Let's see if it still fits.

She almost lost her ground, however, the moment she turned into the emergency room and nearly collided with Jay. In the extended moment in which they stared at each other, Libby weighed dignified silence against their many years of friendship. Apparently, Jay was doing the same, for after a moment he smiled feebly and asked her if she was here to break out the rest of the mental ward. She wasn't sure how to respond to that, but he helped them both past the quip and its more serious underlying truth by smiling more broadly and saying, "I really missed having you around this place."

"Well," she said, removing all traces of combativeness from her posture, "I wouldn't say I missed the place, but I definitely missed you."

"Dr. Dugan missed you too," he added, giving a slight wink, "But he sends his deepest condolences for your brother's death."

"I don't have a brother."

Jay hid a smile. "Such is the nature of death."

From this the tension, though not released, was gradually tolerated. As Libby and Jay moved mechanically through their tasks, he asked no questions and she volunteered no answers. In fact, Libby was surprised at how easily she molded back into the old puppet routine. The script and blocking had never left her and she played her role more elegantly than ever. Still, she did recognize that this was mainly due to the fact that the part of herself responsible for feeling anything was still attached to Andrew, wherever he was. And each time an ambulance call came into the ER reporting a car wreck, she felt physically sick. The backdrop fell forward and she was caught backstage, brilliant character exposed as mere actor.

Then, just as strongly as she had been drawn back to work, she felt pulled away. The first day of the third week without Andrew found her on the Staten Island ferry, wantonly abandoning all reason and embracing an instinct that told her she had to be here.

She leaned over the guardrail and gazed out over the expanse of purely blue water, watching as the sunlight glistened like static on the surface. Somehow, in its entirety, the water seemed pristine. When looking down at the churning waves beneath the bow, however, Libby could see it for what it truly was: murky and filled with the waste generated by the huddled masses both beneath its surface and teeming at its shores. It was simultaneously repulsive and beautiful.

Once on the island, the recognition that this was not the most impressive of her recent plans struck her. She was sure, at least, that Andrew had come here to race. What she did not know, however, were the essentials: when and where?

Partly in an attempt to hide her confusion from the tourists piling out of the ferry, she moved purposefully through the terminal parking lot and onto the main road. Just one block ahead was a small park, the sort of place one could linger without raising suspicion. She made it her destination.

Once there, she found a bench beside the baseball diamond and sat down to study the only resource she had – the map of Staten Island on the back of the ferry brochure. *If I*

wanted to race, she asked herself, *where would I go?* Clearly,
the single longest road on the island that was both relatively
straight and far from public detection. Her eyes combed the
map, fooled by expressways, residential streets and frontage
roads. What might have been two or three hours later – Libby
felt the change in the gradual diminishing of the oppressive
afternoon sunlight – she had it narrowed down to a fairly
decent pick. There were miles of access roads winding through
the Fresh Kills Landfill. Though it had once been home to a
garbage heap so massive it was visible from space, the area had
been cleared out to make way for future parklands. Currently, it
offered the stretches of pavement, sharp turns and seclusion
that Libby was sure Andrew craved.

      Soon, night began to fall in heavy pieces, painting the
surroundings with different palates that moved from golden
hues to soft gray tones. Libby pulled her aching body away
from the park bench and moved through the park, past
lingering teens throwing Frisbees by the lamplight, mothers
hurrying their children home to bed, and lovers huddled
together on blankets, so wound together that she perceived
them as one being until she drew nearer. At the corner, she
called for a taxi and waited with the uneasy swell of being in a
place she didn't belong and facing a situation she didn't
understand. This sensation was never more acute as when, after
climbing into the cab, she directed the driver to take her to the
landfill. He looked at her, clearly withholding the urge to ask
why. It was just another fare.

It's a big city, Libby thought, regretting her decision as the cab pulled away from the curb. *How can I expect to find one person?* But then she remembered the cigarette-smoking woman in the bar and how Ray had looked towards the Heavens and mused at the convenience of her having been drawn to him. Suddenly, as Libby watched the stretches of homes and business rolling by, she no longer saw things as individual entities but imagined the multitude of ways in which they were all connected. Infinite lines stretched this way and that over the image of the Staten Island map she still held within her mind.

The driver took her as far as he had the patience for and then abandoned her on a service road. It was late now, and Libby was only saved by a half-moon rising and the light of her cell phone, which offered more comfort than illumination. She walked along the broken roads, passing long stretches of abandoned clay fields still pungent with the odor of the rotting garbage that had infiltrated the soil. Abandoned construction equipment lay here and there, coming at her like beasts out of the shadows.

Then, sounds that her mind had previously filtered out as background noise began to strike her consciousness. The rumbling of engines. An occasional shout. She stopped in her tracks, bewildered at her own ability to actually find him and wondering if the ability was even ultimately hers. She moved forward until, bit by bit, the scene was revealed: the distant glow of headlights, dark figures crossing through their beams. Figures, she realized as she approached, who might not be entirely receptive to her sudden entrance into their private party.

Her anxiety faded, however, when she saw the familiar sight of the purple Corvette. Its hood was popped and several of the men were circled around it. As she neared, she recognized a head of tousled hair and saw broad shoulders bending over the thrumming engine.

Not wanting to startle him, she tried to approach with as much stealth as the situation allowed, but one of the men looked up and caught her form emerging from the darkness.

"Hey!" he shouted, causing the others to turn menacingly towards her. For a moment she was afraid she was going to get shot. "Whose bitch is this?"

Libby struggled with an answer, then gave up entirely and looked at Andrew for help.

"Shut the fuck up Nately," Andrew muttered, pushing forcefully past the man who had spoken and coming nearer to her. Once out of the earshot of the others, he bowed his head and asked, "How the hell did you find me?" He was close enough for her to detect the strong sweet odor of alcohol on his breath. Instinctively, she drew back.

"Don't tell me you were going to race," she hissed.

His eyes flashed. "What are you doing here?"

"It's been three weeks, Andrew. I'm sick of wondering where you are."

"I told you, I needed time to sort things out."

"Oh, I see," she gestured angrily to the car behind him. Several of the men turned and looked at Andrew suspiciously, most likely wondering why he hadn't gotten rid of her by now. "So you thought the best thing to do would be to come down here, get drunk, and then drive around at a hundred miles an hour?"

He laughed bitterly, sending a wave of foul breath in her direction, and then bent his head closer to hers to whisper scandalously, "Don't let these assholes know but I just put in a Lingenfelter twin turbo kit, Libby. I'm pushing 160 at least."

Libby thrust herself away from him once again. "Jesus, Andrew, listen to yourself. What are you seriously going to do here?"

He rolled his eyes, as if she'd missed the point several times. "Nately's got a Supra he can get to 150. I know if I get my hands on it, I can modify it to…"

"*Stop*," she grabbed him by the front of his shirt and pulled him further out of the earshot of the others, "I don't care about your stupid cars. I want to know how you think you can even drive straight at this point."

He gave her a sloppy grin. "It's not a straight course."

"Okay, that's enough. We're getting out of here." She attempted to pull him further aside, but this time he resisted.

"I'm doing this race," he said darkly, all traces of his former drunken mirth eradicated. "And you know you can't stop me."

"No," she said, "I can't. Just tell me this. Is getting shit-faced part of the normal procedure for you or did you pick tonight as a special night for that?"

His eyelids narrowed. "What are you saying?"

"I think you know exactly what I'm saying."

He stared at her through the haze, still at a loss to understand her presence here. It hardly seemed real. "Why do you care anyway?" he asked, pulling away. He turned back to the others, but Libby's fingers suddenly wound around his arm.

"Look at them," she whispered sharply, "I think they know exactly how fast your stupid car can go, and I think they're excited as hell because they know you're going to drive off the road."

Beneath her hands, she felt his body slacken. "That's sort of the point, Libby," he murmured. She felt him shudder as a breath fought its way into his chest, "This isn't supposed to end well."

Stinging heat went through her, igniting pain in her chest and in the space between her eyes. But she couldn't break down. Not here, not now. She turned him around, "Andrew, look at me. I can't physically stop you from doing this, but I'm begging you not to. I can't leave here knowing that I'll never see you again."

"Get over it, Libby. Just walk away."

"Come with me," she pleaded, "You're giving away a whole lifetime. Just give me one more hour."

"What for?"

"There's something I need to tell you."

After a long silence, he nodded. Libby searched for relief in his eyes, but the glow of the headlights was swallowed entirely by the unchanging pupils. She pushed him forward and he allowed the movement, even climbed into the passenger seat on his own accord once she released him.

As she closed the door behind him, the man known as Nately demanded an explanation. Libby didn't have to fight too hard for an excuse: "His brother was killed."

The men didn't look convinced, but although each of them was twice her weight, Libby barreled through their cluster, slammed the hood down over the whirring engine, and then climbed into the drivers' seat. They hovered in front of the car, adopting menacing stances. Libby glared back, then shifted into drive and rammed her foot down on the gas. Caught in their bluff, the men scattered, coughing in the wake of the dust kicked up by her screaming tires. Andrew watched lazily from beside her as she took the Corvette through its paces, careening onto the access road, needle pushing 100.

"It's good, ain't it?" he said, head lolling as the inevitable stupor fought its way into existence within him.

"I'm only doing this because we're escaping from hoodlums," she said, and though it was a lie, she bristled with annoyance when he laughed dismissively.

If she could have seen what he had, however, she would have understood. Her light came back to him like a pet drug, coursing through his clouded senses. The laughter had overtaken him, joy surging from a dry reservoir so suddenly filled.

He dropped his head and pressed his temple onto the cool glass of the window. Gradually the jerking bumps of the access road gave way to the smooth pavement of the freeway and thus soothed, he passed into a detoxifying slumber.

*

When consciousness returned, his first awareness was of a familiar smell: mustiness combined with cat-urine and human sweat. Beneath him rolled a familiar brown carpet. Libby's apartment building. She was beneath him, struggling to support his weight, hissing reprimands in his ear. Humiliated, he took his weight off of her and struggled in crooked steps to navigate the bucking hallway. He didn't remember the hallway ever doing this before.

Then he was prostrate, the scent of laundry soap close to his nose, the singular texture of a terry cloth towel pressed against one side of his face, the acrid taste of vomit burning the back of his throat. He gagged and heard her voice above him, whispering words he couldn't comprehend. Her small fingers were in his hair. He reached for them, captured their coolness in the palm of his hand and pressed them into his boiling skin.

"Fuck, Libby. I'm sorry," he rasped.

"Shhh," she soothed, "Close your eyes."

He obeyed. Gradually, the bucking heaves of his stomach submitted to the taming of her touch. The dizziness waned and consciousness followed.

*

As Libby sat with him, the night grew old and weary and then retired to watch dawn take its first unsteady steps to climb over the city. But the new dawn proved weak, casting only a dreary sheen of gray. The cool, damp overture of rainfall drifted through the cracks in Libby's windowpanes, chilling her even as Andrew sweated in her arms.

While the city awoke, Libby played audience to the changing traffic sounds. First, the periodic *swish* of a car rolling by beneath the window gradually increased to a steady rush, followed by distant car horns and the distinctive sigh of the city's rapid breathing. Early risers no longer monopolized the grand streets, as from every corner the daily rush emerged. They were the same people, tracing the same weekday routes, holding cups of coffee in one hand and folded newspapers in the other, discovering the characteristics of this particular new day.

When Andrew began to stir, Libby unwound herself from him and went to the kitchen to put on a pot of coffee. The couch springs complained as he rolled over several times, unconsciously aware of the loss of her warmth. Watching over the breakfast bar, Libby felt guilty for the night of stolen moments.

Soon, Andrew was sitting as erect as his weary body allowed, nursing the lip of the steaming mug of coffee and dreading the needed act of pouring the tarry brown liquid into his quivering stomach. Libby sat on a kitchen chair facing him, watching his slow awakening.

The longer she looked at him, the sicker Andrew felt. What was he going to say to her? Her pregnant silence wasn't making this easy on him. The pungent odor of vomit and alcohol steeping from his skin was enough to fill him with the more potent toxin of shame. He had let her see him at his worst.

"How do you feel?" she finally broke the silence. He looked at her, wondering if the question had been legitimate or merely a jibe. Her concern was apparent, however, and it increased the intensity of his shame.

"I don't usually get like that," he attempted an excuse, though he knew he could never deliver the lie with as much strength as it required. There was a lot he had done to himself that she was better off not knowing about.

He stared at her and she stared back. The look she gave him seemed deeply familiar, like a distant memory mostly hidden but occasionally aired. He thought of his first memory, one which had long ago gone dark but was, no doubt, still within him. Newborn, he had laid beside his mother and stared into her eyes. The nature of her love was the first thing he had learned in this world. I am yours now, her eyes said, and you are mine. Love is as simple as that. And yet from that moment on, he had spent a lifetime forgetting.

The hung-over feeling intensified as his mind brought him back to his mother's funeral wake. Her eyes closed, her pale skin withered and painted gaudily like a china doll. It had been so easy for her to take herself away from her. Her own choice, her own free will.

Libby's voice came to him from what seemed a great distance. "I know you think you're doing this because you want to be god of Andrew for once, and trust me, I know what that's like."

"You don't," he muttered.

She let it slide. "Andrew, if this thing drives us to cross that line, who's really in control?"

He glared at her, and then felt terrible for it. His eyes stung and he didn't know why. "Libby, you have to understand." He stopped and let a deeply drawn breath fill him: chest, back, stomach. "When I first saw you, I thought you were an angel. I thought, thank God, I'm finally getting my Clarence. Do you know how strong that feeling is?" The breath caught in his throat. She watched him with eyes both patient and blazing. Softly, he continued, "You're wasting yourself on me, Libby. I know you're meant for so much more."

She was silent for a moment, but in her eyes he could see her sudden anger. In him, regret and triumph had an awkward convergence. He looked away, but her words drew him back.

"Bull shit." She spat.

Then, within the space of a blink, the anger in her eyes drained, leaving softness like he had never seen before. "I am meant for you, Andrew. Everything I am is yours."

Giddy joy pushed the corners of his lips back as she held out her hands and showed him the heart he had abandoned in the bathroom three weeks ago.

"So when do we see this priest?" he asked.

Her eyes traveled to the clock, inviting his to follow. Eleven after eleven. He felt her smile in the heat of her light, swelling beneath corporeal fetters.

He wondered if maybe she couldn't give it away after all. Perhaps it was he who held the only key.

*

Father Gabriel's church, St. John-of-the-Cross, was a mere three blocks from Libby's apartment. Libby and Andrew chanced the walk, pushing through a stagnant fog that was washing colors away from all that it touched. They moved through the streets in silence, descending into the surreal.

St. John-of-the-Cross soon loomed over them, penetrating them with coolness that radiated from the damp gray stone. Andrew pulled open the heavy wooden door and admitted them into the darkened entryway, which greeted them with an overwhelming stillness. Their senses were paralyzed by the ubiquitous aura of church, something like the quiet of reverence and the scent of dust, incense and sweet smoke. In Andrew, the smells awoke dormant memories. Back when she still had hope for her son's soul, Andrew's mother had taken him to church obsessively. Before Justin's murder, it had been to confirm his sainthood. After, it had been to plead for an exorcism. Summer sunlight had been pushed back by the heavy wooden doors that enclosed him in stuffy entryways such as these. This would give way to the confession box and hours of being locked in the dark coffin, asked to speak of things he hardly understood, commanded to save his soul by stumbling through Hail Mary's. Daily he would be plucked away from muddy-kneed pursuits – bike rides and imaginary battles – and made to pray. He would sit in the center of his mother's bed and click through the rosary beads that she took from the top drawer of her dresser, all the while guarded by the saint candles she would light for his soul: St. Amabilis and Dymphna – patron saints of lunatics and the demonically possessed. *Hail Mary full of grace, the Lord is with thee. Blessed are the…blessed are…*"art thou among"…*art thou among…among…*

"He'll be in the confessional," he said, abruptly returning.

"What?"

"The priest," Andrew started to explain, but thought it better to simply show her. He extended his hand and she took it, allowing him to lead her through the arched doors that led into the church proper.

Libby was struck first by the immensity of it; then, a penetrating serenity came through her with the cold. She had never felt anything like it before and was grateful for the support of Andrew's hand as they walked between the rows of pews, stepping across flecks of colored light cast from the many stained glass windows. They were like rose petals leading them to the gilded altar, where mounted stone figures beckoned to them with outstretched hands and permanent pity painted in their eyes.

"This way," Andrew whispered, pulling her short of the altar and towards a warped wooden door set into the high stone wall. The door led into a tiny room, which, in contrast to the church beyond, was oppressively small. Two tiny windows admitted narrow beams of light into the dusty air. The walls were lined with fading tapestries which reeked heavily of mildew.

The most impressive thing in the room was a large wooden cabinet that was ornately decorated with angels carved in bas relief. She gathered this was the confessional, and through one of the two narrow doors, she glimpsed the silhouette of the priest.

Andrew came to a sudden halt in front of the second door and she saw that the hard lines of his jaw were lost. He held one hand outstretched towards it, like the beckoning hands of the stone saints, eyes painted with the same sadness. A word formed on his lips, then dropped. He opened the confessional door and stepped inside and, unsure of what to do, Libby followed.

Inside, it was dark and cramped and Libby felt a familiar anxiety - closed-throat, palms sweating. She pressed herself into the corner, hands feeling for the seam of the door, which admitted a breath of cool air. But Andrew knelt before the mesh window and bowed his head. She watched his shoulders expanding, preparing himself for something. Then he lifted one hand and feebly drew the sign of the cross, murmuring in a voice she hardly recognized.

"In the name of the Father and of the Son and of the Holy Spirit. Amen. Bless me Father, for I have sinned. It's been – ten years since my last confession."

A low, musical voice returned from beyond the mesh. "Blessed are the clean of heart, for they shall see the Lord."

"These are my sins." Andrew said, and then his head dropped and he said no more. Libby held her breath, waiting. She would do anything to be out of this box, away from this heavy silence.

"Son?" the priest urged.

Andrew spoke without moving, without releasing the breath. "These are my mortal sins. I have committed murder. Twice."

Sweat dropped into Libby's eyes, bringing tears. She turned her face to the crack in the door, sucking in the cool air. *I want out. I can't leave him. Oh my God, why is he doing this?*

Still frozen beneath her, Andrew felt consumed by the heat of his shame. It flushed over his face, entered his lungs, set his stomach on fire. He was acutely aware of Libby's rapid breathing and knew he shouldn't have dragged her in here. He shouldn't have said these things. *Why did I believe you, mom? Why did I believe that I could be saved from Hell?*

And then the priest said his name.

12

Andrew's eyes lifted to the mesh screen, straining to see through it. He could hear Libby's hard breathing accelerate, and fighting with his own breath, he weakly demanded, "How did you know my name?"

The priest bowed his head closer to the window, near enough for Andrew to make out the pale tone of his skin and the soft cottony gray of his hair.

"Come, my son. We'll talk outside."

Libby slid the door open forcefully and hurried out. Andrew lingered a moment before stepping out after, still struggling beneath the weight of his confession and the sins which would continue to go unrepented. He turned and stared down at the silver-haired priest, suppressing an urge to ask him how many Our Fathers it would take to absolve a murder.

Still, as he found nothing familiar in the priest's face, he was consumed with the greater question. *How does he know me?*

"Father Gabriel," the man said, extending his hand to Libby. She took it tentatively and said, "We know."

Andrew stepped out of the confessional, looming his imposing height over the priest.

"It seems as though you know me too, Father."

Father Gabriel's eyebrows lifted, "You come here often to have your blades consecrated, do you not?"

"My *what* consecrated?" Andrew asked over Libby's question: "His blades *what?*"

"You don't recall?"

Andrew remained silent.

"Ah, I see," Father Gabriel smiled wryly, "You've told me before that you black out and seem to become someone else. Now I wonder…"

"If I'm that someone else?"

"Well, yes."

Andrew looked toward the door and his body twitched, urging him to get away. Seeing this, the priest stepped closer to him and outstretched his robed arm. "Let's have a seat," he said, "I think there is quite a lot I need to explain."

Father Gabriel went to the door that they had come from and turned the lock. He then walked up to one of the more faded of the tapestries and ducked behind it. Libby's heart rate doubled when she saw the wall give way at his feet.

"Follow me," he said, voice muffled.

Andrew seemed frozen. Libby grabbed his wrist and drew him towards the tapestry, gripped the heavy woven cloth and pulled it away. Behind it, a rough doorway was cut into the stone. They entered it and passed into a narrow tunnel of gray-cemented stone, dimly lit by the lamplight in the room at the other end. As Father Gabriel walked ahead of them, his head passed only within a few inches of the rough ceiling. Andrew had to bend considerably in order to clear it. With him stooping over her and the narrow walls closing in, Libby could hardly breathe. If it hadn't been for the light ahead, she would have panicked.

The room they stepped into was not unlike the one they had just left. While that room had been nearly bare, however, this room was filled with packed shelves and towering piles of papers and books. Four wooden chairs were arranged around a small table, whose warped legs were nearly collapsing under the weight of the books stacked upon it.

Father Gabriel carefully cleared away several layers of manuscripts from the desk and then sat down on one side, gesturing for Libby and Andrew to take the chairs across from him. Libby sat on the very edge of her seat, concentrating on breathing. It was close in here. Hot and stifled and chaotic.

"I'm not even sure where to begin," Father Gabriel said, folding his hands on the table in front of him.

"What am I?" Andrew asked. His voice was tight, as though part of him had tried in vain to resist the question.

"That's a far more complicated answer than I am sure you are ready for." He shook his head slowly and his eyes wandered to the space behind Libby and Andrew, tracing the stacks of books.

"Let us start with something that you, as a member of this atheistic society, may understand. Men have tried to explain the origin of the universe using modern physics, seeking a single theory that will explain the properties of all things. Many feats of mathematics later, they have come to something called string theory. I will spare you the details and only relate what is relevant to my explanation, which is that string theory came into being partly to explain an interesting mathematical problem. Using the laws of physics as we knew them led to a mathematical flaw. There are theories to explain the movements of the wider cosmos and theories to explain the movements of the tiniest particles within it. When combining these theories to describe all things, however, mathematicians have come across a problem. The results of their calculations contain infinity, an endless value. This is typically a sign that the math is flawed. Some variable is incorrect. In fact, there is – or was – a flaw in the entire way these mathematicians looked at the laws of physics. Do you follow?"

Libby wasn't entirely sure she'd moved past the first few sentences, but beside her, Andrew enthusiastically nodded.

"The solution to the problem is string theory," the priest continued, "or a redefinition of the way we see matter. Instead of being made up of particles, matter is made up of small, coiled filaments, like those that compose a guitar string. When this string is plucked, per se, it vibrates at a certain frequency. In conjunction with other strings, the combined frequency of vibration is what determines the property of matter. Think of an A flat as an electron and a B sharp as a proton. An entire symphony then becomes water or wood or you and I."

"And that's where we come in," he continued, beginning to pronounce his words more carefully, "String theory, or its wiser brother M-theory, solves the mathematical discrepancies by adding more dimensions; instead of three or four, we need eleven."

He fell off into silence, allowing them to consider this. *M-theory*, Libby thought, trolling her mind for the explanation of why the word seemed familiar. *Of course, the nut job at the elevens meeting talked about that.* But the significance wasn't in the number. It was in the existence of dimensions beyond the ones she knew. As a strange M.C. Escher-like scene filled her mind, she wondered what they might be.

"Here is where I depart from the physicists," Father Gabriel began again. "While they continue to search for reasonable mathematic explanations, they are not aware that the tools they use are not creating truth, but rather glimpsing it through clearer and clearer lenses. I, and many others, have already known that there are eleven dimensions. We know exactly what they are. Perhaps, given time, the primitive tools of mathematics will allow ordinary men to see what they are, but until then, the secret is known to very few. You both, I believe, were once privy to that truth."

"Okay," Andrew backed away visibly. "See, this supernatural sci-fi stuff is where you start to lose me."

Father Gabriel raised his pale hands yieldingly. "Patience, my son. I will illuminate this more fully in time." He drew his hands back beneath him and fumbled with the desk drawer. From within, he pulled out a yellow sheet of lined paper and a pen. "The dimensions," he began, writing this label across the top of the page and then proceeding to number the margin from 1 to 11. "Bear with me, please. This is information you must understand in order to see your unique place in this world."

Libby shook her head with frustration and looked up at the overhead light, driving her eyes into the core of the dim bulb. It wasn't hard to understand. It was just hard to believe. She was about to find out just how much occupied the space she couldn't perceive.

Andrew's chair scraped against the stone floor as he moved forward to watch Father Gabriel write. Libby looked down, but the bulb had burned her retinas, casting squares of darkness across the page.

Father Gabriel moved his pen with a slight tremor, speaking as he wrote. "The dimensions are contained within each other like concentric spheres, so that all things have the first dimension, but only one thing has the eleventh dimension. The first dimension is energy, which drives all living things and holds together the particles of all non-living things."

"The second dimension is more to your intuitive experience. Space, or the x, y, z plane that you so often encounter. This paper is 11 inches tall, 8 inches wide, and has a miniscule depth. Following this is the third dimension: volume, or what fills that space. Do you follow so far?"

They nodded in unison. Libby glanced quickly at Andrew, the fading blind spot dancing across his cheek. He was poised in eager anticipation, fully understanding – and wanting to understand. Not just humoring her or his twisted self-loathing.

Father Gabriel continued, "Another familiar dimension – the fourth – is time. Whether time is something that moves, or whether or not we move through it, it has a value. This paper before you has not changed its energy, space or volume in the last minute, but it has in fact changed. It has become 60 seconds older, and is therefore a different entity."

"The fifth dimension is the last which you may easily understand, and that is because it resonates with what scientists have discovered. We call this dimension property. As I have just told you, science now believes that property is endowed by the different frequencies of vibrating strings. We are more general. Property is a dynamic state, just as a block of ice can become a pool of liquid and then a cloud of gas. The components are the same, but the property – as well as the preceding four dimensions – have changed their value."

He paused here and drew a thick dark square around the five dimensions he had already written, going over it several times.

"This is what you can gain from worldly experience," he enforced, "But for what I am about to tell you, you must try to see all things in a larger picture, one that lies outside of your perception."

"The sixth dimension is relation. Scientists have tried to characterize the quantum entanglement of particles without getting beyond mere theory. Science fiction writers have come closer, speaking of cause and effect and how an individual who goes back in time and steps on a particular flower may change history. Even without a degree in particle physics, it's not too difficult to imagine how all things near and far can intersect in some way."

Intersection. Libby thought about the man she had stalled on the street. She had done ridiculous things for 26 years because she believed they would affect others. Now, as she thought back to all of her rituals, she could begin to imagine how they might have led to one outcome or the other.

Father Gabriel continued, somehow in sync with her thoughts, "From the very day you were born, the choices you made have affected everyone else's lives just as theirs have affected yours. Say you are driving down the highway and decide to put in a tape. But something happens. Perhaps you drop the tape and unwisely choose to pick it up while still in motion. Regardless, this action leads to your slight deceleration. As a result, you arrive at a particular point in your journey three seconds later than you would have had you not decided to play the tape. Likewise, the car behind you will reach the same point three seconds later. This doesn't seem to matter much until that car passes through an intersection where, exactly three seconds ago, an inattentive driver had run through the stop sign."

Libby felt a chill, the sensation she always had when things worked out or endings had twists. Andrew, however, was less convinced. "How is that not simply a coincidence?"

Father Gabriel's eyes drifted briefly heavenwards, "It is never a coincidence. All things are related, and though all humans make free choices, God knows the result of all these decisions and uses this knowledge to determine how these choices will interact. Where human interaction fails to bring about the greatest good, God guides the angels to intervene. I quote Ephesians 1:11 'In Him we were also chosen, having been predestined according to the plan of him who works out everything in conformity with the purpose of his will.'"

Libby felt her skin prickle under the imagined touch of a divine guiding hand.

Father Gabriel tapped his pen on the page, regaining their attention before continuing, "I will expound on that in just a moment. First, we have more dimensions to cover. And where were we? Ah, yes. The seventh dimension is multifaceted. It includes the rather abstract concepts of awareness and emotion. Emotion is often a memory of a *property*, such as fear when seeing something we deem to be dangerous. It can also be a result of a *relation*, where harmonic relations lead to what we call love and non-harmonic are aversive and lead to hate. Despite this simplification, emotion is a vague and ethereal dimension. A computer can be programmed to delineate properties or to discover relations, but it cannot be programmed to feel emotion, even though it may be programmed to express it at appropriate times. Scientists would like to believe that our chemical nature programs us to express emotion appropriately as well, but this cannot give us the ability to feel more than just the physiologic response. Our bodies respond in the exact same way whether faced with a lover or a delicious meal, but I would say that we feel very differently towards one versus the other."

"The eighth is meaning. Look at what I have written. These letters are symbols that mean a word, the word means a concept. How do things differ when you look at them from the lens of *why* rather than the lens of *what*? Well, to answer that, let me ask you a question, Andrew. When you walked in here and saw the stained glass windows, did you think they were beautiful?'

"Sure."

"And why is that?"

"I don't know. Good combination of colors, I guess. And the shapes spiral together well."

Father Gabriel laughed softly. "You have explained to me what makes it beautiful, but you haven't yet told me why those things denote beauty. Or, for that matter, why you are capable of feeling beauty. The stained glass is here in this church because it allows ordinary people to see the why. Beauty is an imprint of order: frequencies of colors that are in harmony and patterns of shapes. Order is an imprint of God. Without the force of God, chaos would result. The reason we see beauty is because it allows us to see God. Order is beauty because it is essential to life, even as everything in the universe is driven constantly to chaos. You have seen the signs, I presume. Can you see now how many find 11:11 to be a beautiful number?"

"Wait," Libby shot forward, happy to finally find something to grab onto, "We were told that 11:11 was demonic."

"In the wrong hands, yes. Before you knew any of this, you saw the numbers and believed they had meaning. Because you don't know the true meaning, however, you can be lead to perceive them incorrectly. The elevens can be used to lead the blind away from the truth, or they can be used to confirm the sight of the enlightened.

"So how do we know what's the right meaning?" Andrew asked.

"That is something that is often beyond the human experience. We do not know the meaning of life. If we did, it would allow us to make all the correct choices as we journeyed on that life. And yet humans sometimes have a perception of this truth. This is the ninth dimension, or intuition. That is, to say, knowing something without objective experience. There are cases when humans have guided their fate by making a choice that seems to have no basis other than a sensation or a gut feeling. It is how some recognize love at first sight, or how many avoid accidents by changing their normal patterns."

"A combination of human intuition and the work of the angels leads to order, the tenth dimension. Order includes wisdom, which allows God and the higher angels, including the archangel Lucifer, or Satan, to know what causative forces will lead to effects. The devil uses this wisdom to create chaos. Our side counteracts with order."

"The final dimension is the knowledge of why, and it is the place of the creator alone. God knows why the chosen consequence is the best. Why the universe exists. Why one life must be spared while another can be taken. Why humans make the choices they do. The 'why' of existence allows God to perpetuate the one good path."

"Forgive me for saying this, Father, but it doesn't seem like our side is doing very well," Andrew challenged.

"No, it doesn't seem that way to you, does it?" Father Gabriel smiled. "But what you fail to realize is that God is not so concerned with our time on earth as he is our eternal salvation. Perhaps it is a better thing that, as they say, only the good die young while the bad are given ample opportunity to accept their salvation."

Libby let out a sudden puff of air, preceding what she hoped would be a forceful transition, "This is all very interesting, but I'm more interested at this point in how Andrew and I fit into this sermon."

Father Gabriel made a wide sweeping gesture across the piles of books that flanked him, "This is what I too am trying to understand. I believe that you two are meant to be angels – caretakers, as you will. In your true form, you once set order into motion and destroyed the chaos-makers: demons who manifested themselves in bodily form or who possessed a living human."

"All my life, I've never been anything but this," Libby said, looking pointedly at Andrew, "I don't black out like he does."

"All of your lives, you both have not been in your true form. Ordinarily, as angels, you could embody whatever form you wished while in the human realm, though no mortals would be able to see you. If your body was fatally wounded, you would be resurrected. It is my understanding that if you are killed while under demon possession, however, the process is disrupted. You are reconceived and born into the infant form of your human body, unaware of your true nature. Your angelic identity is still within you, however, manifesting itself in a variety of ways and typically leading to what others perceive as mental illnesses. Some have multiple personalities, where another self is the angel. Others, like Andrew, black out and become more like the angel.

"In your case, Andrew, your angel self is just as confused as your human self. He tells me that he blacks out as well and loses time. He is distantly aware of how to recognize demons and knows basic methods to kill them. I have helped him along as best as I can, consecrating his blades, giving him holy water, and allowing him to glean as much information as he can from my books on demonology. I feel as though that self is becoming more aware. In fact, the last time he came to me, he told me that he recognized someone from his past angelic life. Someone who he felt strongly attached to, though he could only remember her name."

"Meg," Libby breathed.

Father Gabriel looked surprised.

"It's me," she explained.

"Ah, yes, that would explain why you are together today as well. Something has drawn you closer, even in your non-enlightened states."

Libby looked sidelong at Andrew, wondering if he was doing the same. It was too hard to tell.

"That is, I am afraid, the extent of my knowledge in the subject. Andrew, while you are dissociated, you are trying to carry out your tasks. And Libby?" He looked at her expectantly.

"Obsessive-compulsive disorder," she said, praying he wasn't going to start talking about washing hands.

His answer pleased her. "Ah, yes, that's a common manifestation. Many of the rituals you perform – though not all of them – are actually attempts to carry out causative force missions. You are setting things in the right time at the right place. And many of your compulsive thoughts or delusions are shadows of the intuition and wisdom you once had. You may find these things I have told you much easier to accept, given your history of believing in the extraordinary."

She didn't answer, but instead looked at Andrew, searching for the same doubtful expression he had worn during their encounter with Ray. His face seemed neutral, however, perhaps buffered by the respect he held for the holy man. She had a feeling, at least from what she'd seen in the confessional, that Andrew still placed a lot of stock in the rituals and power of the church, going so far as to hate God before suggesting that his existence was a lie.

"So how do we get back to normal?" he asked, unaware of Libby's eyes on him.

"Once you die naturally in this world – barring possession, of course – you will be resurrected as usual. As in, from my understanding, you will return to your realm and be able to refashion your visceral bodies. You will undoubtedly regain the knowledge of all your past stints on earth, including this rather unsuccessful one."

"But we're being hunted," Andrew insisted, "My brother is being possessed."

Father Gabriel seemed ready to dive into a ready answer, but suddenly drew back. "Yes, I've forgotten. In your current state, you are unaware of how to manage him."

Andrew looked up, and his eyes seemed to swallow the glow of the overhead light. "What if Jon comes after me when I'm dissociated. How will I know not to kill him?"

"I wouldn't worry about that. Your other self knows how to deal with demon possession. In fact, you would be better off if you were to remain in that state, although…"

He trailed off, allowing the pregnant word to hang over them. Andrew's fingers curled tightly around the seat of the chair. Losing this consciousness would take away everything: his mind, his being, his memories. He would become this mad non-entity, a person without a past. He would hate his brother, and hardly recognize Libby. His other self seemed reckless, unfit to steer the vessel of his body. How could he let himself go?

"What if you taught me everything?" he asked.

"I can certainly try, to the best of my knowledge."

"Then maybe I wouldn't dissociate anymore and we could do this angel thing together," Andrew turned to Libby, expecting to see enthusiasm that reflected his own. The dark sadness he found instead silenced him.

And yet he knew what she was thinking. If they survived, it was only to spend the next sixty years as half-entities. Past that, it was an eternity of angelic duty. They were not the ordinary people who lived self-aggrandized lives filled with the rituals of mowing lawns, grocery shopping and 40 hour work weeks separated by dinner and drinks, sports bars, children's soccer games and Sunday drives. But he could see that she wanted that, even as deeply as she had always understood that this life was never meant for her. And he wanted, so much, to be able to give it to her.

Father Gabriel supported his weight on the edge of the table and slowly rose.

"I'll give you some time to mull this over," he said, then went to one of the shelves and ran his finger along the ancient spines, releasing a shimmer of dust.

"I'm afraid your other self has borrowed the authoritative Key of Solomon, but you might want to look this over," he said, and pulled a thick text off of the shelf and handed it to Andrew. Stamped in faded gold on the cracking leather cover were the words: Candidus Brognolus. "Brognolus was one of the leading authorities on the recognition of demonic possession and the subsequent treatments. It's quite complex, though I have translated much of the important text between the lines."

Andrew held the book out to Libby and gave her an expectant look. *Right*, she thought as she took it, *he does the stabbing, I'll do the reading.*

"The simple fact," Father Gabriel continued, "is that without a successful exorcism, the surest way to chase a demon out of its victim is to make him fear that the possessed body is in mortal danger. If the body dies, the demon is empowered by the victim's emerging soul and is quite terribly destroyed."

Libby remembered her decision to keep Andrew's knife out of the equation when an apparently possessed Jon had attacked her. How might it have played out differently had she threatened him with it? Could she, a person who hid her eyes during horror movies, really pose a convincing threat to something from Hell?

Father Gabriel moved to the doorway and stood beside it, angling his body towards them. "There is little else I can give you now other than primitive protections. Holy water and the crucifix will drive some lesser demons away and weaken most. Take a look at Brognolus and, please, come to me any time. If your dissociated form returns, Andrew, I will be sure to explain this situation to him. Otherwise..." he trailed off and opened his palms to them.

Libby set the heavy book down and rose to her feet. It was like rising into a cloud of fog and she felt suddenly sick and disoriented. This was too much. This was letting go of a hand, toddling across a room unsupported, facing ninety-nine ways to fail and only one chance to succeed. Andrew rose beside her and, seeing her unsteady posture, looped his arm over her shoulders. She leaned into him, grateful that he was there and that he wanted her there. The ghostly lover's arms had held her through 26 years of lonely nights. How strange that it had now become embodied by a spirit. And she too – a spirit. She stepped forward, weightless, queasy.

"It was nice meeting you, Father," Andrew said, tucking the book beneath his free arm.

"You can find your own way out, I trust?"

Andrew nodded and ferried Libby into the tunnel, his shoulders arcing over hers as he bowed his head. They moved towards the line of dim light that passed behind the tapestry. Then through the narrow opening, into the musty room, turning to pull the secret door shut, fighting for breath in the dusty air.

"Come on," Andrew murmured to Libby, going for the door and passing the confessional with an accusing glare. All those years he had spent apologizing for doing God's work. His mother had been right all along and what had it gotten her? She had turned her back on it all, effectively taken her own life. Would God have mercy on her faithless soul?

He remembered the last day he had seen her – the day before she died. He had walked into the bare room at the institution to find her hunched in a chair, the white robe hanging off of her frail body. She hadn't eaten for several days, and would lash out at anyone who came close. But she had called her sons forward, first Jon and then Andrew. He was afraid to see her, sensing somehow that her madness was due to her fear of him. But she lifted her bruised hands to his face and framed it, staring deeply into his eyes – eyes that had always been so bright, which now reflected her darkness. She whispered that she loved him and then lowered her head and told him coarsely that tomorrow she was going to Hell.

Andrew, too young to understand, saw only the thirty years she had lived on earth weighed beside the eternity she would spend burning in Hell. Her hands dropped from his face and fell into her lap and her eyes, now pale and lifeless, moved to a distant void. And at that moment, her son - hands balled at his side, eyes now muddy - inherited her hatred against God.

Now, as he and Libby passed into the church, his eyes found the familiar figures on the stained glass: beloved martyrs, St. Sebastian pierced with arrows, St. Justin...*Justin.* Hot tears stung the corners of his eyes. Now he knew the truth: he hadn't taken a life. He was an angel and his mother was like these martyrs, an unintended casualty of belief. But knowing this didn't bring his family back.

He only had what was before him. And Libby. She knew his sins and loved him anyway. He would do everything for her.

"Are you okay with this?" he asked her, feeling her strength wane beneath his arm.

"Yeah," she exhaled the word. "I just don't know where to go from here. It's a lot to think about."

Ordinarily, he would have lost his mind behind the wheel of a car. But there was another space, one where he had sometimes gone to place his tempest-tossed thoughts in perspective with the complexities of the world. He tightened his arm around her and felt her ease into him. Then, driving a smile through his taut expression, he told her that he knew just where to go.

*

He took her through the tunnel into Jersey and headed
south on the turnpike. To their left, the city skyline dissolved
into the fog while Libby's mind was consumed gradually by its
own haze. She lost her senses to the steady rush of the
pavement beneath her and his steady hands rocking the wheel.
She didn't ask where they were going. She only hoped they
would never stop.

But as soon as the city was out of sight, Andrew pulled
the car off the road beneath an overpass and came to a gentle
stop. He drew the keys from the ignition and then turned to her,
half-smiling.

"We're stopping here?" she asked.

He nodded. "Get out. I'll show you."

She wanted to ask him if he was crazy, but that was the
fundamental question that they were trying to avoid asking.
They climbed the hill, leaning over knees and digging toes
deep into the moist ground. At the top, a guardrail curled off of
the overpass. Andrew sat down on it and slid over to make
room for Libby.

Six lanes stretched beneath them, dark pavement
interrupted in flashes by the vehicles speeding by. They
screamed, colors blending, shapes expanding. Libby felt
breathless in the rush of wind.

"Cars go fast," she said, then immediately realized how
stupid that must have sounded.

Andrew laughed, his deep voice resonating into her
through the junction where their shoulders touched.

"I mean, it seems like you're going so much slower when you're actually driving," she clarified.

But he'd moved on. "I come here to think."

"Think about what?"

"About what we've done to ourselves. How fast we go. How little we see."

She lowered her eyes to the ground, picking apart the contours of a long-dead dandelion. She was – apparently – eternal. All this misguided life she had tried to match pace with the rest of the world, catapulting from one milestone to the next. It had never seemed right to her and now she knew why. She was always on the edge, watching passing cars and incoming subway trains.

"We're selfish," she murmured, eyes returning to the road. "All those years I was alone, I used to tell myself that the only reason people fell in love was because they wanted someone to love them in return."

Andrew laughed dryly and leaned over his knees, folding his hands tightly, knuckles whitening. "Yeah, well, that's not always the case."

"I guess." She looked at his hands, wanting to soothe them.

He turned his head to her. The hair fell away from his eyes, allowing her to see the glow that rose to the surface of his dark pupils as he smiled. "I don't know why I love you, but it's not for that."

She couldn't remember if she had ever heard the words before, but it felt good. She felt a warm satisfaction, like an itch being scratched, like hands being washed, washed, washed...

"Before we died, do you think the two of us had – a thing?" She looked down. Why was it so hard for her to say the word? He had said it, hadn't he?

"What kind of thing?" he teased.

She prepared herself to answer, but when the word *thing* began to form on her lips again, she quickly closed her mouth.

Andrew smiled and shook his head slightly, his eyes rising and following the horizon, inheriting the light willed away by the now dying sun. Somehow it aged him, first to a possibility, then to an eternity.

It drew the word from her, softly. "Love."

His shoulders rose and fell. Then he turned his eyes on her – the touch of sunlight –and every part of her instantly bloomed.

"Amor vincit omnia," he said softly, then smiled, "Have you heard the phrase?"

Her eyebrows furrowed, just briefly, just long enough for the words to seem familiar and then become strange once again.

"Maybe. What does it mean?"

"Love conquers all."

She filled her lungs and looked up at the deepening sky. Twenty-six years of waiting for the dues ex machina, the God out of the machine, to tell her that no, this was not the way things were supposed to be. Did love conquer all? Did it conquer the fear she had always had of embracing it? She looked at Andrew, taking in the hard contours of his face and the boyish softness in his eyes. She wished she could look into him and see the child he had been – see all of him, and what he had been to her before they had died. Then she would know why she had been drawn to him above anyone else. Why it would be safe to say the word *love* and give her heart away.

"We should find the room," she said, as a sudden inspiration struck her.

He laughed, "What? We should get a room?"

"No," she glared. "The room with the red panels. We both have the memory, so it must have been significant to us. Maybe if we go there, it'll trigger something."

"So what's your plan? Open up every door in town until we find it?"

"It's the reception room off of the church of St. Augustine."

His smile dropped abruptly. "Oh."

He figured that a church made sense, but why a reception room, why a photograph? *Why now?* He felt Libby's fingers curl around his and heard a contented sigh rise within her. His eyes traveled with hers and found the sun, which in its descent could no longer hide its form beneath a blinding fire. At once, each decided it was time to stop looking away.

*

As Andrew drove back into the city, Libby fought with the necessity to call her mother. After all, just knowing the name of the church wasn't enough. Her mother had been there, not knowing that the child in her belly had been there before her.

"Just call her," Andrew said, trying to hide his impatience as she had opened and closed her cell phone for the third time.

"She'll want to know what I'm doing."

He laughed. "I'll give you fifty dollars if you tell her the truth."

Scowling, she pressed her fingertips into the buttons, dialing with the courage that had come as an ancillary effect of her anger. This situation was precarious enough without Andrew's constant vacillating.

After several rings, her mother picked up, with the sort of breathless hello that indicated she had been in the middle of something. *Great*, Libby thought, as her mind rapidly began auditioning plausible excuses.

"Hey mom, it's me."

"Elisabeth? Is everything all right?"

Libby consciously reduced the urgency in her tone. "Yeah, I just had a quick question. You know that pic…" *Wait. Think.* "A friend of mine is looking for churches for her wedding ceremony. I know you mentioned that St. Augustine had a reception room. Do you know an address or at least a general location? They don't seem to have a web site."

Andrew's lips twisted before a repressed laugh. Another piece of her mind had been revealed to him; it thrilled him. He couldn't help himself. He slid one hand from the steering wheel and wrapped it around the back of her neck, fingers crawling up through her dark hair.

As he did, an electrified wave of warmth swept over Libby, leaving goosebumps in its wake.

"Goodness, it's been so long," her mother mused, "It's on the lower East side, a little ways south of Grand, a few blocks east of the FDR. Hope that helps."

"Yeah, it does," Libby said, then pulled the phone away and repeated the directions to Andrew.

"Who are you talking to?" her mother asked.

Libby bristled. "No one."

"Fifty dollars." Andrew whispered, ruffling her hair now in a teasing way.

Angrily she grabbed his wrist and pulled his hand off of her. But when their fingers contacted, she found it hard to let go. Their hands dropped together onto the center console. His fingers curled over hers, exploring the contours of her hand, soothing the raw, red skin.

Meanwhile, her mother spoke. "Elisabeth, I'm sorry for making you upset before. I don't mean to pry."

Libby, having never heard any such words from her mother before, hurriedly turned her attention back to the conversation.

"I know I've been hard on you," her mother continued, "I just – I wanted the best for you. I wanted you to be happy"

"Mom, I *am* happy."

"Are you?"

Libby hesitated, searching within for the familiar

gripping anxiety. The truth was, she was still terrified. Her fingers tightened around Andrew's, but he didn't flinch, didn't pull away, didn't murmur the teasing comment she half-expected. A wizened serenity settled over them, for they had all the reason in the world to be afraid, but all the reason in the universe to be strong.

"I am now," she said.

"I believe you. And I do love you, Elisabeth."

Libby broke into a smile. She breathed through it, felt tears drop into her eyes.

"Mom, you have no idea how long I've waited to hear that," she said, euphoria inviting words she would have normally repressed.

"It's been too long," her mother said, and Libby heard the catch in her voice. It was infectious, Libby found, strangling her own voice as she spoke: "Love you too, Mom. I'll talk to you later."

"Goodbye sweetie."

Her mother hung up, but Libby hesitated before pulling the phone away from her ear. She wanted to hear more. There was a lifetime of validation to be had.

"Why does it matter so much what our mothers think of us?" she asked rhetorically.

"They say you never forget your first love," Andrew replied, his voice detached and pedagogic. As if he knew. As if he had not, for all these years, dodged the truth with pretended ease and careless humor, deluding himself with ready-made answers for the questions he was afraid to ask. He wished it could be as simple as it was for Libby. A phone call: *Mom, you were right to love me. I'm not a demon. I'm an angel.* An angel. He considered it. Was there really some cloud filled realm beyond the universe? Would she be there, flitting on wings, strumming a harp? Smiling the way she used to when he caught her eye in the audience of the Christmas pageant and stopped being the third Wise Man long enough to wave and mouth 'hello'?

If all of this were true, then she had to be there. And if so, she already knew.

*

They circled past the church twice before it finally captured their attention. It lacked the intricately carved stone façade of many of the city's older churches, and instead possessed a square tan front centered by a squat steeple. Like all the buildings on the semi-residential street, it was set close to the sidewalk. A thin strip of weedy grass was wedged between the crumbling concrete and the plastered exterior wall.

As Andrew killed the engine and stepped out of the car, Libby threw the Brognolus book onto the dash. But halfway through the car door, she reconsidered. Though hardly expecting passers-by to be tempted into breaking in and stealing it, Libby had found special comfort in being within reach of her only weapon against the minions of hell. Clutching it in front of her like a shield, she stepped into the church's shadow.

"Door's locked," Andrew said, drawing her attention to him. She found him half-heartedly tugging on door handles he suspected wouldn't budge just because he was persistent.

"What are we going to do?" she asked hesitantly, carefully navigating full out anxiety. Despite her lack of recognition of the church's unremarkable exterior, she sensed that a vital clue lay within. This wasn't the sort of question that could wait until Sunday to be answered.

But Andrew didn't seem to be fazed. "Please tell me you've got a hair pin on you."

She shoved the book unceremoniously beneath one armpit and began to dig through her purse, fishing through change and old gum wrappers until her fingertips finally found the familiar ridged surface of a long-abandoned pin. She gave it to him, raising her eyes with a skepticism that would release her from future disappointment.

Andrew grinned and held the pin aloft, briefly admiring it. He then took a small utility knife from his pocket and opened the pliers. With this, he got to work on the pin, twisting off part of one end and – with considerable force – bending back the very tip of the other. He then dropped on one knee to the ground and rapidly ran the bent tip back and forth against the sidewalk.

"What are you doing?" Libby couldn't help but ask.

But he remained silent, and instead sprung to his feet and bent over the lock, working the pin in through the slit. Less than a minute later, he drew his hand away and then, in a grand gesture, turned the previously frozen lock.

Then, as if the whole act had been effortless, Andrew
flicked the pin onto the sidewalk behind him and gestured for
Libby to follow him inside. She hesitated, watching the pin
bounce and settle at her feet.

"How did you do that?"

He lifted his eyebrows and looked at her like she should
have known. "I wasn't exactly an honor student in high
school."

She narrowed her eyelids. "You know, you're lucky I
came along to straighten you out."

"You have no idea," he laughed, then extended his hand
to her, "Come on, God will forgive us for breaking into his
house."

Libby ignored his gesture and strode pointedly past
him. He stayed close, pressing his shoulder into hers as they
passed with increasing hesitation into the darkened entryway.
Once inside, Andrew gestured for Libby to hold open the door
while he fumbled for the lights. As his fingertips moved along
the wall, he upset a crucifix, which titled on its nail and then
dropped to the ground with an echoing thud. Libby's breath
came sharp and she clutched the book more tightly.

"Sorry," Andrew murmured. He flipped the switch and
then retrieved and hung the cross reverently.

As he turned back to Libby, he found her still in the
half-open doorway, clutching the wood frame tightly, features
frozen.

"You coming in?"

Libby stepped forward mechanically, her eyes never straying from their lock on the chapel doors. Andrew followed her gaze, but saw nothing shocking in the set of plain wooden panels.

But Libby was hearing the music and seeing in her mind's eye the two men beckoning to her from either side of the doorway. Yes, the doors were ordinary, but she would have recognized them anywhere. After all, she had seen them night after night, leading her into the recurring dream. The images, once confined to her subconscious mind, were now before her. She felt the tangible rush of blood draining from the center of her skull and briefly wondered if she was going to faint. Instinctively, she dropped her head and reached for support. Andrew's voice came from a distance, though she felt the pressure of his hand in the small of her back, steadying her.

Yet she moved forward, drawn automatically to the doors, opening them with the same feeling of anticipation that had strangled her once-unconscious breath. And then she was there, beneath the same ceiling, standing before the same aisle, though the altar was bare of its floral adornments and the pews abandoned. She stepped forward, head down, eyes tracing the carpeted aisle – seeing, in flashes, the scattered white petals. In pieces, the vivid images in her mind seeped through to reality. She moved towards the altar and saw in shadow the man standing there, as he always had, waiting to receive his bride. Another step and she perceived the lost echoes of violins that had been slowly dying in the cathedral ceiling since that day – the day which, she now knew, had been real, had been hers.

The picture sharpened, leaving her senseless, moving on legs that hardly felt the weight of her body. Another weightless step. The room brightened and the air grew heavy, displaced by the presence of the congregation that was slowly settling into place. There was no rush to the altar as in her dream, but instead she took slow, unveiled steps. The man lifted his face, watching her. She could see him clearly now and could make out the deep brown hair, which though cut close to his head here, still managed to escape in insolent wisps over his forehead. The hard line of his jaw softened as he smiled and his dark eyes glowed brilliantly in the building light. She stumbled, and even as she now fully saw Andrew's ghostly form waiting for her at the altar, she felt him behind her as well.

"Say something," he pleaded, voice unusually tight.

But she shook her head listlessly and moved forward, drawing him to the altar. As she neared it, the pressure of Andrew's hands on her shoulders anchored her and chased away the images of the dream. But she knew it now as if she had always known it. She stopped in front of the altar, staring without really seeing. *'Til death do us part. No.* She smiled. *Not us.*

"Libby," Andrew insisted, gripping her shoulders and forcing her to turn to him. She met his eyes lazily. "Libby, what do you remember?"

She lifted her hands to his and drew them from her shoulders, then held the fingers within her own. Not long ago, she had offered him her broken hands and he had cradled them. She had felt his skin, soft and familiar. Now she knew why.

"Do you remember?" she asked, voice barely breaking above a whisper.

He stared at her for a moment and then threw his head back, eyes lifting to some distant point beyond her and then falling to the altar. She watched them change, pupils widening, swallowing light from the stained glass windows and losing it in brimming beads of color.

"I've seen it all before," she said, voice breaking, "I think – I think we were…"

But he silenced her, dropping his head and catching her stammering lips between his own. There was a rush; her breath being drawn from her, followed by her senses, her strength, her fears. She remembered this, all of it. She remembered falling in love. She remembered watching him die.

Tears rolled down her cheeks, beading on her lips. He pressed them away, pulling her so close now that her pounding heart could have influenced the beat of his own. There had been others like them, friends and families. But he had stood out among all the rest, thrillingly different, comfortably familiar. They had fallen for each other and settled into the obvious love, teasing it out and then firmly embracing it. But he had been possessed and they had killed him. She had watched, wounded, her earthly body already failing. And after he had faded in her arms, the demon moved from him and into her and she lost the strength to fight.

They were never meant to forget, but for all of their lives they had lived apart from each other, hungering and never fulfilled, waiting for this. Her fingers moved expertly through his hair, drowning in the dark waves, then to his face to feel the slackened jaw, the corners of his lips – relaxed, perpetual smile stunned from him. He was open now and she poured herself into him.

Andrew's head dropped suddenly, his temple pressing into hers. He had felt it, her light – all of it. It had hit him like the first breath of smoky autumn air after a long summer, awakening sweet memories and tantalizing him with the promise of what was to come. *I remember this. I liked this.* He closed his eyes and relaxed into her, hardly daring to believe that anyone would let him get this close. He felt a thrill deep within him that was more gripping than the one that reached up from a grinding engine. It was like fire, overwhelming backdrafts rolling over him, heated plumes erupting from deep within. He was losing himself to it, but he let it come, wanting to know where it could take him. As the blaze drove him senseless, he searched for an anchor and held her fast.

Then, a muted footfall reached him. Though it was weak, it went through him like a cold knife. He drew away from Libby, eyes penetrating the shadows.

"What is it?" she gasped, as his fingers tightened on her shoulders.

"I don't know," he said, "I thought I heard a…"

There. A glint of colored light in a patch of shifting darkness. Something was coming. He pressed his eyelids together tightly and fought for his strength and sensation to return. Another footfall reached him, unmistakenable this time. His eyes flew open and he looked around. *What do I have?* No weapons, no font of holy water. Libby had dropped the book onto the front pew, but there was no time to read it. *Shit.*

The darkness shifted once again and from it emerged a growing shadow, cast onto the floor by the light of the stained glass. He could see a pair of eyes now, glowing red in the darkness. *That can't be good.* He lifted his hands to Libby's shoulders and his body tensed.

Libby felt it acutely and her heart sprang from its slumber. She saw his eyes, dark again, locked on something behind her. But when she tried to turn back, he held her fast. Her heart beat faster now. She felt her knees, weak, on the verge of collapse. Then, a sudden electrical surge through the back of her neck warned her of a close presence. Her eyes dropped and she saw the shadow, swelling behind her own, arm lifted and ending in a very sharp point…

"Get down," Andrew murmured.

She resisted, frozen, "What?"

"*Get down!*" Andrew's weight came down on her shoulders. Her knees buckled and she fell to the floor. Her palms stung as they slapped the cold marble. The sensation intensified the current already surging through her neck. Something was there, still behind her. A booted foot came down close to her head.

She rolled away, tumbling down the altar steps, somehow managing to get on her feet. The attacker was as real

as it was unreal: hairless and cloaked in black, with skin gray
and speckled, eyes as red as blood, and a toothless mouth
gaping as he faced Andrew, swinging a long curved blade in
wide arcs.

Andrew dodged swing after swing, but Libby could see
the increasing delay in his movements. The demon, fueled by
inhuman strength, would outlast him. It was only a matter of
time before...

Brognolus.

She grabbed the book and rapidly tore through the thin
yellow pages. The ink was dark and blotted and the priest's
notation was miniscule, wrapped along margins and impossible
to read. Andrew cried out and she looked up to find him falling
hard on his back. Then the demon was on top of him, pressing
his hand over Andrew's face, blackened fingernails digging
deep. Andrew's body arched, chest struggling to draw in air
past the obstruction. Libby's desperation mounted. She looked
back down at the pages, squinting at the tiny writing. It was
useless. Even if she could read the words, she wouldn't know
which ones to say.

Andrew's strength was waning. His arms dropped, no
longer fighting to push the demon away. Libby could see the
color rushing out of his skin. He thrust his arms out to the side,
reaching desperately, clawing the ground. While she sat here,
the demon was killing him.

Fuck it. Libby grabbed the book, sprang to her feet and
did the only thing she could think of. She brought the useless
thing down hard upon the demon's back.

He howled, an utterance that sounded like the desperate cries of a thousand of Hell's prisoners. Now turning his fiery eyes on Libby, he sprang off of Andrew and lunged for her. The blackened fingernails sliced the air just inches from her face. Andrew drew a deep renewing gasp and then wrapped his hand around the demon's ankle. Libby could see the slits within the red eyes narrow suddenly, before Andrew lifted his shoulders and flung the demon to the ground behind him. At impact, the blade slipped from the demon's fingers and clattered past Andrew, who rolled to the side and snatched it out of its trajectory. Together they rose, facing each other, the demon's red eyes boiling, inviting the attack.

Andrew raised the knife to make a wild swing, but caught himself mid-arc and lowered his arm. Libby watched, torn between confusion and understanding as he slowly turned the blade over in his hands and regarded it fearfully. He let it roll down his palm and it turned over once and stopped, loosely caught in the curve of his fingertips.

The demon's throaty hiss rose in pitch as his excitement mounted over discovering the helplessness of his prey. Andrew felt the weight of the knife acutely, knowing what it would mean to use it, fearing that he might enjoy it, knowing that he could never go back.

The demon, advancing, was unaware of the dark object descending until it struck. As he stumbled beneath the blow, Brognolus fell to its feet and arced open. Loose pages fell out and slid across the marble, pentagrams spinning. *The hated things!* The thousands of whistling screams buried within his chest intensified. This was it. This infernal thing was what they had sent him for.

He snatched it up hungrily with his long fingers, feeling the aching burn he had experienced since entering the holy place concentrating now in his fingertips. So the priest had consecrated it. No matter. It would be destroyed in no time. A sharp howl of triumph erupted from his sunken chest. Hearing this, Libby came to a sickening realization that the book was worth more to them than just a convenient trajectory.

"Get the book!" she cried to Andrew, vexed by his inaction.

Andrew turned to her, arms wide as though inviting suggestions. Libby looked pointedly at the knife in his hand. Taking advantage of their inattention, the demon crouched low and then sprang into the air, arcing over both of them and landing behind Libby. Before she could even turn, it had delivered the blow of retribution, striking the back of her head so forcefully, the image of the world before her seemed to tilt and fall out of frame, leaving a buzzing darkness behind. Blindly, she stumbled forward, catching herself on Andrew's shirt. He slowly lowered her to the ground then pulled away, unwinding her fingers from him and laying her limp hand on the back of her head. She lowered her neck and pressed her fingers into the already swelling lump, driving away the pain and dizziness. *Where is he?* Ground rocking still. *What's going on?*

Her vision cleared and she looked up to see Andrew drawing a deep gash in the demon's shoulder with the whole arc of the knife, his eyes glowing with as much ferocity as the scarlet ones before him.

At the insult, the demon uttered a sound like screeching tires and then reached up with lightning speed, wrapping his long fingers around Andrew's throat, lifting him off his feet. Andrew struggled to drive the knife home, but in one swift motion, the demon catapulted him towards the wall. Andrew's body crumpled at impact and he fell to the ground. Pieces of the wall fluttered down from the edges of the crevasse he had left behind.

Libby shifted, torn between going to him and chasing the demon, who was now tearing up the aisle, stolen book still clutched beneath his corpse-like fingers. No. It was too late for that. He'd be gone before she figured out how to stop him.

Andrew coughed as the sudden rush of heated pain roused him from the brief unconsciousness. Libby knelt beside him, anxiously checking for injury. But he crawled to his knees and resisted her restraint.

"Where'd he go?" he rasped.

"Who?" Libby stalled.

Andrew shook his head and then leaned his weight on her, using her as an unwilling crutch. She wanted to pull him back, to tell him to lie down, elevate his feet and take an Aspirin.

"You've still got my old knife, right?"

"Yes." Libby looked back to the altar and saw her purse teetering on the edge of one of the steps. It was still there. She should have used it. Should have...

"Then take these."

She looked back, and saw Andrew holding the keys to the Corvette out to her.

"Why?"

He jangled them impatiently. "Get in the car and go back to your place. I'll meet up with you there. If anyone comes after you, use the knife."

Libby took the keys and stared at them. A leather strap extending from the key ring had the name *Scott* stamped into it. What did he want her to do? Leave him? The demon...

She looked up suddenly. Andrew was already limping down the aisle, clutching the curved blade tightly. He was going after it. They had to get the book back, didn't they? But he couldn't. It was too strong for him. It had – her eyes were drawn back to the crater that his body had left in the wall. He was hurting, weak.

She called his name and ran after, stooping to grab her purse. As her cries became more desperate, he slowed his steps and turned, allowing her to catch up to him at the door to the church.

"Libby, please," he began.

She handed him the purse. "Take the knife. It's consecrated."

He shook his head, causing sweat-moistened strands of hair to fall in front of his eyes so that she couldn't see them and know whether or not she could trust his motivation. "You need it more than I do," he insisted impatiently.

"And what are you going to do to the demon?" she snapped, "Let it kick your ass until it gets tired and falls over?"

He shook the hair out of his eyes, but before she could read them, he turned sharply, found the crucifix he knew was there, and ripped it from the wall. "There's no time," he muttered, holding the cross before him like it was a torch, "I'll take care of it."

And then he left her, bursting through the church doors and out into the still gray afternoon. She followed, screaming his name. But he had spotted the demon darting through traffic a block ahead and was after it, blade raised like a madman.

Libby fought queasiness as she watched him go. He was always leaving, always teasing her with dreams and then fading with the onset of reality. The euphoria lingered, but he was lost.

She stumbled to the wall and leaned back against the cool stone, soothing the ache in her back from where she'd fallen. *Damn you*, she cursed Andrew's blurring form. She pumped her fingers into fists and turned her head rapidly towards the church door, determined not to let the tears fall. *It knew we were coming*, an insistent voice urged her. She fought it. *Devils be damned, let them have the book*. But she knew it mattered and sensed that whether or not Andrew managed to chase down the demon, more would come.

She went back into the church and gathered the few pages of Brognolus that had scattered onto the floor before the altar. This was it. She was standing at the altar where she'd been married and the man who held her heart had just run off to possibly get himself killed. All she had between her and Hell was a handful of drawings. She had to hope that one of them contained the information she needed.

Libby tucked the papers into her purse, beside the knife and the keys to the wagered car. *Unreal.* It felt odd, climbing into the drivers' seat. She cupped her hand over the wheel, imagining Andrew's hands there. In her peripheral, the passenger seat lay empty. He'd been here once, sick, drunk, despairing. She couldn't get him out of her head. *Bastard.* But despite all of it, despite the horrible sensation of emptiness in her chest and the sickening thought that she'd never feel him living beneath her fingertips again, she smiled. This had been their life, these moments of terror soothed by moments of passion, and for the first time in her life she felt like she could stop moving.

13

During every endless hour that he didn't call, Libby sat
at her kitchen table, dim overhead light shining down on the
old manuscript pages. Her eyes passed over them without
really comprehending, instead settling on those things which
forced her to acknowledge what she was determined to ignore.
The glowing cell phone display incessantly reporting no missed
calls. The vase of dying flowers on the kitchen counter. The
stark absence of the coffee table in the center of the room. Her
eyes lingered on the last, burying into the fibers of the carpet.
Blood and glass, still there. *I should clean.*

No. She shook her head and lowered her hands to the
table, framing the pages that lay before her. Most depicted
drawings of circles containing complex combinations of
sketches – stars, animals, unrecognizable symbols. One of the
pages she had saved, however, was filled edge to edge with

spotted writing, a chaotic mix of Latin and Hebrew which left little room for the priest's feeble translation. *Construction of the circle.* She pulled a sheet of blank paper closer and began to copy the text in her own handwriting.

Take the knife, consecrated after the manner which we shall deliver in the second book, and trace two concentric circles. Within the space between, trace the four quarters of the Earth, the symbols Tau, and the four names of God (tetragrammaton) within hexagonical pentagrams while speaking the following Psalms...

She lifted her pen. This involved a whole host of knowledge she didn't possess, the least of which was a basic understanding of geometry. *Names of God?* She didn't even know he had one, much less four. She checked her phone again. No missed calls. *Damn him.*

She reached for her laptop, wagering on the assumption that Father Gabriel wasn't the only one who knew about these things. Bit by bit, as one webpage linked to another, she began to decipher some of the symbols. This success sheltered her from further distraction and as the clock rolled unnoticed past eleven minutes past eleven, she had managed to draw her very own protective circle. What the circle was for, she had no idea. But it was there, in front of her, written in Bic pen on the back of a grocery list and it wasn't going to do a damn thing about the fact that Andrew should have been back by now.

Somehow, between the abrupt return to worry, the sweating palms, and the three shots of Jack Daniels, she collapsed onto folded arms over the table. She slipped into the recurring dream, clear now, yet haunting her more deeply than ever as night slipped into morning without him.

*

A stiff neck and a painfully full bladder woke her. The room was stark and bright with the afternoon sun. She pushed the blur out of the corners of her eyelids and checked the clock. When she saw that it was nearly noon, her heartbeat became palpable. He hadn't called. Surely if he was all right, he would have called by now. She lifted her hand to her mouth and caught the loose skin of her knuckles between her teeth. She had let him go. *All night, reading these useless papers.* She dropped her head to the surface of the table, pressing her aching head to the cool wood and staunching tears of frustration. He wasn't dead. She felt like she would know if he were dead. But still.

The table vibrated madly. She looked up and saw her phone dancing across the surface. Heart rate doubling, she grabbed the phone and opened it hungrily.

"Andrew?"

But the voice that responded was Jon's. "Libby, it's me. Do you – have you heard from him?"

She dropped her head back down the table, conserving strength and gathering breath for the casual lie. "No, Jon. I haven't. I thought you were him."

"Look, I - I thought maybe we should meet."

Libby's wearily unwinding spool suddenly retightened. Was he still possessed? Did he want to get her alone in some back alley and finish her off?

"Um, I don't know if that's such a good idea."

"Libby, please. I know I said a lot of terrible things to you, but I've thought things over and I know I was wrong to push you away. Andrew really needs both of us right now. It's better if we work together." His voice hitched, "I'm really worried that something terrible has happened this time."

Me too, Libby thought grimly.

"Okay," she sighed into the phone. She had her knife and knowledge on how to draw a magic circle with it. With any luck, that was all she needed to counter a possessed Jon. If he was clean? Well, that was a different story. What could she possibly tell him? Meanwhile, as she wasted time padding the truth for Jon, Andrew could be out somewhere in the city, clinging to life.

"Did you have lunch?" Jon asked. Libby fought her way back into the conversation.

"No."

"Then why don't you meet me at the IHOP north of Madison Square Garden. Can you get there by noon?"

"Sure."

She threw her head back, grimacing at the ceiling. Her world was falling apart and Jon wanted to take her out for pancakes. Without waiting for Jon's goodbye, she lowered the phone from her ear and snapped it shut. Her head swam. This was a bad idea. She would tell him that Andrew hinted he'd been racing in Staten Island – no, New Jersey – and Jon would leave to city to find him. Then she'd comb every street looking for him. If he'd dissociated, he might have gone back to Father

Gabriel. And there was always that spot above the interstate on the Turnpike… Her shoulders collapsed as something withered in her chest and her empty and whisky-irritated stomach became heavily tangible. Those eyes. *I don't know why I love you…*

But there wasn't time for this - for withering, for breathing in the ether of these images and letting them drug her into inaction. She methodically collected her transcriptions, folded the design of the circle and slipped it into her pocket for comfort. Then she snatched up her cell phone and dropped it into her purse beside the tube of lip gloss, the coupon for one free Lean Cuisine with the purchase of four, a small hair-clogged brush, a wad of five-dollar bills and a consecrated butcher knife. She was ready for anything.

*

She couldn't take the Corvette; Jon would wonder where she'd gotten it. Still, it felt strange getting into her own car as if it were an ordinary day. She kicked aside a balled up McDonalds bag that had wedged beneath the gas pedal. Something smelled: a wad of old cinnamon gum stuck to a Coke bottle in the cup holder. All vestiges of a life she had lost, for better or worse. So much importance placed on ordinary things.

As she drove into the shadows of the taller buildings, her sense that she was heading into doom was heightened. To combat the pregnant silence, she sought the mindless drone of the radio, tuning to her oldies preset. Familiar songs, familiar jingles. *Just another day.*

But it could never be that. Trumpets and drums heralded in the next song, one which she recognized far too easily, one which had often left her stuttering down busy streets every time the word repeated -

Stop! In the name of love…

Her head swam as her heart kicked in double time. *Now now,* she pleaded with herself. But inevitably, the familiar compulsion consumed her.

She turned up the volume. Hot tears stung the corners of her eyes and stole her breath.

Stop! Before you break my heart…

Her foot tapped the brake. A mere hiccup, but it was enough to incite a protest. The piercing howl of the car horns drove through her. She felt sick, Jack souring in her stomach. But she was unable to resist, couldn't change the station. Her foot was on fire, she had to keep…

Stop!

…on going. Before all of this, she would have sat rocking with the car on its axels, telling herself that someone would die – that God was watching. Now she knew that he was. A tsunami was brewing in China every time the dopamine charged her brain to…

Stop!

But it still hurt her deeply to know that several dozen cars were backed up on 3rd Avenue because of her, and that the drivers behind her, now weaving to the side to see what was the cause of the hold-up, were discovering nothing before her but empty road and a green light beckoning for her to go…

Stop!

The song broke into the instrumental bridge. Libby gripped the wheel and floored the gas, determined to make it through the intersection before the chorus returned. Ahead of her, pedestrians had begun to trickle out into the crosswalk. Now, they darted back to the safety of the curb, robotic affects dismantling briefly into scowls.

Yet one man continued unaware. Libby was signaled by the glint of his pressed white shirt in the sunlight as he stepped out from the shadows of the buildings and entered the intersection. *Shit!* Libby stood on the brake and felt the tires skid. The man froze, looking at her with the lazy resignation she had seen on Andrew's face in the emergency room. She screamed to him futilely as her car slid past the point beyond which she believed she would stop in time. At the last second, she yanked the wheel sharply to the left and felt the body of the car wrenching. Adrenaline rushed through her like a paralyzing poison, taking away all motion and sense and leaving her to feel little else but a heart beating madly in a block of ice. She felt the tires leave the pavement as her momentum catapulted her into the intersection, and the world spun in all directions – up and down, right to left, in and out of her.

Then, a metallic crunch exploded through her and the car came to a hesitant stop. Her head slammed back into the headrest and black flecks, edged in light, descended in her peripheral vision. She struggled first to fill her deflated lungs and then pressed her fingertips hard into the corners of her eyes to clear her vision. When she opened her eyes again, she found that she was completely turned around in the intersection. The man she'd nearly killed was still frozen in the intersection, staring at her with a dull expression, unaware of the cars already beginning to inch around him. As Libby looked at him, she was captured by a sudden feeling of déjà vu. Yet there was nothing familiar in his face. He was just another clean cut office clone, unremarkable from the hoards that teemed past her daily.

He broke away from her and walked on, lifting his arm casually to flip her off. As he did, his shirt sleeve fell open at the cuff and she saw, as clearly as if it had been inches from her face, a phrase tattooed on the inside of his forearm. Amor Vincit Omnia. She smelled sweat and saw in a flash an advertisement curled on a subway stop wall – Try Sodium Bicarb.

A loud tapping to her left startled her. She looked over to see a round face hovering in her window. *Right. I've hit a car. I'm somewhere in the middle of a busy New York City intersection.*

The man facing her tapped again more impatiently. Libby forced him back by opening the door. He was bouncing on his ankles, cartoonishly anxious. Cars were trying to work themselves around the scene, each driver offering choice words which seemed to increase the man's edginess. She glanced at his license plate and saw that he was from Iowa. No wonder.

Libby brushed past him and went to inspect the damage. It was minimal: a dented fender on her end and a busted headlight on his. His car, a tan Supra that might have once been brown, looked as though it had seen better days. He couldn't possibly mourn the loss of one headlight. Besides, in New York City, the unwritten rule regarding car accidents in traffic was that if no one was dead, things were handled quickly and quietly.

Libby felt the man bobbing behind her. "Busted up light," he muttered, which Libby assumed was an attempt to elicit her to offer her insurance information. Of all the places Libby didn't want to be today, this was the worst of them. Impatiently, she dug her insurance card out of her wallet and handed it to him. He hesitated to take it, asking her tersely if she had a pen.

"Just keep the card. I don't need it."

This was too much. Jon was waiting for her. Andrew was probably dead. Now suddenly she'd crossed paths with this tattooed man who she knew she'd seen before, and had to wonder if that meant she was supposed to kill him.

"Do we – do we call the police?" the man asked, snapping her attention back to him.

She looked him over. "Are you hurt?"

"I…" he paused, rubbing his hand on the back of his neck and sizing her up. He seemed to be asking himself how much he could get out of her if he really tried. But Libby's fierce expression must have deterred him, for he dropped his hand and muttered no. "Just banged my hand on the dash."

"Let me see," Libby said. He lifted his other hand and dangled it in front of her. She saw displacement in the metacarpals and a ring of swelling.

"Look, I'm a - doctor," she said, struggling with the word. Had she abandoned that along with everything else in her life? Still, she knew a fracture when she saw one.

"I think you should go to the hospital and get an x-ray."

"Really?" he winced and drew the offended hand close to his chest for protection, "I'm supposed to meet a realtor at an art gallery. I flew all the way here for this."

"Fine. It's your choice," Libby interrupted him, already moving back to her car.

But he lingered, looking at her with a pathetic helplessness that she couldn't ignore. She sighed and wrenched open her back door, which was slightly impacted from the collision. Beneath the seat, next to the tennis racket she hadn't used in years and several thick textbooks, was her first aid kit. She'd never even opened it since the day her mother had insisted she keep it in her car. Now, she was grateful to find a small roll of bandages inside.

She went back to the man and indicated for him to hold out his hand. Gingerly, he obeyed.

"Why don't you just get this taken care of first?" she said, carefully winding the bandage around his wrist and hand. "Call your realtor and tell him to meet you later."

He nodded slowly, still somewhat in a daze. Libby cut off the bandages and gave his hand back to him. "Keep it elevated," she instructed, "And get your car out of the intersection before one of gets shot, okay?"

He nodded and backed away, injured hand raised above his head. Libby got back in her car and restarted the engine.

Forget Jon, she thought, as she wound through the knot of cars in the intersection and headed south. She had spent her life giving into her fears of ordinary things. Now, faced with the extraordinary, her anxiety was surprisingly dormant. But despite this, she knew it wasn't enough. Whether or not she needed Andrew or he needed her, he was out there somewhere and if she had to go down every street in the city, she had to find him.

*

He awoke with the sense of movement. Cracked leather under his palms, dim light, tinny Middle Eastern music. He was in a cab, going God knew where. He laughed and lifted one hand to his head to soothe the burning behind his eyes. The hand, he saw, was sticky with fresh blood, oozing from a terrible gash across his palm. He tried to remember the last time he'd been conscious. *Right.* He'd followed Meg in the limousine, gotten into a fight with that bastard, and blacked out before he could finish it.

He wasn't used to waking up in cabs. It had always been in that same house, usually alone and locked in. Before that, there had been a different house, filled with people who kept photographs of him on their walls. But he always woke up alone, and never knew who they were or what they were doing with him. Now, one of them of them was keeping Meg prisoner.

He patted his pocket, feeling for the hip flask. It wasn't there. Instead, he found a heavy book resting across his knees. The cover was spotted with the blood from his hand, but he could still make out the gilded title: Candidus Brognolus. *What is this?* He opened to a random page and found pentagrams drawn between handwritten Latin rites. It looked like something of Father Gabriel's, but he hadn't seen it before and didn't remember taking it from him.

He'd being seeing Gabriel for a year now, after the priest had found him filling bottles of holy water from the font of his church. Before Gabriel, he'd done everything on instinct. It told him where to go, what to say. And even though the priest had told him who he really was, he had a hard time remembering his past. He hardly understood his current existence, which came in bursts and then disappeared into what appeared to be days or even months of lost time.

But that had all changed the day he had seen Meg in the alley. He recognized her as if there had never been any time lost between them. She was the one link he had to his past life, but unlike him, she seemed completely unaware of her other life. He'd tracked her down and followed her, only to find her with *him* - with his captor, the man she called Jon. He knew then that the man was a demon and he was trying to keep them apart.

He set the book aside and looked out the window, cringing when he recognized the familiar street that led to the house where he was being imprisoned. Whatever he'd managed to do since the last time he blacked out, something had led him back here. He had no idea how many minutes of consciousness he had left, but perhaps it would give him enough time to figure out who this man was and what he'd done with Meg.

The wounded hand was still oozing blood. He pressed it into his knee, generating searing currents of pain that radiated from the broken skin and fried his arm. But there was more pain in seeing the naked finger. After encountering Meg, he'd started to see flashes of the day she'd slipped the gold band on that finger, and now remembered more than anything the content feeling that came from knowing that his life would be complete. But he had lost it all: his name, his identity, his power, and his love. He was left utterly alone, living a lifetime of stolen moments that channeled years into mere hours.

The cab pulled to a stop in front of the house. He placed a wad of bills into the driver's outstretched hand and stepped out onto the street. The man's car was gone, but the truck he had been using – the black Durango – was still parked on the curb. Preserving the book in his good hand, he pulled open the trunk with the other. His bleeding flesh stung as it came in contact with the metal handle. He swore and threw the book down angrily, then pulled up the corner of carpet that concealed his supplies: consecrated knives, relics, crosses, bottles of holy water, and several of Gabriel's dusty volumes. He tucked the Brognolus book in beside the others, then grabbed a cross and his favorite knife, already having laid out a plan. He'd sneak into the house and carve the devil's snare on the ceiling. By now he knew by heart how to conceive the protective circle and pentagram. If a demon walked into the trap, it couldn't walk out. There, he'd be free to do whatever he willed to it. Whatever it took - he fingered the cold edge of the knife - to get his wife back.

He was halfway up the front steps when he heard the sound of a sputtering engine at the end of the block. He froze with his hand extended towards the doorknob. *Shit, there's no time.* He jumped the porch rail and crouched down behind a bush, pressing himself into the dirt and watching through the lattice of the bush as the car pulled up to the curb and stopped. He held his breath as the man called Jon stepped up onto the sidewalk. Even from here, he could see the inhuman darkness saturating the man's possessed eyes.

"*Tu autem effugare, diabole,*" he murmured the protective rite, and the demon's eyes, blood red now and boiling, snapped to him. Concealing the knife at his side, he rose.

*

Libby stepped through her apartment door and then stepped out again. She stepped in, then out, in, out, in…*stop.* It was the stress. It got right at the cracks in her foundation. She'd fought the traffic for hours, but he wasn't out there. And if he was dead – *bastard* – then he was up in some ethereal dimension plucking harp strings and leaving her to face whatever Hell could throw at her with little more than what she had learned watching The Exorcist. In the meantime, she'd have to go in and out eighty-two times. *See if you can*, her mind had challenged. Then, it became a threat. *If you don't*…

She took a moment to examine what dwindling sense of control she still had, then forced herself to step all the way into the apartment and slam the door behind her. It gave her a sense of freedom, but her body felt fettered by the exhaustion that was catching up to her now.

Somehow she made it to the couch and collapsed, pressing her face into the cool leather. It had retained the smell of him: engine fumes and church incense. She inhaled, but the breath was staggered as the dam broke behind it and all the thoughts she had tried to keep out of her mind came rushing in. All the possibilities, the realities, the consequences. Desperate to silence them, she turned on the television. Droning voices discussing ordinary things filtered in past the unwanted thoughts and freed her to slip into semi-consciousness.

For hours, the murmur of voices skittered on the surface of her awareness until, very suddenly, a familiar burst of music penetrated through. Startled by the rapid return to reality, she shot upright, sending a searing pain from her neck down into her shoulder. The music came to another crescendo, offering a fanfare to the 5:00 news. Libby checked the clock impulsively, confirming what she hardly believed was possible. It had been three hours since she'd collapsed. She listened with some disinterest.

"This is NBC-10 news at five. Good afternoon everyone, I'm Sherry Dodger...."

"And I'm Jim Jones. Looks like the clouds are clearing up, but we may be in for rain showers this evening. Ken Mullins has more on that later with NBC 10 Weather. But first: we've all had one of those days, haven't we, Sherry?"

"Yes, Jim, we have. But sometimes a little bad luck can

be a lifesaver. Here's Karen Smith, live on location in
downtown Manhattan to bring us the remarkable story of an
accident which averted disaster."

"Thanks Sherry. I'm standing here at the site of an
explosion, which took place just a few hours ago near 60th and
7th. This building was once home to the art gallery Vibe, which
went out of business several months ago. Fortunately, no
paintings were present in the building at the time of the
explosion, nor were there any casualties. But that, you will see,
is nothing short of a miracle. I'm with Iowa native Theodore
Mason, who is here to share his incredible story."

Libby bolted forward on the couch. The red face that
filled the screen had once been bobbing in her car window. It
was like looking at an optical illusion, seeing something right
in front of her that shouldn't be.

"Well," the man began, "I was on my way to the gallery
to meet with my realtor when I was involved in a fender
bender. I smashed up my hand pretty bad and decided to go to
the hospital, so I rescheduled the meeting. If I hadn't..." he
glanced back at the building, his crimson face paling to rose,
"We would've been in there when the explosion hit."

The reporter pulled the microphone away and turned
back to the camera, "Fire investigators have attributed to blaze
to faulty wiring and have confirmed that no arson or terrorist
activity is to blame. Clean-up crews expect to have the rubble
cleared from the street by nightfall. Back to you Sherry."

"Thanks Karen. Well, Jim, that gives you something to
think about when you're having a bad day, doesn't it?"

"Yes it does, Sherry."

Libby lunged for the remote and turned off the television before anything else could be said. When she was little, she'd done the same when watching forbidden horror movies late at night. But this was real. This was her work, her doing. She felt God's fingers sending electrical surges down her puppet strings.

At that moment, her cell phone rang. She watched it buzzing on her side table, skirting a bit into the ceramic bird her mother had got her as an apartment-warming gift. If she just didn't answer, she could stay here for the rest of her life and never have to face any of this.

But on the third ring, she grabbed it and checked the display. Her heart sank when she saw Jon's name flashing on the screen. She imagined the conversation. He'd ask her where she'd been. She'd find a way to lie.

On the fourth ring, she answered. "Hello?"

"Libby. It's Jon."

From the sharpness of his tone, Libby knew the reprimand that was coming. She'd shirked the pancake pow-wow and raised his suspicions of her even higher. She decided to lay it out on the table before he could make the accusation.

"I'm sorry I didn't meet you," she said. "I got into a car accident on the way over and it shook me up."

But he went on as if she hadn't said a thing. "I thought you should know, I found Andrew."

Everything within her seemed to halt for just a moment, a brief loss of power before the lights and buzz returned. "You did? Is he okay?"

"I had to call the police on him."

"What? Why?"

"I think he was trying to kill me," Jon faltered, and she heard the withheld tears strangling his voice, "He must have knocked me out pretty bad. I'm having a hard time remembering what happened before I came to. But he was out cold on the lawn next to me, and – and he had a knife."

Libby let the phone drop. Andrew was okay. He was dissociated and trying to kill his brother, but he was still alive. And Jon, if he truly couldn't remember what happened, had been possessed. She wanted to reach through the phone and shake him. It had been so easy for him to do what he had once vowed never to do.

"Where is he?" she demanded, chasing away images of straight jackets and sedatives. They'd hurt him, ruin him, drain him slowly.

"They took him to the hospital."

"Are you out of your mind? They're not going to let him go after this, you know that don't you? He's going to end up like your mother."

She could hear his muffled gasps as the tears broke through. "What was I supposed to do?" he cried, "He's going to kill me. I can't stand there and let him do it, can I? But if I try to stop him, I'll hurt him…" he trailed off, giving in to the tears.

Libby mind was spinning, but she seized control and drew everything to a halt. "Jon, listen to me. I haven't been completely honest with you, but I'm not sure that you'd believe me if I told you everything. Everything seems like it's spinning out of control, but believe me when I tell you that it's not. Is there any part of you that believes that your mother might have been right when she said Andrew was an angel?"

"I don't know. I want to believe that. But he killed…"

"He killed demons, Jon. They exist, and we – Andrew and I – we try to stop them. You're being taken over by them. Can't you feel it? Don't you wonder why you've lost time? Something made you stab Andrew, you broke the table in my apartment when you pushed me into it, and just now, when you blacked out, it was because you were going to kill me at IHOP and he was trying to stop you."

The sound of his gasping sobs diminished as the phone dropped from his ear. She cried his name, wishing she could run to him and take his hand as she had in the limousine and spark that hope and stolen happiness she had seen in his eyes. He was so much a part of this, but so far removed.

"Jon, we're going to fix this," she beckoned him back to the phone. "Listen to me. I'm going to go down to the hospital and get him out. Just wait at home. We'll come and talk about how we're going to stop this."

"Libby, I can't. What if the demon comes back? I don't want to hurt you."

"We can handle ourselves, Jon. Don't worry about us. Don't worry about anything. Your whole life you've been taking care of someone, but now, no matter what happens, I'm going to take care of you. Now breathe."

He inhaled, shuddering. It was hard to let go. But the first moment he'd seen her, he'd known he could trust her. He breathed again, this time more smoothly, and then murmured a goodbye in response to hers. Her voice was soft and maternal. It was all he'd ever prayed for.

She'll get Andrew back. His eyes moved across the room, passing over the photographs of his brother, the abandoned video game controls, the bloodstain he had scrubbed at for hours and hours. *It'll be okay.* He sat down on the couch and pulled his knees up, tucking them under his chin, holding himself. He couldn't remember the last time someone had held him like this. But it would all be okay. They would come here, explain everything, and together they would end this madness.

Something darted across the ceiling. He looked up quickly, but saw nothing but empty corners. *Just getting antsy.* But a moment later, he felt the movement again followed by an intense heat on the back of his neck. He screamed and lunged forward, falling onto all fours on the ground and turning in time to see the buzzing cloud of darkness as it compacted itself to a point and rushed into him.

*

The lights outran Libby as she walked down the psyche ward corridor and approached the nurse's station. Channeling her anxiety, she asked for Andrew's room with the impatience of a doctor in the middle of a busy day. The nurse before her looked up from her computer screen and down again.

"Andrew Calahan?" she confirmed, then leaned in closer to the screen. Her expression deadened for a moment, then sprung up into a tense smile. She looked up. "I'm sorry, ma'am, but he can't see anyone at this time."

Libby struggled to hold onto her false composure. "I have orders to run a neurological screen. Is there a better time I can come back?"

The nurse's smile dropped slightly. "No. Actually, his doctor has requested that he have no visitors."

"Visitors? I'm a doctor." Libby tried to laugh, but it was lost in her panic. Clearly, they'd been warned about her. Jay had known all along that she'd broken Andrew out the first time. She couldn't expect him to stand idly by while she did it again.

She murmured a feeble thank you and walked back to the elevators, mind assaulting her with suggestions and concerns. *Wait until no one's looking and open up every door until you find him. Spot on the wall – touch it, once, twice, three times. Stop. Or have the hospital operator connect you to his room phone. Hands dirty, shouldn't have touched the wall, was it blood oh God oh God it was...*

The elevator doors were sliding open to her right. She fell through them and stabbed the button for the ER floor until the doors closed. *Jay.* She threw her head back into the elevator wall and shoved her burning hands brutally into her pocket. She couldn't do this again without making him understand.

The doors slid open. She lifted her head and rebuilt her composure, then walked towards the nurses' station at the

center of the department. Just like any other day at work. She
leaned casually against the counter and looked for Jay, but
heard his voice first. Barely visible behind the chart rack, he
was seated with the phone cradled on his shoulder, squinting at
an x-ray film that he held up to the light.

She came up behind him and placed her fingertip on his
shoulder. He darted forward in his chair, professional tone
faltering. But when he looked behind him and saw her standing
there, he stopped speaking altogether.

"Hello?" came a muffled voice from within the
receiver.

"I have to call you back," Jays said mechanically, then
laid the phone back in the cradle and stared at her expectantly.

"I have to ask you a favor," she decided on directness.
"I need you to release Andrew Calahan."

Jay stood up and grabbed her by the crook of her elbow,
then dragged her to one of the empty exam rooms. When he
stopped and turned to face her, she saw that his stunned
expression had hardened into anger.

"Libby," he exhaled slowly, calming the frustration,
"You know I can't do that. You're having a mental breakdown,
and it's scaring the Hell out of me. What's going on in your
head?"

"Believe me, Jay, I've never thought more clearly in
my entire life."

"That's what you think," he shook his head and stared
up into the overhead lights. He never thought it would come to
this, but he should have. "You've *learned this*. Patients believe

so ardently in their delusions, they're willing to give everything up. Let me help you."

She was prepared to argue, but for a moment his words got to her. Memories of the past few weeks came to her in flashes, and she began to question them the way he wanted her to. What if Ray and Gabriel were crazy too? What if Andrew just had a lot of people mad at him for winning their cars? What if everything that had happened was really just a disturbing series of coincidences, with connections perceived simply because she wanted so ardently to find connections?

But she shook her head. "I feel this, Jay. This has to be real. Why can't you trust me?"

"Because it doesn't make any sense."

She gestured pointedly to the x-ray films, which he still held at his side. "And a thousand years ago, you would have said the same thing if I told you that it was possible to take pictures of the inside of the human body. Are we so proud that we can't imagine there are things out there we don't yet know?"

He balked. "So what are you going to do?"

"There are bad things out there and Andrew and I are trying to stop them. Please, you know me so well, Jay. I wouldn't put your ass on the line for nothing. Look at me. There's a reason for all of this," she made a sweeping gesture with her hand and then laid it on his shoulder, "And for *this*."

His eyes bore into her, pupils swelling and retreating before he looked away. "Go outside," he murmured.

"Jay, please."

"No," he looked at her sharply, but then his eyes instantaneously softened. "Wait by the ambulance bay. I'll bring him out to you."

Tears pricked her from within. "Thank you."

He looked away and moved slowly to the door, but before his hand could touch the knob, he turned and looked back at her. "What's going to happen, Libby?"

"I don't know," she said, because truly she didn't. She and Andrew couldn't go on living these half-lives. It was a truth she had been afraid to admit. But now, looking at Jay, she felt a tug of sadness. More than likely, the days of their casual friendship had been spent. There would be no more beer pong in frat house basements, no study sessions at Starbucks that disintegrated into conversation and Chinese checkers, no chicken salad sandwiches shared in the hospital cafeteria.

"Whatever happens, don't you ever think for a moment that you made a mistake here today," she said, and he nodded slowly and reached for the door. She waited until it had swung shut behind him to let the tears fall freely. They coursed to her jaw line before she drew them back and ran the back of her hand against her face. Her skin felt abrasive, but familiar. Yet everything familiar to her now was about to be lost, and she wasn't sure she was prepared to abandon it all. If she had clung to any delusion too ardently, it was reality itself. Now, it was time to let go.

*

Low gray clouds had swallowed the sky. The wind whipped through Libby as she stood, hugging her arms in the ambulance bay. When she saw Andrew, her body instantly forgot the cold. He jumped up from his wheelchair and she ran to him, letting him wrap his arms around her and draw her in so deeply she might have lost part of her being within his own.

"Are you okay?" she asked, pushing him away and checking him over.

"Just this," he lifted his hand, showing a fresh line of sutures running across his palm.

"For all the hell you put me through, you could at least be dead."

She laughed at the expression in his eyes and held him again, breathing his scent in deeply, glad to feel his pulse strong against her fingers as they crawled up his neck and plunged happily again into the currents of his hair. It was like putting on a favorite sweater that had been packed away for the summer and settling into the old fit.

Jay coughed and they both turned to look at him.

"You might want to get out of here before someone notices that you're not where you should be," he said.

Andrew broke away from Libby and extended his hand to Jay. "Thanks for doing this, man."

Jay pressed Andrew's hand firmly. "Don't make me regret this. Take care of her."

Libby pushed Andrew aside and embraced Jay, tightening her face into a grin to keep the tears from falling. "Thanks Dad," she laughed, "I promise I'll be home by curfew."

She pulled away and looked at him, trying to imprint his image into her mind. The way he carried his shoulders high to compensate for his mediocre height. The way his thick eyebrows dignified his boyishly bright eyes. The way the white coat fit so well, so much better than her own.

She knew how much he had given up for her. Trusting in her now meant abandoning everything he held sacred: reason, logic, science. Yet there was something familiar in the way he looked at her, some lost innocence surfacing in his eyes. She hadn't seen it in him since their first few years of college when the only chemistry they knew was that of mixing drinks and quantum mechanics was best applied to squeeze a term paper into the hour before dawn after an ethanol-fueled night that was lost in a blink.

He had given her something; but as she looked at him now, she knew she'd given something back.

*

As Libby pulled the car out of the hospital parking lot, Andrew frowned at his haggard reflection in the vanity mirror. All he wanted was to go home for a long hot shower and a change of clothes, but had gotten the sense that Libby had something else in mind.

"Where are we going?" he asked, falling wearily back against the seat and looking at her. She looked just as haggard, though there was still that ethereal glow pulsing beneath her pale skin. The corners of his lips lifted into a brief satisfied smile.

"We're going to talk to Jon. He knows what's going on, and we're going to figure out what we're going to do next. There are a couple of protective circles we can draw at least to keep him from being possessed again."

"Protective circles?"

"Yeah," she smirked. "While you were out carousing, I was home doing research."

"Okay," he let it slide. "So what do we need to do?"

"Everything should be in the book…" she trailed off, suddenly struck by the fact that Andrew was empty-handed. "Which is *where*?"

Andrew looked down at his open palms with a puzzled expression. "I thought I had it."

She swore. "Andrew, we need that book. What the hell were you doing last night?"

He scowled and then mimicked her abrasively, "While you were home doing research, I was busting my ass trying to fight a demon from *Hell*…"

"Okay, stop." She cut him off before their shared anxiety and exhaustion could fuel a full-blown argument. "When was the last time you had the book?"

"After I left the church, I tracked the demon for about ten blocks until I finally cornered it." He laughed bitterly at the memory, "Of course the thing had me overpowered in no time. I probably would have gotten myself killed if Ray hadn't shown up."

Libby pictured the disgruntled man as she had left him in the diner. "How'd he know you were there?"

"Ray's a mysterious guy, Libby. He got the demon with a cross bow, which by the way was fucking *awesome*, and we got the book. I was pretty messed up, so he took me back to his place for his cure-all, four fingers of bourbon and a Montecristo. I tried calling you, but my cell battery was dead. So I passed out for the night and when I woke up I called a cab and headed back home to get my charger. That's the last thing I remember before blacking out."

"So you never made it home?"

"Well," he faltered, "Not as me. But I had the book in the cab and I have to assume that my dissociated self is smart enough not to just leave it there."

"Well then we'd better hope he left it some really obvious place at your house."

"From the little I could see while the cops were manhandling me, I can tell you that it's not anywhere on the front lawn."

She didn't answer, instead concentrating on edging between a double-parked car and a taxi being loaded with baggage. Inch by inch, with the entire swell of the city building behind her. She breathed into the tension and wished she could tell Andrew how glad she was that he was still alive.

As they turned on Jon's street, their breathing increased together and Libby lifted her foot slightly from the gas. It was the last chance they had to back out. She imagined slipping back into the pretense of her ordinary life, following scripted dialogue and clinging to familiar props. There was a chance they could go on living without ever facing this unknown.

No matter how many books they read, they'd never have the knowledge or skills that they once did. Embracing this reality would lead to a lifetime of near misses, recovering with bourbon and fine cigars in Ray's apartment and letting the puppet strings guide movements that seemed irrational.

Libby pulled the car to a stop behind the Durango and killed the engine. Jon was sitting on the porch steps, as he had been the night the limo brought her back home. The Brownstone didn't seem to swallow him today; if not more massive, he seemed denser. She swallowed hard and stepped out of the car. Andrew seemed more hesitant. Halfway through the car door, he stopped and looked up at his brother.

"This isn't going to be a sting operation, is it bro?" he shouted, half-serious.

Jon said nothing, but merely lifted his head and looked at them weakly. Andrew's smile dropped, his expression matching his brother's weary sadness. He joined Libby at the foot of the sidewalk and offered a murmured apology.

Without changing the dull expression on his face, Jon spoke. "No apology needed...*bro*." He slow rose and took a step towards them.

Libby felt Andrew's body tense suddenly. His fingers curled around her wrist with a painful urgency. She looked first at him and then at Jon, whose face was contorted with an odd pleasure. *He must have lost his mind*, she thought. Then she saw his eyes:

Black, soulless.

14

As Andrew and Libby drew back, Jon's pace towards them increased. Libby felt her pulse quickening beneath Andrew's fingertips.

"Do something," he whispered urgently.

But she couldn't. In the space of time between now and when Jon reached them, she would need to find the book, search it for a protective pentagram she only assumed existed, and then trace it around them with a consecrated knife they didn't have.

Seeing that Libby wasn't jumping into action, Andrew began to plead with his brother. "Stop, Jon. I know you can hear me. You're still in there."

But the demon within Jon answered shrilly. "This man is my puppet now. He cannot stop himself from playing the part I have so elegantly conceived for him." The dark eyes bulged, glowing as if there was flame behind them. "It is in fact the very first tragedy known to man. One will die at the hand of his brother."

Libby crafted a threat, but as her jaw fell loosely open it spilled out and she faltered. In a flash, Jon had a knife raised. She felt Andrew's fingers tighten on her wrist and release, and then he charged his brother. Libby eyes zeroed in on the glinting point of the knife.

But Jon simply extended an arm, brushing Andrew aside in a casual gesture that sent him stumbling to his knees with the unmatched momentum.

Libby stepped back, feeling the hairs on the back of her neck rise to attention as if an entire invisible demon army was building behind her. Jon's dull expression broke into a jagged smile as he moved towards her.

"Seems like we've been in this position before, sweetheart."

"Who are you?" Libby asked, stalling for time.

"It is of no consequence."

Libby pleaded with herself not to say the words until they came tumbling out of her mouth: "You think we're going to break a sweat over a demon who admits he's just another one of Hell's pawns? We've faced your type before."

The demon laughed harshly, tearing through Jon's vocal cords: "Honey, I know you break a sweat over having to use a public restroom."

Libby tried not to let her shock register, but the demon caught the slight flinch. "Oh yes, I know all about you. I'm not just a pawn. I've survived on this earth for over a century. It is my own pawns that are ordered to occupy the dying bodies of your kind. My own pawns that were in you nearly thirty years ago when you died, *weeping.*"

Andrew was on his feet now, watching the exchange with a panicked expression. Libby kept her eyes locked onto Jon's black pupils, but lowered her hands and mimed the opening and closing of a book. Andrew's eyes fell to her hands and he nodded.

"Is that what you're going to do to us now?" Libby asked the demon, keeping his attention away from Andrew as he began a chaotic search.

"You could only *pray* to get off so easy this time," the demon snarled. "I know that you won't harm this man's body. You will struggle, but you won't fight. And when you are vulnerable, I will call my demon pawn into you and force this body to put an end to yours."

Before Libby could make another retort, Jon was on top of her. His fingertips pressed into her shoulders, forcing her arms to extend as pain rocketed through them. She could feel his inhuman strength, and though she tried, she couldn't look away from the dark eyes. The blackness was alive, pulsating like a dense swarm of insects, swelling as he lifted his hand and struck her across the face. She heard the crunch of impact, and the vibrating *clunk* of her teeth coming together. Her vision blurred, leaving her unable to see the course of the second blow until it struck her from above. She had never felt such pain before; it was skull-splitting, blinding. Her stomach heaved and she gagged, falling forward, clinging to Jon's body for comfort.

Andrew saw her falling out of the corner of his eye and he froze, in agony to help her but knowing that he needed to find the book in order to do so. But how he could hold back? His body wrenched forward with hers as the demon grabbed her by the arms and threw her towards the street. She came down on her back, skidding on pavement, arms flailing lifelessly.

"You son of a bitch!" Andrew screamed, rushing once more at this brother. This time he was ready. He would do whatever it took. Twist his neck if he had to.

But the demon caught him under his arms and easily sent him rocketing face-forward to the ground. He caught himself on his outstretched hands; the concrete sidewalk ripped apart the freshly sutured wound. He gritted his teeth to barricade a scream and rolled onto his back, staring up at the gleaming metal body of the Durango, hyperventilating fumes of rubber and exhaust. Beside him, he heard Libby breathing in short high-pitched gasps.

He pleaded with his body. *Get up. Get up!* Fighting the searing pain in his arms, he reached up and hooked his hands over the back bumper, using it to support his weight as he stiffly rose. *Where is that goddamned book?*

He looked back for Libby and found that the demon had pulled her to her feet. Though she could barely stand, the demon was recoiling for another blow. Andrew turned away and leaned against the trunk, pressing his forehead into the metal and letting its coolness settle the incendiary fear. *Damnit, Andrew, think!*

His eyes drifted downward, coming to a focus on a dark spot on the silver trunk door handle. *What is that*? He leaned closer to it. It was crusted brown, roughly wedge-shaped, interwomen with the twisted parallel lines of –

He lifted his bleeding hand and saw the fresh blood, now oozing into the cracks and lines of his palm. *I was here.*

Libby was screaming. He forced himself not to look at her and carefully opened the trunk door. The inside was empty, but a spot of dried blood at the corner of the interior alerted him to a loose edge in the carpet. He hooked his fingers around it and pulled the carpet away, revealing a deep cavity. It was filled with unimaginable things - things he had never known were back there: weapons of every sort, books, bottles of holy water, crucifixes and saint icons. *Dymphna.* Resting beneath her was the book.

He pulled it out with his bleeding hand and used the other to grab a dull gray pistol. Its weight threw him off at first, but the grip fit nicely in his hand. He flicked the safety off and lifted his arm, steadying it before stepping out from behind the cover of the Durango and approaching Jon.

"Let her go, or I'll shoot," he warned, advancing towards his brother in steps that felt like they were through quicksand.

Libby was on her knees, coughing blood into the grass. "What are you doing?" she gasped, lifting her weary eyes to him.

The demon laughed. "You wouldn't dare kill your own brother."

But Andrew's arm never moved. "You have no idea what I would do for her."

For a moment, the blackness in Jon's eyes retreated. But it swelled again as he sneered, "I have found that big words seldom represent the man."

Andrew extended his arm, eyebrows furrowing together. His finger curled around the trigger. It felt natural to him. He sensed that his aim would be true.

The demon lunged towards Libby and pulled her into air, then forced her body into the trunk of a tree. He held her suspended, supported only by a hand that was wrapped around her neck. Her arms and legs flailed desperately and then fell limp as she was overcome with the struggle to breathe. Her gasps, high pitched and intense, cut through him. But his finger slid off of the trigger as the power of the gun seemed to explode within his hand and through his mind. *I can't do it.* The weight of the book under his arm reminded him of his uselessness. *I'm not the one who should be doing this.*

Libby's naturally pale skin was now an unnatural shade of gray, her light fading into darkness. He couldn't kill his brother, but there were other ways. Slowly, he advanced the chamber to an empty round and depressed the trigger. The gun exploded in his hand, a convincing enough sound. The demon howled and flew back, beginning a slow descent. A buzzing black cloud began to stream through Jon's open mouth as he fell.

Libby hit the ground, falling forward onto the cool grass. She got to her knees and doubled over, forcing her diaphragm to contract and push air into the deprived lungs. The black cloud hovered, buzzing over her like a mad swarm of bees. Andrew screamed her name and her eyes met his. "Take it!" he cried, and she looked down to see him holding out the book and the gun. She crawled over and took them, fighting with the awkwardness of the warm pistol. She'd never held a gun before, much less used one. Why was he giving this to her?

The buzzing increased, each thrumming surge of current becoming an individual scream, different pitches, different miseries. She looked up and saw it channeling into a dagger-like point, saw Andrew spread his arms and open his mouth wide.

"What are you doing?" she cried, but he opened his mouth wider and let the cloud pour into him.

She crawled away, blindly running into Jon, who was still in a heap on the ground. The impact stirred him awake and as he moaned she grabbed him and pulled him with her. Andrew howled and approached with impossible speed. Libby didn't know what else to do. She raised the pistol, hands shaking as she felt the explosive power in the belly of the weapon that she knew would rip through her when it tore through him.

But Andrew continued towards her, completely undeterred. "Fool me once, shame on you. Fool me twice, shame on me."

Then his hand closed around her neck and she was lifted again, vertebrae separating, breath choked out her, blood pounding in her temples. He forced her into the tree. Lights danced at the corners of her vision and burned in the center of his eyes.

"Please, stop," she gasped, "Andrew, please. You have to fight, you have to – "

He lifted her further, choking off the sound. Dizzy now, she lifted her hands, curled her fingers around his wrists, and pressed her skin into his. *Remember this.* Her vision began to fade, but she locked her eyes onto his and let him see her. He had to see her.

Then the dark swell retreated, just briefly, long enough to allow the hand around her neck to release. She dropped to the ground and crawled away, pleading with him: "Fight it!"

Andrew's hands lifted to his forehead, pressing his temples. "I can't," he gasped, stumbling backwards, "The gun, Libby. Shoot me."

Her blood instantly ignited and she stumbled forward, the gun slipping down into her fingertips. "No," she faltered, "You're out of your mind."

His head snapped up. The eyes were his: intense, desperate. "Please, Libby. I can't stop myself from killing you."

This demon thought the bullet was a blank, but she knew enough to know that it was real this time. He would die again possessed and be lost to her forever. She would remain blind in this sphere, he blind in another.

"I can't..."

Andrew yelled in anguish and fell to his knees. When he lifted his head, she saw the inhuman darkness once again filling his eyes.

Libby got to her feet before he could and ran to the car, rapidly taking in Andrew's inventory. *What do I need?* She pulled out a knife with a thick squat handle and a Bacardi bottle filled with a clear liquid she could only pray was holy water and not rum.

She ran back to Jon, stopping to grab Brognolus even as Andrew lunged for her. She twisted off the cap of the bottle and took a swig, then handed it to him.

"Drink this!" she demanded.

He looked puzzled.

"It's holy water. It wards against possession," she thrust it at him, and then added, "Probably."

Jon took the bottle and drank a large mouthful. Libby sensed Andrew behind her and threw her weight into Jon, pushing him away. As they both fell, her knee pressed into the hard body of the gun. She picked it up and handed it to Jon.

"Keep him busy," she commanded.

He eyed the gun with fear, "No. I can't do that."

But she pushed it into his palm and then pressed her lips into his ear. "I said distract him," she whispered, "Don't *kill him*."

Jon nodded and his fingers closed around the handle of the pistol. As he raised it, Libby slipped away. She threw herself behind the cover of the Durango and pulled Brognolus open. Praying for a table of contents, she tore through the first few pages. *There* – somewhat of a list at least. *Recognition of the state of daemonical presence, concerning the arts and construction of the circle, the confession, prayer, the holy pentagrams...*

"Libby!" Jon's desperate scream reached her.

She grabbed pages in chunks, tearing through the sections. There were pages and pages of circles, most containing a star and some form of script or symbol. Protection, healing, *obedience.*

"To be used when evoking a spirit," Father Gabriel had penned, "During exorcism, e.g., and to cause that spirit to be trapped within its bounds, rendered obedient."

She ripped the page from the book and grabbed the knife. Jon was pinned to the ground, screaming her name.

"Kill me," the demon cried, "Go on, do it."

"Hang in there Jon," she yelled, putting one foot on the back bumper and hoisting herself up onto the truck. Balancing on the very edge, she placed the pointed edge of the knife onto the roof of the car and began to scratch the circle into the black paint. It came out as an oval. She cursed herself, but continued, tracing the second circle within it. This inner circle she divided into fourths, and then began the daunting task of mimicking the Hebrew letters and symbols that occupied each quadrant. A curved line, looking like a broken lasso. Two words. A bisected circle. And in the space between the concentric circles, a star and the words that Gabriel had written out in the margins: *quo a facies tua fugiam.*

"Libby," Jon gasped, his voice raw and strained. She turned and saw that Andrew had him pinned to the ground, one hand wrapped tightly around his throat. She slid off the car, tore a second page from Brognolus and then ran towards them.

"Get off of him," she demanded, drawing the blade of the knife across Andrew's shoulder as deeply as she could stand. The arm recoiled, giving Jon time enough to roll away. The demon howled and swung at Libby, breathing in shrill gasps. It sickened her. There was evil in Andrew, evil staining his eyes, evil contaminating his soul. The fire ants erupted within her, drove her hands to his shoulders, and gave her the strength to pull him towards her and to kiss the howling lips.

Blindly, she held him into her until she could feel the tension in his lips softening into submission. As his own strength surged back into his arms, he no longer pushed her away but instead pulled her hungrily into him.

But she fought her way out of his arms, looked into his eyes and saw once again the desperation and the sickness. Then in a whisper, she told him to drive.

He didn't understand. She thrust him towards the Durango. He faltered and looked back, lips parting in a silent plea. But then as though he'd been kicked from behind, he stumbled forward. His hands rose to frame his temples and he dropped to one knee and screamed in bitter anguish, fighting the swell of the demon within him.

Libby ran to him and pulled him to his feet. The eyes were still his own, but he was growing weaker. "There's no time," she said, pressing her mouth close to his ear. "Trust me."

He stumbled to the car, threw open the passenger side door and climbed through it to the drivers' seat. The keys were on the dash. The demon was winning back control. He could feel it rising like vomit from his gut, unstoppable, burning, suffocating. The engine kicked in, thrumming beneath him. Both hands clasped the wheel, white knuckled, and his foot came down hard on the gas.

As the Durango rocketed forward, Libby pulled Jon to his feet and ran after it.

"What is he doing?" Jon screamed.

Libby had no answer. It had felt right. For all the times she had told Andrew he'd get himself killed driving, the demon would have to think the same thing. And yet as the Durango sped in a blur to the end of the block, the black cloud did not appear and she was stricken with the realization that the demon wasn't going to call her bluff.

Then, as Andrew barreled through the stop sign and into the intersection, Libby caught sight of a tan car approaching with speed from the left, not prepared at all to stop. She froze, eyes locking onto its deadly trajectory towards Andrew's car, seeing every detail as though it were inches before her eyes: the Iowa license plates, the busted headlight.

The collision was massive, pulsing though the ground beneath them. In a tempest of breaking glass and crunching metal, the Durango span several times in the intersection and then slammed into a power line. The cables swayed violently

like captive beasts fighting against chains. One snapped free
and arced through the air before slamming onto the ground
with a sizzling explosion of sparks. It fell again and again, each
popping explosion rocketing it into the air and propelling it
closer and closer to the car. Yet as Libby and Jon ran towards
the Durango, Libby's eyes were not on the arcing wire but on
the buzzing black cloud that had poured through the wrecked
roof and was now hovering over it, trapped by her hastily
constructed snare. *Got it.*

As she ran, she held up the page from Brognolus and
screamed the words aloud: *Exorcizo te, immundissime spiritus,
omnia incursion adversarii, omne phantasma, omnis lego, in
nomine Domini!*

The cloud seemed to swell, and then with a sudden pop
that ricocheted like a sonic boom it collapsed into a single
thread. This thread danced for just a moment within the snare
before it slid down the body of the Durango and drained into
the earth.

Libby threw the page down and ran to the driver's side,
fighting the heaviness in her arms and legs that grew as her
fluttering heart denied them blood. She threw open the door
and saw Andrew slumped forward over the wheel, bright red
blood streaming down the side of his face. She laced her
fingers through his hair and pulled his head up, screaming his
name, barely hearing her own cries – or Jon's, or those of the
man in the other car who was now stumbling towards them
with a cell phone in his hand. She could feel only the rapid
thrumming in his neck and the warm stickiness of his blood.

Jon pushed her away. *Not like this*, he thought, as he grabbed his brother's shoulder and shook him. *Just like waking him up for church.* His knees felt weak. Libby gripped his arm and gently tried to pull him away.

But as Andrew's eyes opened, they both froze. Jon laughed euphorically and he began to chant, "You're fine. See, you're fine. You're fine..."

Andrew nodded, grimacing in pain. "What about the demon?"

"It's gone," Libby said. She pushed Jon back and reached for Andrew, compulsively drawing folds of his jacket into her fingers – fold once, fold twice, fold three times, can't let go, can't ever let go. "You're okay," she took over Jon's chant. "You're okay."

But as she pulled him towards her, he flinched - teeth bared, eyelids pressed together tightly. Her last heartbeat seemed to echo in her head as everything within her froze but her eyes, which moved downward to the large metal shear and followed it from the spot where it had ripped through the dashboard to the spot where it had entered his chest.

"Oh God," she pulled away, her eyes meeting his, tears pooling when she saw the resignation there. He was going to die. He was going to leave her here. "Call an ambulance!"

But Andrew shook his head and laid his hand on Libby's cheek, stopping the tears in their course. She clutched his arm and turned her face into his palm, whispering to him, "You're going to be okay." But even as she said it, she could feel the strength waning in his arm. "Don't be an ass," she cried, "Don't give up like this." But she couldn't feel what he did – the falling apart, organs into cells, cells into molecules. He couldn't hold them together. Pieces were floating away in a current of blood. "Please," he begged, "Let me say goodbye."

He pulled his hand away from Libby and his eyes met Jon's. His brother's mouth fell open, but no words came.

Andrew smiled and felt tears flooding the corners of his eyes. "Looks like I won't be a pain in your ass anymore, bro. Promise me you'll go out and get yourself laid."

He flinched. Jon grasped his hand and squeezed it tightly between his own. All these years spent trying to keep his brother alive, he had never been able to hold on tightly enough to keep him from slipping away unseen. Andrew closed his eyes and his head fell back, jaw tightening as his barricaded a scream.

"I promise," Jon whispered. And he released his brother's hand.

Andrew felt the fire building in his chest, the hot swell of blood within, choking each breath, each heartbeat. He closed his eyes and tried not to think about any of it: the video games he hadn't beaten, the Corvette he hadn't detailed, even the cans of Campbells soup still uneaten in the cupboard at home. Jon didn't like split pea. What would he do with all the split pea? And Libby…

He opened his eyes and looked at her intensely, willing himself to keep her image with him so he could find her again someday.

But Libby looked away, finding unexpected fury. Did he think that he could just leave and she would be fine? How would she find him again? How could she do this alone?

But when he whispered her name, she turned back. He held his hand out to her, the golden light in his eyes streaming now in the pool of tears that had gathered there. She took it and let him caress the stinging skin, let his soft touch draw the words from her as she looked at him and said she loved him, to which he laughed in staggered gasps and said "Yeah, I think we might have a thing."

A sudden loud electrical pop startled Libby and she drew away, catching the last of the sparks as they fell from the dancing wire. She became suddenly aware of a pungent odor. Burning rubber, or – or gasoline.

As she realized it, the others did too. The man from the other car dropped his cell phone and began to stumble backwards, screaming to them. "Get away from the car!"

But she and Jon remained. The wire was on the ground, bucking closer and closer. It would kill him; for real, now, instantly. For one eternal moment, she, Jon and Andrew looked at each other in frozen silence. She was aware of time running out, felt it as water dribbling through her fingers. When the last of it was gone, Andrew mechanically released her hand and told them to get back. They remained still, staring at him with obvious terror. But he couldn't let them see his own. They'd die if they didn't leave him. "Jon, please," he looked at his brother, "Get her out of here."

Libby tensed to resist, but as she watched a lifetime of moments spent and lost pass between the brothers, she no longer had the will to resist as Jon took her arm. She was numb, eyes chasing the distance between she and Andrew as Jon dragged her back, back to the curb, back to the sidewalk, back to the world. The arcing wire lifted to an impossible height, biting and snapping at the air. She was leaving him.

Sparks were illuminated in the pooling gasoline, but her eyes were on Andrew as he settled back in his seat, hands framing the metal shear that pinned him there, eyes watching the falling wire in the rearview mirror - eyes resigned, as always. Always ready to end the show, to cross the line. Jon's fingers pressed deeper into her shoulders. She felt withheld sobs quaking within him. But she couldn't cry. It wasn't supposed to end like this.

As the wire began its terminal descent, Libby pulled out of Jon's grasp and ran to Andrew, ducking through the shower of sparks and holding fast to the twisted metal of the doorframe.

Andrew turned to her, eyes wide and pooling with tears, pierced lungs struggling to support a breath as he gasped, "No, Libby. *Go.*"

The wire cracked loudly, poised now like a snake ready to strike the deadly blow. But very softly she shook her head and smiled.

Her gaze locked onto his, searching once more the dark depths of his eyes. His fingers wrapped around her neck, gently pulling her in, holding her fast to him with the last strength he would possess, letting her see once more the boyish light in his eyes as his smile matched hers. Then they held their breath together as the wire came down.

The very last thing Libby saw was all the light that his gaze had ever captured streaming to the surface of his eyes and exploding into the space around them. It coursed with a musical rush like strong wind, intensely hot, blindingly bright.

In his light, she felt her own.

Epilogue

Outside Solomon's tavern, the city was slowly settling into the pace of the evening. The sidewalk crowds were noticeably more stooped and disheveled as they returned from their various pursuits, worse for the wear and eagerly focusing now on questions behind which no fortune could be won or lost: dinner choices and TV lineups.

A few of the hapless souls had peeled off from the commute and stepped into the dreariness of Solomon's, where it had been night since eight that morning. But those with loosened ties and five-o'clock shadows were out of place among the bar regulars: a grisly crowd with thick calico beards and secondhand clothing, who sat around the lacquered table marking time by glasses emptied and cigars smoked through. They were the crowd that had been swept under the rug by the city, clearing the stage for the cream of the crop, top of the heap. Most who entered after five o'clock strode to the bar and downed a quick drink or two without turning around to notice this silent unwanted crowd.

At the very end of the bar, Jon sat alone. His elbows were resting in something sticky and one hand was wrapped around his fourth drink while the other distractedly knotted and unknotted the stem of a cherry. His concentration, for the moment, was on the acrid haze of blue smoke drifting from the cigarette held by the man beside him. He breathed deeply and held the sting in the back of his throat, defying the reflexive rejection. This, he thought bitterly, he could hold onto.

The cherry stem dropped. He lifted the sweating glass to his lips and took another sip, filling his mouth with the thick bourbon. As it generated heat, his eyes burned. He set the glass down and ran his tongue over his lips, peering through the smoke cloud, hoping she was still there – the pretty young girl with golden hair. As his mind swam in more bourbon than his teetotaler physiology was used to, he could only think to make the comparison that the color of her hair was like that of the night light that had hung above his grandmother's bathroom sink. He'd been watching her for a while as she gnawed buffalo wings with a lack of etiquette that was strangely appealing to him. Yet after rejecting several of Andrew's corny pickup lines, he had reached a familiar breaking point. It was better to spare her the pain of his awkward introduction.

"God, we're a bunch of losers," he said aloud.

The man next to him responded by downing his shot and slamming the glass back onto the bar. He gave Jon the slightest of nods, then pressed his cigarette into the ashtray and stood up. After blinking back the haze from the whiskey, the man departed to the back of the bar. He knew in the way that he always knew – *it's time*.

His steps were uncertain as he dodged drink trays and stumbling patrons, yet his eyes focused with a steely darkness on the curtain that separated the bar from the back room. As he neared it, he let the concealed knife slip down into his fingers.

He pushed through the curtain and stepped into the smoky darkness of the back room. No one was at the pool tables, though several empty bottles littered the surface. The girl was nowhere in sight. He felt a brief panic, wondering if he'd been set up. They'd never been wrong about anything before. Eliminate the target, chaos reins. *All in a day's work.*

Out of nowhere, something heavy came down on the back of his skull. He stumbled forward, grasping the edge of the pool table for support. Several of the bottles dropped and began to roll. He lifted his hand to shield his face and turned to see the source of his attack. A tall man with thick brown hair was standing over him, pool cue raised in his hand. *Of course,* he seethed, *one of* them…

He ducked under the swing of the cue and drove his fist into the man's face with a force that knocked him off of his feet.

"Andrew!" A girl with short dark brown hair and pale features stepped out of the shadows. "You okay?"

Andrew stood, spitting blood from his mouth and bouncing his shoulders to loosen them. "We're just getting started."

The demon lunged for one of the fallen bottles and smashed it against the side of the pool table. He swung at Andrew with the jagged ring of broken glass left in his hand, pupils now like boiling tar. Andrew dodged the swing and cracked the pool cue over his knee, then held the two broken ends up in the shape of a cross. The demon was thrown back as though he'd been lashed across the chest with a whip, falling spread-eagle onto the pool table. Andrew advanced with the cross, forcing the demon back further, writhing and twisting towards the edge of the table.

He looked at Libby, summoning her back out of the shadows. "Go for it Lib."

Libby nodded and began to search for something heavy, eyes finally connecting with the large stuffed elk head mounted above her. She reached up and yanked it from the wall, guiding its fall towards the demon. It came down on his head and then fell to the ground, antlers separating. The demon lay still.

Andrew dropped out of his menacing stance and threw the pieces of the cross aside, then retreated to explore his swollen jaw. He was getting tired of this.

"Are you okay?" Libby asked again.

He nodded and spat another mouthful of blood. "Just do the thing."

Libby took out the holy water and drew the cross on the demon's bleeding forehead, feeling the skin sizzle beneath her touch. The body began to jolt as she began the exorcism and the demonic soul was torn from the other. Andrew watched, still amazed even after all he had seen, as Libby's words drew the black cloud from the possessed man's lips and banished it to Hell.

When it was over, they walked back out into the bar.

"I feel bad about the elk," she said. He smiled and drew her over to the end of the bar where his brother was still sitting. "Don't worry," he said, looping his arm over her shoulders. He could feel her heart racing. She still got so frightened. "You need a drink."

"No," she shook her head. Her eyes were on Jon, watching him sadly. She wished Andrew would look. It had taken something out of him when they'd walked into the bar earlier and seen him here, drowning in bourbon.

"Well, I need one," Andrew said. He took his brother's glass and downed what was left of it.

Libby looked back at him sharply. "What if someone saw that?"

Andrew set the glass down gently, following his brother's gaze to the golden-haired girl. "He's not looking."

She saw his jaw tighten. They didn't need to see him like this. She knew how hard it had been for Andrew to watch his brother collapse into solitude while he was unable to do anything but offer the signs of his presence that had gone unnoticed.

"Let's just go," Libby said, looping her fingers around his arm. He settled into her touch, but didn't move with her as she pulled away.

"Just wait a moment."

He reached over the bar and took a cocktail napkin from a stack beside the register, then casually slipped a pen out of the pocket of a man walking by. He began to write on the napkin, hiding the words from her.

"Andrew, we can't do that," she said, wishing she didn't have to. They'd pushed the line before, with Jon - with Jay. But no direct communication was permitted.

"I'm not," he shook his head and pushed past her. As he walked by the girl, he slipped the napkin in front of her.

Libby joined him as he lingered near the door, curling her hand around his as together they watched her discover the note and followed her gaze to Jon, who was now staring inquisitively into his suddenly empty glass.

The girl stood. Jon's attention moved from his glass to her, features frozen as she began to make her way towards him. He jolted back, eyes frantically finding the exit. *I can't do this.*

But she slipped into the space beside his stool and held out her hand.

"I'm Julia."

"Jon," he shook it gently, "Nice to meet you."

There was a long silence. He watched her face change, expecting disappointment. Instead, she smiled, showing a row of perfectly white teeth. "So," she laughed, flute-like, "I figured I'd break the ice."

Color flamed into his cheeks. "Was I that obvious?"

She touched his arm lightly and smiled, "Well, at first I thought you were just a psychopath. It's not often that you find guys worth talking to in this dive."

He felt hinged on the moment and quickly thought back to what Andrew might have said. "I suppose I should ask then, what's a pretty girl like you doing in a place like this?"

"I'll admit it. Kroger's *Times* review rates their wings as the best in town."

His heart jumped. "Yes! Second only to – "

"Leeland's," she finished with him. "I still have some left. Would you like to join me?"

Sweat trickled down his brow. Her wide eyes focused on him with a quiet intensity, waiting. He thought about what Andrew might have said and then made the words his own, his uncertainty tilting them with an inquisitive inflection that made her smile. "Only if you'll let me take you out afterward to test Kroger's analysis?"

He waited for her expression to fall apart into panic, disgust, pity. But her smile held, and for the first time in a long time, he felt himself smiling back.

She put her hand on his arm and spoke softly, "You know, your brother underestimates you, Jon."

Instantly, Jon's smile dropped. He felt his heart pounding differently now. "My what?"

"Your brother." She unfolded a cocktail napkin and laid it before him. Scrawled in his brother's uniquely tilted handwriting were the words: *My brother loses his tongue around pretty girls, but he would like to know if he can stare at you up close instead of from across the room.*

"You look a little sick," Julia said, her voice edging towards concern, "Are you going to be okay?"

He felt weight on his shoulders and heat behind the eyes that welled with tears as he looked past her and saw the bar door, opening and then closing seemingly by itself. Blinking the tears away, he looked back at her and told her that he was.

THE END

"Writing is a socially acceptable form of schizophrenia."
E.L. Doctorow

In the past, 24-year old Wisconsin native Laurie Knapp has sung in castles in Germany, worked in a giant hot dog suit, driven a gondola (into other gondolas...), taught Arabic to thousands of strangers, made animated movies using dollhouse people, conducted research on squirrels she caught in the forest, worked in a hospital as an occupational therapist, and written over 25 novels.

In the future, Laurie will be pursuing a PhD in history in order to become a college professor or a consultant for the film industry. She also hopes to complete the album of her one-woman band, get a dog, visit every continent, and of course continue devoting every quiet moment to dreaming up new stories to tell.

Laurie may never decide just what to do when she grows up, but she's come to the conclusion that this is the very best way to live.